Walking with a friend in the dark is better than walking alone in the light.

— Helen Keller

All I can tell you today is what I have learned... And that is this: you can't do it alone. As you navigate through the rest of your life, be open to collaboration. Other people and other people's ideas are often better than your own. Find a group of people who challenge and inspire you, spend a lot of time with them, and it will change your life.

— Amy Poehler

novel women

3

Silk Scarf Publishing
Hardcover ISBN: 978:1-7322666-6-7
Paperback ISBN: 978-1-7322666-7-4
eBook ISBN: 973-1-7322666-8-1

Printed in the United States of America
First Edition

Cover Photo Credit: Denise Panyik-Dale

To Between Friends Book Club

We thank our sisters for the cherished memories, the
laughter, and the comfort you so lovingly give.

Praise for Novel Women 3

Settle into your favorite chair, grab your beverage of choice, and prepare to be entertained and moved by Novel Women 3, the latest entry in the saga that celebrates the power of female friendship, resilience, and the beauty of new beginnings at any age. I cheered—and you will, too—for each member of the Novel Women Book Club as they navigate romance, family heartbreak, bad bosses, and self-discovery. A great addition to the series.

—Mally Becker, author of the Agatha Award nominated Revolutionary War mystery series

Third time's the charm for the ladies of Novel Women book club! Life continues to challenge them, but having each grown through this three-book series, they face down new obstacles with grace and aplomb. And the end with make readers smile!

—Michelle Cameron, author of *Babylon* and *Napoleon's Mirage*

"Kim Harwanko and Between Friends Book Club's latest book is yet another 2025 Official International Pulpwood Queen's Timber Guy Book Club Reading Selection. It's all about the story and boy, is this a good one. Five Diamonds in The Pulpwood Queen's TIARA, my highest mark."

—Kathy L. Murphy, CEO and Founder of the New Brand -Kathy L. Murphy Big Book Love Reading Initiative in Celebration of our 25th Anniversary

novel women 3

• BETWEEN FRIENDS BOOK CLUB •

PREVIOUSLY IN NOVEL WOMEN 2

The enduring ties of friendship and sisterhood began for six women when they formed a book club. *Novel Women 3* is the final installment of the trilogy that traces the journey of these middle-aged women grappling with life's trials. Through their shared love for reading, they built unbreakable connections as they navigated the intricacies of aging parents, adapted to empty nesting, and maneuvered through unexpected challenges, including divorces and layoffs. Their book club became more than just a place to discuss books. It was a sanctuary, a refuge, a place where they could be vulnerable and real with one another. After all, book clubs are so much more than just reading.

Brianna Lambert

Bri founded the Novel Women book club. Navigating the challenges of her new job in event planning, she grappled with feelings of inadequacy and frustration. She struggled to meet the demands of her role. Her insecurity was exacerbated by a lack of proper training and support from her colleagues. Bri's mounting stress and exhaustion were compounded by the pressure to perform in a high-stakes environment. And her interactions with her boss, Nicole, highlighted the toxic dynamics within the workplace.

Madeline Miller

Opinionated and always thinking she was right; Madeline had been friends with Bri since their children were in elementary school together. A series of unexpected events triggered a flood of memories to resurface, leaving her with a sense of unease and longing for control. She grew uneasy when she saw her husband's partner having lunch with an attorney, and her worries intensified when she received an invitation to a family gathering. Her husband's partner did, in fact, betray them, tainting her husband's reputation in a way that affected their lifestyle. Despite her inner turmoil and past traumas resurfacing, Madeline remained determined to support her husband and face the challenges ahead.

Staci Hughes

Divorced from her suffocating husband, Staci met her soulmate when she ventured to Burlington, Vermont, to reinvigorate her long-stalled writing career. But John wasn't ready for a relationship and his friend, Maryanne, warned her to stay away. Trying to rebound, she went with fellow book club member Charlotte to a singles event. Throughout the evening, Staci wrestled with her insecurities about being single. John eventually called, coming to her house in New Jersey. Staci's ex-husband barged into her house during John's visit, causing tension and confusion. But by the end of their weekend together, Staci's had a renewed sense of optimism and excitement about John. However, the relationship with her mother, who had always been on her ex-husband's side, deteriorated, frustrating and hurting her. Staci accompanied John to Maryanne's daughter's wedding and was confronted by the mother of the bride.

Charlotte Egan

Finally feeling whole again after her disastrous marriage, Charlotte falls in love with the man of her dreams. As happy as she is, she's uncertain about meeting his adult children. The encounter validated her fears, proving less than warm. During the visit, Maxwell grew somewhat distant, telling her that their children want their parents to get back together. She is incredulous, unable to believe she trusted him. Her college roommate came for a visit. But instead of helping to ease her anxiety it only aggravated an already tenuous situation with Maxwell.

Ava Aguiar

Ava's twenty-year marriage had fallen apart due to Paul's gambling addiction, leaving her single with their two children. Neil, the man Ava had fallen deeply in love in her early twenties, comes back into her life, convincing her to date him despite her hesitation. He still seems like the charming man that she had dreamt about all these years. But after being in the relationship for six months, something felt wrong. Had he always been this self-absorbed?

Hanna Feldon

Last summer, Hanna had reached a boiling point, taking care of the children, the house and the dogs as her jet-setting workaholic husband, Mark, was never home. As her resentment peaked, she decided to indulge herself in running lessons with her daughter's soccer coach. A couple of months later, the two became quite close and one day the coach kissed Hanna. Her husband arrived home that same night, having had an epiphany while in Japan, swore he would be a better husband and father. But Hanna is tortured by that kiss. Should she have told her husband on the night he returned? Should she tell him now?

Chapter 1

MADELINE

STANDING ON BRI'S front porch waiting for Stan, a sense of calm washed over me. I breathed in a long, slow breath of crisp December air and watched it float back out into the world. The book club holiday party was exactly what Stan and I needed tonight. Looking at the night sky sparkling with millions of flickering stars added to my feeling of serenity or maybe it was all the champagne I drank. It's amazing how reading had brought us all together. The group was more than just members of a book club; they were my friends, especially after they'd stood by us during Stan's legal troubles with the Attorney General. Thankful for their support, I vowed to be a better friend myself.

My feet were screaming in my high heels, and I was grateful when Stan offered to get the car. He drove up the driveway and I walked down Bri's front steps.

"Honey, thanks for coming tonight," I said, pulling my seat belt on. "You looked like you had fun."

Stan clicked the left blinker to turn out of Bri's development. "I did – a very nice time. Just what the doctor ordered after everything we've been through."

Feeling affectionate, I put my hand on his thigh. "Hopefully, everything will return to normal." That asshole, James, Stan's long-time friend with whom he had shared an office, had been arrested for fraud. If that weren't bad enough, the state's officials had also suspected Stan. It took a while to straighten everything out and clear his name. Unfortunately, it devastated his company.

"Sweetheart, normal is long gone. Things will be different now." His voice sagged with resignation.

"Hey, cheer up. Don't worry about it tonight."

He mumbled, "We have to downsize. I've lost too many clients to keep our home." The sadness in his voice made me shudder.

"Who cares? I don't need a big house. All I need is you and our beautiful daughters. What else is there? Besides, it's time we downsized anyway."

He looked at me. "I knew you'd say that. And I love you for it." He reached over and grabbed my hand.

"Whatever it is, it is. Believe me, I've been through worse." I winked at him. "Let's get home and commiserate some more."

He grinned. "You got it."

My phone vibrated. I looked at the car's clock – 12:45 a.m. Who the hell was calling me at this hour? Interrupting this moment? "Some person has been calling me for the last three hours. If this is some kind of scam caller, I'm gonna give him a piece of my mind." I yanked the phone from my purse. "Yup, it's that same number."

"Just answer it," Stan said.

The vein in my neck pulsed as I said, "Who is this? How dare you call me this late at night!"

"Mom," a faint voice said.

The air rushed out of my lungs as I recognized my youngest daughter's voice. "Sarah, is everything all right? Why are you calling me from this number?"

"Mom... uhm... well... I'm at the police station," Sarah uttered, barely audible.

I raised the volume on the phone and put it on speaker. "What?" She cleared her throat. "Mom don't get mad. I made a mistake." "Did you say you're at the police station?" I held my breath. She started to weep.

My stomach roiled. "For God's sake, what is wrong?"

"You have to pick me up. I'm at Chester police station."

Stan said, "Hold on." He did a K-turn in the middle of the street, heading back to the center of town. "Sarah, honey, we'll be there right away."

"Sarah, what the hell are you doing at the police station?" A surge of fear and anger rushed through me as she spoke. A man's voice in the background was saying something to her.

"Sarah, you tell me this instant what is going on."

"I got arrested." She was still crying. "A DUI."

What? I shook my head, struggling to comprehend Sarah's words. Memories that I had long buried began to resurface. I gripped the car's console tightly, a sense of worry and dread washing over me. My surroundings blurred as images from my past flooded my mind, like a raging river, drowning me in the pain of those awful years. I shook my head again, trying to expel them. But as Sarah's voice faded in the background, the haunting image of my alcoholic father loomed before me. Cigarette in one hand, drink in the other sitting in his usual spot in my childhood home. *Jesus. I thought all that was behind me.* A shiver ran down my spine.

Chapter 2

BRIANNA

PACING OUTSIDE OF Starbucks, trying to keep my breakfast down, I practiced over and over my opening lines to Shelby, the owner of Elevated Events, where I'd worked for a few short months. My direct supervisor, Nicole Crestfield, the senior planner for the company, had fired me for making inappropriate remarks and gestures to a client, which couldn't be further from the truth. But I'd waited until the holidays passed, knowing how busy the company would be. Also, it gave me time to think about how to handle this conversation.

Bolstering my courage, I turned and quickly walked into the office. "Hi. I have an appointment with Shelby. I'm…"

"Bri, come in," Shelby yelled from her office.

Her receptionist pointed out the way.

Hyper focused, I walked in. My stomach churned. "Thank you for seeing me."

She sat behind her desk. "Well, I was surprised at what happened and I'm glad we have a chance to speak."

Comforted by her words, I took a deep breath. "I wanted to give you my side of the story, because… well, because it's important to me."

"Go on." She leaned forward in her chair.

"We were setting up the annual accountant's holiday event for Steve Lousse. Jane and I had everything ready by the time he arrived." I cleared my throat.

"Where was Nicole at this point?" Shelby asked.

Nicole hadn't made my job a pleasant one. "Finishing another event. Ah…" Her question threw me, and I momentarily forgot what I was saying. I shook my head to clear it. "Oh, Mr. Lousse asked if Jane and I were changing into something more alluring." *God, it galled me to use his title. Should be just louse, period.* "We didn't response, so he asked when Nicole would arrive."

"Did he touch you inappropriately?" she asked.

"Ah, no, not then." I thought back to that night. I wanted a clear picture, as I explained what happened next. "I left the dining room to check on the food preparation in the kitchen. Half an hour later, I returned to the banquet area and saw him in the hallway. He'd been drinking at the bar." I shifted in my seat. "He cornered me and grabbed my arm when I tried to pass."

Shelby nodded; her face neutral. "Was anyone around?"

I shook my head at her question. Did she doubt me? "No," I replied firmly, remembering how he reeked of garlic and whiskey. The memory left a bad taste in my mouth and I tried to swallow it down. Why did she ask that? "He moved closer to me, put both hands on my shoulders and told me I smelled good as he slid his hands down my arms." I shuddered.

"Did he try to kiss you?" Shelby asked.

I still couldn't tell if she believed me. "No. I moved quickly through the kitchen door. He grew angry yelling at me, saying 'Don't be a tease.' I'm sure the kitchen staff heard him."

Shelby shuffled some papers on her desk. I wondered if it was a file on me. "Were there any other incidents with Mr. Lousse that night?"

"Not that I know of. Nicole told me to leave a few minutes after she arrived." I wanted to tell her to speak with Jane, my co-worker, but Jane had made it clear she didn't want to get involved.

"Okay. I have Nicole's notes about the incident." Shelby picked up one of the pages.

"But she wasn't there when this happened," I protested.

Shelby's brow furrowed. "Do you have anyone who can corroborate any of this?"

"Don't you believe me?" I sat back in the chair, wondering why I'd bothered. Why didn't someone call that asshole out on his behavior? Anger bubbled up inside me and all the anxiety I'd had about this meeting faded away.

"Bri, it's not that I don't believe you. But accusations like this are impossible to prove without corroboration." Shelby dropped the page and closed the file on her desk.

"So, that's it?" I sat straight in the chair.

"I'm sorry that it happened. You're a lovely person and no one should make you feel uncomfortable. Mr. Lousse clearly has boundary issues. But Nicole said that her decision to let you go had nothing to do with that incident. It had to do with your skills. She felt your organizational skills and your interactions with others weren't strong enough for the job."

My mouth fell open. "Really?" Nicole had to be the worst boss I ever had, and I'd worked for litigating attorneys.

"You just said yourself a few minutes ago that you were in the kitchen speaking to the staff for half an hour. That should have taken you five to ten minutes. Tops. In this business, speed and organization are keys to success." A tight-lipped smile stretched across Shelby's face, and she stood. "Again, Bri, I'm sorry this didn't work out. I wish you all the best in the future. I have a meeting I need to prepare for in a few minutes, so I have to get back to work." She held out her hand.

I stood and returned her weak shake.

*

Frustration bubbled up inside me as I drove to the mall. What could I have done to deserve getting fired? I had stressed over it for weeks, trying to figure out where I had gone wrong. But nothing was clear-cut. All I wanted was some closure and a chance to make things right. But no one, including Shelby, seemed to care about my side of the story. They didn't care about how hard I'd worked, just my alleged mistakes. Shelby used something as trivial as being in the kitchen for thirty minutes as a reason to let me go. It was ridiculous. Just like how Nicole blamed me for the late buses after one of our programs. How was that even my responsibility?

Even after the meeting, I could not understand why I was fired. Shelby's explanation was vague at best. Of course, and as an at-will employee, I knew the company didn't have to justify their reasons. Her feedback rattled me, calling into question what I had always believed were my strongest qualities - my interpersonal and organizational abilities. Had I truly been deficient in those areas all this time?

I pulled into a parking spot and turned off the engine. Tears streamed down my face as I sat there, lost in thought. The idea of going inside the mall to buy a present for Trudy's shower this weekend felt like an insurmountable task. All I wanted to do was crawl back into bed and hide from the world.

My phone rang, and I took a few deep breaths before answering. "Hi honey. How did it go?" Eric asked.

I sniffled. "Well, not what I expected. That's for sure." I held my phone tight to my ear, holding back any more tears and relayed what happened.

Eric talked, but I didn't hear a word he said.

I was grateful he still loved me after all these years of marriage. But how long would he want someone who couldn't hold a simple job? *Christ. Listen to me.*

"Bri… Bri."

Hearing his raised voice brought me out of the fog I had sunk into. "Sorry, honey. I'm very upset. I don't know what I expected." "It was a stupid-ass job with crazy hours. Quite frankly, I'm glad it's over."

His comment pulled me up short. "Well, I'm sorry I disturbed your sleep on those late nights. But…"

"Wait a minute. I'm not talking about my sleep. I'm talking about all those hours you worked for someone who didn't appreciate them or you. But she certainly charged fees for your alleged inadequate services and then took all the praise your hard work garnered."

"Oh." My mind was still trying to process what he was saying.

"Bri, you have so much talent. So many skills. Don't let this bring you down."

"Yeah." Not truly believing him. He's supposed to be supportive. I pulled down the visor, reaching for a tissue to wipe away my tears. But it was nice to hear it anyway.

"I'll see you tonight. Let's go to Redwoods and have dinner. Don't cook. Okay?" he said.

"Okay." I ended the call and looked toward the mall entrance. It seemed like such a daunting distance to walk.

Trudging from one store to the next for a shower present turned out to be a much-needed distraction. I felt more focused by the time I purchased a KitchenAid mixer for Trudy. I knew she'd love this. I asked the salesperson to wrap it and deliver the mixer to Trudy's home by Saturday. It was too heavy for me to carry to the car.

As I passed by a bookstore, my feet slowed down as if on their own accord and before I knew it, I stepped inside.

The smell of books never failed to comfort me. As I perused the shelves, my eyes landed on two titles that piqued my interest – *Starting Your Own Business* and *Discovering Your True Potential*.

I grabbed both books and headed toward the register. These would guide me on this journey toward finding a new direction for myself.

Feeling slightly lighter with my purchases in hand, I made my way back to the car. The drive home was filled with conflicting emotions – sadness over losing my job but also excitement about starting a new chapter in my life.

I called Charlotte on my way home. "What do you think about me starting my own event business?"

"That's a fantastic idea," Charlotte said. "I guess the meeting didn't go so well."

"No, it didn't. It made me feel worse. I'd tried hard not to show it but being fired crushed me. I hoped that things would work out today. Totally idiotic thinking on my part."

Charlotte paused, and then said, "You is kind. You is smart. You is important."

Her words registered a minute later, and I laughed out loud. "Thank you," I choked out between chuckles. Ever since we read *The Help* in book club, when one of us is down and out, someone always uses these words as a talisman. Did Kathryn Stockett know how many people she influenced when she wrote that touching scene?

"Let me know if you need any help," Charlotte said.

"Thank you." I clicked off, wondering where to begin.

Chapter 3

HANNA

OW. *THIS IS actually happening.* I watched my father help the driver put my parents' suitcases into the back of the SUV. They had decided to go home to California. Ashley's remission and her renewed strength convinced them that it was safe. I could almost guarantee that it wouldn't be for long. Within a year, they'll be living here. There's no way they'd stay so far away when one of their children was sick.

Dad walked in the front door and yelled, "Bags are in the car. Let's go."

The dogs blew past us and jumped on him like they hadn't seen him in years, not minutes.

I shouted, "Down," grabbing their collars and pulling them away.

Mom had been speaking quietly with Ashley and her husband, Josh, on the couch. The commotion made her look up. Her eyes were red and moist.

She wrapped her arms around Ashley. "Honey, you call me immediately if you don't feel well. We'll be on the next plane."

We all followed our parents outside. Ashley's kids hugged their grandparents first, followed by my kids. When it was my turn, my vision blurred and my hand trembled. *What the hell?* Am I getting sick?

"Are you okay?" Mom asked.

"Yes, of course." I smiled at her, not sure how convincing I was. "I didn't get much sleep last night. That's all."

Mom gave me another hug and joined Dad in the car. As I watched them pull away, I had the urge to scream *Stop!* It shocked me. The last few weeks with Mom had been the best in my life and I didn't want to lose that. Maybe if we'd had more time, I'd have told her what had happened over the summer, when I nearly had an affair. The memory tore me up inside because it showed the cracks in my marriage. But instead, I had closed up like a tulip before a storm, keeping the secret to myself.

"Hanna, Josh and I are going to get some steaks for dinner. We'll be right back," Mark said.

"Oh, sure." I walked into the house, half in a daze. Mark had been great since the summer when he came home from that Asian business trip, swearing that he'd be more attentive to his family and home. Saying how stupid he'd been to put all his time into his job and not in the people he cared about most. And what did I do? I welcomed him with open arms like nothing was wrong, pretending everything was fine and not addressing any underlying issues. But deep down, I knew there were cracks in our relationship that I had tried to cover up with a thin layer of denial.

Within two weeks after his return, Ashley had been diagnosed with cancer, and our lives had turned upside down. My parents moved in with us and our focus shifted to my sister. Despite the distraction, the guilt I had buried resurfaced through tiny holes in the facade.

Ashley asked the kids if they wanted hot chocolate. Screams of yes echoed around the room.

Leaving my thoughts behind, I said, "I'd like one, too."

Together, we made hot cocoa. The kids put it into a large thermos, grabbed some hot cups and ran outside and up the tree house. The dogs circled the ladder, barking.

Ashley and I laughed.

"Are you relieved Mom left?" she asked.

"Actually, no. Shocking, right?"

Ashley sipped her cocoa and then said, "Mom's changed. I never thought it would happen, but it did. That talk you had with her really helped. She's different."

"It wasn't just the talk. It was you getting cancer, disproving her crazy belief that nutritious eating can prevent all illnesses."

Ashley leaned close to me. "Mom's cooking probably helped me more than she thinks. I wonder sometimes if I did this to myself, between my anxiety and my past eating disorder."

"Who knows? Maybe it's genetics. Look at our grandmother," I said. "Honestly, Ashley, there's no need for guilt over what you should or shouldn't have done."

Ashley stood and walked over to our bookcase. "Got anything good to read? What are you reading in your book club?"

"I forget." I pulled my phone out of my pocket and searched through the emails for the name of the next book from Bri.

"Hey, you never showed me this."

I looked up. My breath caught. Ashley had found the picture that Staci had taken of Katie and me over the summer. I had hidden it between some books.

"Whoa. Who's this?" She brought the picture over to me.

Pausing, I looked at it. "It's…"

Ashley sat next to me. "Wow. What's going on?"

Tears welled up. "Ah… ," I shook my head. "Nothing."

She knew me better than anyone and just waited for me to talk.

After a few minutes of silence, I told her about how Jim and I nearly had an affair. My hands fumbled in my lap as I recounted the events of that summer.

She reached over and patted my hands. "So, you had a mishap. It's over now. Right?"

"Of course." But was it? "I'm scared to tell Mark."

Ashley stood. "Absolutely, no way should you tell Mark. Why would you do that? It would just upset him and for what? Nothing. It was just a kiss." She looked back at the picture. "Or was it?"

I shrugged.

"What does that mean?" She paced, looking pensive.

Watching her walk around the room grated on my nerves. Why was she so anxious? "Sit down and relax. You're making me wish I hadn't told you."

Ashley sat in the chair closest to me. She blew out a loud exaggerated breath and said, "I'm sorry. It's just that our families are so happy together now that my cancer is in remission. I just want everything to be perfect."

Bewildered, I just stared at her.

"Sorry, that didn't come out right."

"You think?"

Ashley cupped her face in her hands. When she looked up, she said, "I'm sorry. That was selfish of me."

"I don't want to upset you. You've been through enough. I shouldn't have told you," I said. "I wish I confessed to him when he came home from Asia. He was so contrite and apologetic and probably would have just accepted it. Now, if he finds out, it would be worse because I never said anything. Like I covered it up."

"If it didn't mean anything to you and it just happened, and you immediately broke it off, then it's just a moment in time. I mean, you have millions of beautiful moments with Mark. Why upset everything for one instance? To do what, alleviate your guilty conscience?"

I rocked back and forth on the couch, staring at the floor. "But it wasn't just a kiss. I had feelings for him." I couldn't believe I had said it out loud. But there it was. "Doesn't that matter?"

"Do you still?"

"No."

"See? It's a stupid moment in your life when you felt lonely, and someone was there filling that loneliness. But you're not lonely now. So, move on. Let it go." Ashley opened her arms wide. "Done."

"Would you keep the secret?"

"Hell, yes. Like it never happened. You overthink everything. You always have."

Maybe she was right. I held up both hands. "Okay."

"Atta girl." Ashley sat back on the couch, brushing dog hair off her skirt. "Don't think about it again."

Inhaling, a thought crossed my mind. "You can never, and I mean never, tell Josh. He'll start looking at me funny and stir it up all over again. And what if he slips one day and says something to Mark? That would be the absolute worst thing – me telling you and Josh and not him. So, I beg you. Don't tell your husband anything."

Ashley promised and went outside to join the kids. I stayed behind to clean up. My heart pounded. I wished I had never told her. Trying to push my fear away, I watched the kids through the glass slider as they chased each other screaming around the tree with the dogs in pursuit, barking incessantly. But I couldn't calm down. Leaning on my arms on the counter, I bowed my head and said, "Stupid. Stupid. Stupid."

"What's stupid?" Mark asked from behind me, putting the grocery bag on the counter.

Chapter 4

CHARLOTTE

TUCKER DRAGGED ME through the mudroom, heading straight for his water bowl. "Geez, dog. You're thirsty? It wasn't that long of a walk." I released his leash, juggling the mail and packages I had just retrieved from my mailbox. I hadn't checked it in a week, and now the box was bursting with letters and parcels. A few things tumbled onto the ground and a small package had fallen onto the back steps.

Leaving Tucker to his water, I retrieved the fallen items and brought everything into the kitchen. As I sorted through the mail, I heard Tucker's nails clipping on the hardwood floors. Turning my head toward him, I saw a slobbering mess. The fur on his head and chest was soaked. "Hey boy. Did you get any of that water into your mouth?" I knew I'd find a trail of water from the mudroom into the house, so I brought a roll of paper towels and wiped it, starting with him first.

My son's huge Newfoundland puppy was a handful. The floor under his water bowl was drenched and so was the wall behind it. He must have shaken his big head after he drank. I laughed, wiping away the water. He sat by the doorway, watching me. After I finished cleaning, I tousled the fur on top of his head. "You're a devil."

What a comfort Tucker had been since my younger son's deployment. Chad had Tucker for only two months before he found out he was stationed overseas. As much as I hate him being there, I have fallen in love with this sweet, sweet dog.

Chad swore to me that he'd be safe in Kuwait. But I wasn't so sure. His older brother, Michael, keeps telling me it's not safe anywhere. So, there's no point in worrying. If he meant that to be comforting, it wasn't.

Neither of my sons has met the new man in my life, Maxwell. With Chad's sudden deployment and Michael living in Seattle, I couldn't get everyone together before Chad left for Kuwait. I know they wanted to meet the man they say has ended my "over dating." My sons constantly nagged me to settle down after the divorce. I don't think they liked the idea of their mother playing the field. If they actually knew how much of an "over-dater" I had been, it would shock them. But Maxwell had slowly reeled me into his safe and comfortable arms. And it had been beautiful, better than expected. That is, until Maxwell's ex-wife decided to relocate back to New Jersey.

My phone rang. It was Maxwell. "Hi. How was your business trip?" I purred into the phone. I could hear his exhaustion in that sensuous voice. "You should get some sleep. How about we grab dinner on Friday?"

"OK," he replied.

He yawned. "I'll call you during the week. Goodnight." He clicked off.

A loud crash shattered the quiet night. *What the hell?* I jumped up and headed toward the noise.

Bam, bam, bam.

Running into the family room, I saw Tucker thrashing about. His head was stuck inside a wire side table I had brought in from the deck to clean. Even though he's just seven months old, he's the size of a bear with an enormous head. He'd put his head between the table legs and it got stuck. I tried to get close, but he was whipping the table in all directions to free his head.

"Tucker, it's okay," I said in as soothing a voice as I could, hiding my dismay as my crystal vases flew off the coffee table onto the floor. At least one broke. I grabbed the blanket from the couch and threw it over the legs of the wire table to give me more leverage, hoping to yank the table from his head. It was tight. I had to gently wiggle it from side to side until it finally slid off.

"It's okay, boy." I clutched his collar and led him outside to check him for any broken pieces of glass. "That was scary, huh...?" Petting him, I checked each paw and finger-combed through his fur. "You're lucky, no cuts or glass." I left him outside to clean up the mess.

At least Tucker didn't get hurt. I couldn't imagine telling my son that his sweet dog was injured. The wire table's legs were slightly bent, so I decided to throw it out. Tucker's antics scratched the TV console and the DVDs had been thrown about. But just the three vases had broken.

No loss there. They had been an anniversary gift that no longer meant anything. Grant, my ex, never made a promise he kept. Like "I'll never sleep with another woman again." I was delighted to toss the glass shards in the garbage. It felt wonderful to get rid of this remnant of my old life.

I've never told my sons about the crap their father put me through. They were living on their own by the time we divorced, and I didn't want to damage their relationship with their dad. I don't regret that decision. After the divorce, however, Chad and Michael saw a different side of their father. Without my constant intervention, his narcissism blossomed like a succulent, and he moved his manipulation and belittling from me to them. So, they distanced themselves, seeing him on holidays and birthdays. He didn't seem to notice. Or care.

I looked through the slider and saw Tucker's nose slobbering the window, his tail wagging furiously, knocking a chair back and forth. He didn't like to be left alone. *Maxwell used to be like that.*

*

It was finally Friday night. I raced around, picking up Tucker's toys and straightening the house. Humming a showtune from *Mama Mia*, imagining myself with three suitors… oh, those were the days. No strings, just great sex. Now, I only wanted one man in my life. But that came with a heap of anxiety. *Damn love.*

With a final stroke through my hair and a quick application of lip gloss, I hurried into the kitchen to arrange some cheese and crackers on a plate. Just as I finished, the doorbell chimed. I had made it just in time.

He stood there with his collar up, his hair tussled by the wind, looking better than handsome. I yearned to feel his lips move on mine. He looked exhausted, so I contained myself. "Hi." I gave him a peck on the lips. "Has it gotten cold out?" It was all I could think to say as I ushered him in.

"Yes, very. Though it's warmer than Chicago." He handed me a bottle of white and we moved into the kitchen.

His voice was always my undoing, so melodic, deep like a baritone's, soft and smooth like a piece of velvet. *Oh God, can't we skip dinner? Stop it.* I hoped I wasn't utterly transparent, and he couldn't see my longing.

I picked up the corkscrew.

"Let me do that." Maxwell took the opener and popped the cork, pouring us some Pinot Grigio. "What have you been doing lately?" He took a cracker and some cheese and sat at the counter.

I told him about work and Tucker. As I spoke, his eyes darted out the window. He seemed lost in thought. I stopped speaking mid-sentence.

He looked up. "Sorry, Charlie. My mind was elsewhere. This cheese is good. What is it?"

"Some brie from Kings. I don't know what kind." I placed my hand on his. "Is everything all right?"

"Yes, fine. Everything is fine." He looked away. The intensity in his eyes contradicted his statement, but I let it pass. We ate a few crackers and finished our wine. "Where's Tucker?" he asked.

"I just fed him before you came and put him in his crate. It's hard to get Mr. Excitement into the crate when I have company, so I put him in before you arrived."

"We'd better get going if we're going to make our reservation. I thought we'd try that new Italian restaurant in Morristown. I've heard good things." He rose and inserted the cork into the bottle.

He was quiet in the car. So, I talked and talked and talked. That uneasy feeling crept back. It started when I met Maxwell's kids a few months ago. Emily, the oldest, was downright rude and his son was indifferent. Maxwell told me his kids wanted him to reunite with his wife, Kara. *What?* Eight years had elapsed since their divorce. Most kids would have accepted it by now. When I mentioned that to Maxwell, he grew terse and retorted that all kids were different in how they handled things.

When I worried about it, my friends kept telling me that I was nuts to think that he'd ever consider reconciling with Kara. She'd had an affair and left him. Now, apparently, she was single again and the kids thought it a perfect time to get their parents back together. It was crazy. His kids weren't kids. They were adults in college.

Shaking all these negative thoughts away, I wrapped my arm around his as we walked into the restaurant. Loads of windows looked into an outside area strewn with lights, and the romantic setting made my spirits soar. Maybe my friends were right and I'd been overreacting. *But why is Kara really moving back here?*

Maxwell brightened, talking about his Chicago deal and the

lengths he had to go to close it. "You wouldn't believe how hard this deal was…"

I faded from following the conversation, staring at him, watching how he moved and the beautiful cadence of his voice, imagining being in his arms.

"Charlie." Maxwell waved his hand in the air.

Snapping out of it, I said, "Now, I'm sorry, I spaced out." Smiling at him, my cheeks grew warm.

Then, during dinner, Maxwell brought up his ex-wife. "Charlie, remember me telling you that Kara was moving back to this area? That her job was transferred?"

Transferred, my ass. She looked for a position here to move closer to you. You idiot. Narrowing my eyes, I said, "Yes, I remember." Like I'd forget.

"Well, she's moving into her new townhouse on Saturday. I offered to help." Maxwell reached for the bottle of wine and poured himself another glass. He asked if I'd like one.

Jerking my head up from my plate, I asked, "What?"

"Would you like more wine?" He held the bottle up, ready to pour.

"No! What about Kara?"

"She's moving to her new place this weekend and I offered to help her on Saturday. The kids will be there, too," Maxwell said.

Helping her move in? Are you out of your mind? Or am I out of mine? His lack of concern for my feelings astonished me. *Stay calm,* I repeated to myself over and over as I tried to think of a reply. *Please stay calm.*

But I couldn't find the words. I dabbed my lips with a napkin, trying to compose myself. All I wanted was to leave the restaurant and call for a car to take me home. "I'm speechless."

"Whoa. Does my helping her bother you?" Maxwell reached across the table to take my hand, but I pulled it away.

Pushing my nails into the palm of my right hand, I tried to speak in a mild, level voice. "Yes, it bothers me."

His lashes fluttered. "I'm sorry. I didn't think it would upset you." He frowned, leaning back in his chair.

"I'm confused. If my ex asked me to help him move, I'd laugh. You helping her doesn't make any sense." I held my breath, praying that he'd say something to make my heart stop hammering.

Silence.

He focused on me, but I couldn't read his face. Nervously, I tapped my finger on the wine glass.

"You can't seriously be mad that I'm helping out?" he asked.

You think? Is it my red face or my pleasing disposition? "Yes, I am."

"But why?"

"You can't be that naïve. Unless, of course, you're actually thinking about getting back together." I started to rise. I couldn't sit here with him any longer.

"It's not like that, Charlie." His hand grabbed my arm.

I pulled away. "Then why?"

"I'm just helping. I don't mean to hurt you…"

I didn't hear anything else. I dashed out of the restaurant and sprinted down the street until I reached a nearby movie theater. Struggling to hold back tears, I called for a car to take me back home.

Chapter 5

AVA

Ow! This morning light is fantastic, I muttered as I walked into the house. I pulled my client's key from the front door and closed it. Taking my phone out of my purse, I took pictures to give the photographer some ideas about the angles I'd like. Having only seen the inside of this house in the evening, I was thrilled to see it in the daylight.

The seller recently relocated to Florida after he signed the contract for sale and took some of his furniture and belongings. With fewer things in each space, the rooms looked bigger. I moved furniture around, pulled back the curtains and lifted the blinds. I knew this place would sell quickly. Humming, "Our House," as I slid into my car, I looked at the clock on the dashboard. *Shit.* I was already an hour late.

I got to Alysia's place in Hoboken by noon. Speeding most of the way. *Jesus.* No parking on her street. Why the hell does my daughter want to live here? Circling the block a few times, I got lucky as someone pulled out. The spot was tight, but I'm a Bronx native who could park a dump truck in a compact space. Bri always tells me I'm one scary bitch to drive with. She doesn't know the half of it. I used to drive taxis in the city.

Trudging up the three flights of stairs to Alysia's apartment, I remembered what a pain in the ass it was when I lived in a fourth-floor walkup in my twenties. But hell, I survived and so will she. I didn't like that my twenty-four-year-old would be living on her own now. Her two college roommates had stayed together after graduation, but one got engaged and the other took off to California. Maybe I should buy her a pit bull, to keep her safe

Music thundered through her door, and I doubted she'd hear me knocking. Turning the doorknob, I was surprised that it opened. She definitely needed a pit bull. Who the hell leaves their door open? The music overwhelmed me as I stepped inside. "Alysia!" I yelled, plugging my ears with both hands.

She glanced up from a cardboard box she was unpacking and gestured for me to shut the door. Unable to hear her words over the volume. I complied with her arm command and closed it behind me.

Alysia smiled and flicked off the music. "Hey Mom." She came over to kiss me on the cheek.

"*Querido Dios*," I exclaimed. "You just moved in. You're gonna piss off your neighbors playing your tunes so loud."

She laughed and shook her head. "No, don't worry. They play louder than me."

I wrapped both arms around her as I told her to keep that damn door locked. When I pulled away from the embrace, I thought I noticed something move, but when I turned to look, nothing was there. Should I have gone to bed earlier and not spent hours on the phone with anxious clients and Neil? The clients were easily soothed. Neil didn't need anything other than an ear, so he could tell me about his latest deal. I went to sleep wondering, not for the first time, if he was even more arrogant now than when we dated in our twenties.

Pushing my thoughts away, I looked around at Alysia's studio apartment. It had everything she needed - a tiny kitchen, bathroom, and a living area that doubled as her bedroom. We both went to the window and admired the view: the Hudson River and Manhattan both visible in the distance.

"It's beautiful. Isn't it?" Alysia asked.

"Yes," I replied, before handing her a gift bag I had brought with me. "Happy new apartment."

"Mom, you already bought me everything I need."

"Just open it."

She pulled the pilon from the bag and looked at it quizzically.

"That's your grandmother's. She gave it to me. I'm passing it on to you," I explained.

"I remember. This was on the cupboard in our kitchen," Alysia said, turning it around in her hands.

"Yes, and it's a Puerto Rican tradition – the passing of the pilon," I said.

Alysia walked into the kitchen. "I'm not sure where to put it."

I followed her. "Don't worry. We'll find a place." I remembered when my Mami gave me the pestle and mortar when I moved into my apartment. I didn't have any room either and I don't think I ever crushed spices until years later, when I had a family and cooked dinners.

She placed the pilon on the counter in a corner.

"Ok. I came to help you unpack. Where should I start?" Again, movement from the corner of my eye. I jerked my head around. But nothing was there.

Alysia inspected the boxes and handed me one. "This is kitchen stuff. You can start there." Pointing, she instructed me where to place everything.

"Oh no," I protested. "The cups shouldn't go on top. You use them more frequently, so I'll put them on the lower level." I walked to the cabinet and placed a cup on the lower shelf.

Alysia pulled the cup off the bottom shelf and tried to put it on the top shelf but couldn't quite reach it.

I smirked but kept quiet.

"Well, okay. You're right," she said. "But Mom, this is my place and I'd like to put things where I want them. I have a few more cups in a box in the living room. I'll go get them." Squelching my immediate response, I said, "Sure." Hearing Bri's voice in the back of my mind helped me hold my tongue. *Your children are adults now and don't need you hovering over them. They'll figure it out.*

I put the plates in the middle section of the cabinet and the cups on the bottom shelf. Wiping all the dishware with a moist paper towel, I almost dropped a cup but managed to catch it before it hit the oven. "Whoa. That was close." I turned to grab a fresh paper towel to wipe the cup again.

Reaching into the open cabinet, I stopped abruptly. *Ay Dios mío!* Two dark eyes fixed on me with an intensity that made the hairs on my neck stand up. "Alysia, stop unpacking. You're coming home with me now," I whispered, inching away from the cupboard. I ran out of the kitchen and into the living room, where my daughter was arranging picture frames on an end table.

"What?" she asked, confused. "Why?"

"You have one of the biggest rodents I've ever seen! It's sitting on your plates in the cabinet. Carefully step back and leave the apartment." I whipped my phone out of my pocket. "Give me your landlord's number. This is outrageous."

Alysia walked into the kitchen.

"Stop. Don't go in there." I felt panic. What if it bit her?

"Fergus, you idiot, you scared Mom half to death," she said. I couldn't believe how calm she was. "How did you escape the crate?"

"Don't touch that." I screeched. "It could have rabies."

Alysia laughed so hard that she started to cough. She came into the living room with this thing she called Fergus.

"What the hell is that?" I asked, backing away.

"A ferret. Silly."

"A what?" I watched, horrified, as that thing crawled up her arm and around her neck.

I had to co-sign Alysia's first apartment with her friends but not this time. So, I don't know if she could have pets. "Are these allowed?" I pointed to the ferret as a shiver slid up my spine.

"No. But it's not mine. I was hoping you'd bring Fergus home just for the night. My ex-roommate's mother will pick him up tomorrow morning from your house."

I felt my nostrils flaring. "You've got to be kidding. Tell your friend to do it. What am I, an animal Uber? No way."

"Mom, please. Morgan and Kyle left this morning for the Bahamas. Their landlord doesn't permit pets and went nuts when he saw Fergus."

"Can you blame him?"

She sat on the couch and Fergus curled up in her lap. "It saves Morgan's mom from a trip to Hoboken. I didn't think you'd mind because you were already going to be here."

"You could have asked, not sprung it on me."

"Morgan only asked me late last night. Her mother had to go to Virginia and will be back tomorrow. Even though Fergus would have been fine for one night alone, Morgan wanted to save her mom some driving after I told her you were coming today. It's okay. Right?"

"This is a big ask." I marveled at how affectionate she was with the creature.

"Don't worry. He's getting his exercise now and will be exhausted on the way home." She stood and attempted to put that beast into my arms.

"Don't you dare! Keep that thing away from me," I cried.

She backed away. "Ok. Listen. You don't have to do anything but transport him. It's just one night. The crate has everything he needs in it. No feeding. No exercise. Absolutely nothing." She brought the crate into the living room.

"That crate better not stink. I don't want to smell shit the entire way home." I shuddered at the thought. "So, you're telling me that when I'm ready to leave, that creature goes into the crate, and I don't have to do anything until Morgan's mother comes by in the morning?"

"Yes, absolutely nothing."

"All right. I want Morgan's mother's name and phone number and address. I'll drop off the beast to her in the morning. Tell her that, please."

The afternoon sped by quickly and I kept my distance from the rodent who managed to get into everything. Why the hell would anyone want one of those things? When we were finished unloading the boxes, I looked at my watch. *Shit.* It was five o'clock already. I'd be late for my date with Neil. Damn it. He hates it when I'm not punctual.

Alysia and I had to carefully maneuver the crate down the three flights of stairs and put it in the back of my car. My daughter was right. Fergus slept the entire way home. *Wait until Neil gets a load of this.*

When I pulled into the driveway, Neil's car was already there. *Of course.*

"Did you have a fun day with your daughter?" he asked, giving me a peck on the cheek.

"Yes. I have to bring some stuff inside." I handed him my house key. "Go in and make yourself comfy. I'll be right there."

"Don't be silly. Let me carry your packages." He handed me back my keys, then leered at me. "You didn't happen to buy some sexy lingerie, did you?"

Grinning, I watched him open the backdoor, jump up and scamper backward.

"What the hell is in your backseat?" He pointed into the car. His face was flushed. "It looks like a giant rat."

I laughed. But Neil was clearly not amused. I said hurriedly, to placate him, "Listen, I thought the same thing when I first saw him, but it's just for tonight. The ferret will be gone tomorrow morning.

Alysia's ex-roommate left for vacation and her mother is in Virginia today. Just helping out and saving her mom a long trip to Hoboken."

He glared at me.

"Do you need my help to bring in the crate?" I clicked my garage opener in the car. "Let's put him in the mudroom."

"I'm not staying in this house with that creature." He stormed through the garage and into my house.

Oh, for God's sake. What a baby! He won't carry the damn crate because he thinks it's hideous. But he'll let me do it.

I placed Fergus on the counter by the sink in the mudroom.

Neil was still agitated by the time I found him in the family room, with a scotch in his hand. He started to say something but interrupted himself to go into the mudroom. Flipping on the overhead light, he said, "I hate rodents."

At the sound of his voice, Fergus screeched loudly. I almost laughed out loud. Maybe the animal knows what he's like better than I do.

"That's it. Call me tomorrow when this thing is gone." He opened the door and then paused. "You know... you let those kids of yours run roughshod over you all the time. You need to let them know who's boss." He left.

How dare he! My blood boiled. Who the hell is he to tell me how to raise my children?

Chapter 6
STACI

AFTER NEW YEAR'S, I started packing my clothes and furniture, preparing for my big move. Alleluia! I'm getting out of here. Even though I'd been divorced for half a year, my ex insisted that I remain in our marital home. He wanted me to supervise the renovations needed so that the house would sell well. That way, he didn't have to pay two rents or two mortgages. I agreed, but George kept finding things that needed to be refurbished, like our seven-year-old kitchen, even though it had all the latest appliances. My lawyer had to force him to sell the damn house. Plus, he thought nothing about constantly popping over, using the excuse of some contractor problem or other.

No more house meant George couldn't interrupt my life any longer. Ava found me a nice two-bedroom townhouse in Long Valley, right on the Columbia Trail with beautiful amenities. I couldn't wait to move. Goodbye, old life.

The doorbell rang. I looked through the peephole. *Oh, no.* I opened the door. "Hello, Mother. What brings you here?"

She pushed past me into the house. "I'm here to help, of course."

Yeah, right. I thought back to the family Christmas dinner. Oh, what fun that was. Mom, Grinch-like, she always managed to insult both my sister and me at various times during the meal, while lavishly praising Savannah's husband, Peter. Just like she used to do with me and my ex. Unlike Peter, who knew the score and defended his wife, George ate it up. Whenever Mom complained about me, he'd agree and start grumbling about whatever she was picking on me about too. Now at least I'm not double-teamed anymore.

She stood in the entranceway now, hands on hips. "You know, dear, I just don't understand why you're leaving this beautiful home to live in a tiny townhouse. Do you want me to talk with George? I'm sure he'd let you keep this. He loves you so."

I sighed, closing the door. "First, it's not a tiny townhouse. It's nice. Big. Second…" I halted mid-sentence, realizing what she'd just said. I threw up both my arms. "You're still talking to George?"

"Why, of course, silly. He's my son-in-law." She headed into the kitchen.

Anger sizzled in my gut as I followed her. "We're divorced. He's not your son-in-law anymore."

"Well, you could change that and remarry him, or at least ask him for this lovely home." She twirled around, taking in the kitchen. "The renovations are spectacular. George has great taste. Look at how everything shines." She sat at the counter. "I'm going to miss this house."

I stared at her, unable or unwilling to speak.

"You know, I just don't understand you. George is everything a girl could want. How did you let the situation get to this?"

I put both hands on the counter and bowed my head. "Just leave."

She sighed. "What, dear? Speak up. I can't hear you when you talk into the counter like that."

Raising my head, I wanted to leap across the island and pummel her. Rage pulsed through my veins as I thought about all those years in therapy, shell-shocked by her lack of validation or love. I took a deep breath and walked to the door. "Leave. I don't need your help or your advice or anything from you." I held the door wide.

"Oh, such dramatics. Really, dear? Look around you. You need all the help you can get." She went into the family room and peeked into the box on the coffee table I had started packing with knick-knacks from the bookshelf. "Look how these are packed. There's not enough bubble wrap around that vase. It will break."

I shut the front door with a loud bang. "I'm not staying here another minute with you. If you're not leaving, then I am. You can stay here and pack to your heart's content."

Slamming the bedroom door, my heart pounded. I had hoped I could talk to my mother like Hanna had hers, but her mom wasn't a narcissist, a person who lacked any insight into her own behavior. Why did Dad love her? I couldn't find a single reason. I went into my bathroom and looked at my face in the mirror, grateful I resembled my dad. Such a kind soul. I missed him every single day. Why did he have to be the one to die? He had managed to control her outbursts. No one else could.

I threw on some jeans, boots and a sweater, grabbing my purse off the dresser. I'd drive around or go to the mall. Anything to get away from her.

"Staci," Mother called from the family room. "I left my spare key for the house on the counter in the kitchen."

I had forgotten she had a key. "Thanks. I'll see you." I opened the front door to leave but stopped and walked into the family room. "And by the way, George won't give this house to me. He's not who you think he is." Why did I say anything? Just leave! Christ, I'm as bad as she is.

"Oh, pish. I suppose that janitor you're dating will buy you a big, beautiful home someday." She moved into the kitchen and sat at the counter. "May I have a glass of water?"

"He's a farmer. Mom. You know that. Stop it. And what if he were a janitor? If I loved him, what damn difference would it make?" I pulled one of the few remaining glasses from the cabinet and handed her a glass of water. Her constant belittlement of John made me angry. She's never even met him.

31

"Well, dear..."

"Stop, Mom. I mean it," I hollered. "If you're going to criticize everything I'm doing, get out!" I pointed to the door.

Her face turned scarlet, but she sat silently, sipping her water.

"And for God's sake, get it through your head – we're divorced. Period!"

*

Not even my mother could depress me. I'm getting out of this mausoleum and into John's arms. He'd called late on Christmas night, and we talked for hours. He was the only Christmas present I wanted. After the tractor accident last month, he was slowly returning to work on his farm despite his occasional headaches. It had been weeks since I last saw him, but in a few days I was heading to Vermont.

Cleaning out decades of stuff from the home I shared with my ex and my children wasn't easy. But I was determined to finish and within a few days it was almost completed with boxes for both sons and George. The moving company had brought my belongings to my new townhouse. And the movers would put my sons' stuff in storage for them to go through. George could take care of his own things.

Only a few things remained that hadn't been boxed or moved. Mostly, pictures that littered the family room walls and I wrapped and placed a few of them in boxes for each son. I was wondering if I could photoshop George out of the one picture I actually liked of me when I heard the door open.

"Hello?" I cried.

"It's me."

My heart sank. First, Mom a few days ago and now George. *Ugh.*

"What are you doing here?" I asked. I couldn't keep the snide tone out of the question.

"Relax. I'm having one final look around. The closing is Friday, and the walk-through is tomorrow." He walked over to where I was sitting. "I thought you'd be done by now. The movers are scheduled for later today."

Dear God, it's only hours away from being over. No more George. "I've got two personal boxes left and I'll be gone in ten minutes. You can have the house all to yourself." I placed the remaining family photos in the box and stood to carry it to my car. A huge grin crossed my face and I felt like singing. He won't be able to waltz into my home anymore. He won't have a key. No more surprise visits.

"Why are you smiling? This is amusing to you?" He stood in my way to the door.

"It's freeing." I looked into his beady eyes.

"Of course, it means nothing to you." He looked around the room and pointed to the window. "I'll never make another steak on the grill, or dive into the pool or make friends drinks at the bar. Someone else will be here in my home, using my things."

Naturally, he just cares about losing material things. It's no wonder that he and my mother get along so well. "You'll have another home where you can be the gracious host and impress people." I elbowed my way past him to the door.

Chapter 7

BRI - BOOK CLUB

ARRANGING A TRAY of small sandwiches, I hummed a tune I couldn't get out of my head. "Some will win. Some will lose." *Damn song. Enough already.* I dried my hands, grabbed my phone and started streaming Adele radio. Anything to shake this earworm out of my head.

The doorbell rang. I picked up the tray of sandwiches from the counter and placed them on the kitchen table on my way to the front door. "Come on in," I crooned.

Staci rushed in, twirling around and around in the middle of my family room. "It's over. The house closed. I'm free. Completely free."

"Take it easy. We don't want you falling over a chair," Madeline said, standing right behind her.

"You two came together?" I asked, still surprised at their blossoming friendship.

"How else would she be here on time?" Madeline handed me a bottle of wine. "Her time management clearly needs improvement, so I offered to help."

Staci giggled and shrugged.

"Where is everybody? Do I have to pick them all up to get them here on time?" Madeline asked.

"Relax." I placed my hand on her shoulder. She can be exhausting. "They'll be here."

"I brought champagne for a change of pace." Staci took the bottle from the bag. "Can I put this on ice?"

I guided them into the kitchen. "Yes, of course."

"I must say I thoroughly enjoyed this month's book." Madeline poured herself a glass of red wine from the assortment I had laid out.

"Me too." Staci agreed, as she struggled to free the cork from the champagne.

Madeline eased over and gently took the bottle away. With a quick twist, she popped the cork and poured Staci a glass.

Chuckling, Staci said, "Thanks. You may have just saved one of Bri's windows."

Madeline wrapped her arm around Staci's shoulder. "We all have strengths. I open bottles easily and you're got a big heart."

Did Madeline just say that? What happened on that trip to Vermont? They've been like bosom buddies ever since.

The doorbell rang and I greeted Ava, escorting her into the kitchen. Ten minutes later, I did the same for Hanna and Charlotte.

"Not bad. You're only fifteen minutes late," Madeline chided.

Both women ignored her. I handed them each a glass and pointed to the assortment of already opened wines.

As Hanna poured, she turned to me and said, "Charlotte told me you're starting your own event planning business."

I shook my head. "That reminds me. Can I give everyone a few of my new business cards? You never know when someone might need a planner."

"Of course." Madeline piped in right away.

Everyone took a few cards. I smiled at them all. "Word of mouth is still the best way to get noticed. Thanks, guys, for helping me."

Ava popped an olive into her mouth. "You'd be the first one there for any of us."

Blushing, I ushered everyone into the family room. "So, did you guys like *Ordinary Grace*? I thought it was so good that I'm keeping it on my bookshelf to read again."

"Loved it," Ava remarked.

I turned to face Charlotte. "How about you?"

She seemed dazed as she looked around the room. "Sorry, I didn't read it." She sat in a chair by the fireplace some distance away from the group.

Then, I noticed. Where was her perpetual lip gloss? Bare lips? Charlotte? Never.

"What? Why not?" Madeline started right in.

"That's perfectly okay. I barely finished this month's book myself," I said quickly before Madeline could voice her disapproval. "Is everything okay?"

"Sure. What could possibly be wrong?" Charlotte replied sharply, her free hand waving the air.

Her sarcastic tone made me uneasy as I watched the wine swirl in her glass. Even Madeline bit her lip and let the comment pass.

Hanna broke the awkward moment. "Can we read *The Great Gatsby* next month? Or maybe we should read another classic, like *Anna Karenina*. Though that's a long book. So, let's read Fitzgerald's novel."

"Rather provocative themes for you – adultery and thwarted love." Madeline put her glass on the table and sat forward.

Flushed with embarrassment, Hanna said, "Well, I thought you liked the classics… it's been a while since we read one. That's all."

Even I didn't buy that, so, of course Madeline wouldn't. To her credit, she kept silent, just picked up her glass and leaned back on the couch.

"Sure, Hanna, we can read *Gatsby* next month. I loved that book. Everyone okay with that?"

Charlotte bounced up from her chair. "Adultery. Really. Why in the name of God would I want to read yet another book about infidelity? I need more wine." She stormed off toward the kitchen.

We all looked at one other but said nothing. During their marriage, Charlotte's ex-husband had numerous affairs, even with so-called friends. But that was years ago. I didn't understand why she's upset now.

She returned a minute later with a glass brimming with wine and made a beeline back to her chair in the corner.

I cleared my throat. "We don't have to read that book or any book that upsets you. Is something wrong?"

Clearly uncomfortable with all eyes on her, Charlotte gulped a large mouthful of wine and shook her head.

She was obviously not herself, but I didn't want to push. "Let's give Charlotte some breathing room. We're here for you if you want to talk."

An awkward pause followed. As the hostess, I turned to conversation back to reading.

"Okay, everyone, let's discuss this month's novel." I picked the book up from the table and brandished it. "I can't tell you when I've read characters with so much basic humanity. When the father finished his sermon after Ariel's death, I sobbed."

"It moved me also," Madeline said. I noticed her turn slightly in her seat to keep an eye on Charlotte. She opened her mouth again but said nothing.

I remembered all those times when I should have opened up with this group and didn't. I finally did after that woman kissed my husband last summer. It was such a relief. They didn't ridicule me; they listened and asked what they could do to help.

"The author pulled on my heartstrings. You know, like Pat Conroy does in all his books," Ava said. "It was magnifico."

I nodded. We'd all had some crisis or other to deal with. But it had been years since Charlotte was this moody.

She muttered something.

"Why don't you sit over here with the group? I can't hear you," I said.

"Fine." She plopped into the chair next to Madeline and placed her empty wine glass on the table in front of her. "Basic humanity, did you say? Well, that seems hard to come by."

I wondered where this was going. I'd had one sip of wine while Charlotte had already downed two glasses. Her cheeks were tinged with red. She must be a bit tipsy.

Madeline asked in a modulated tone, "Why is it hard to come by?"

"Oh, don't start with your know-it-all attitude. Please. I don't have the strength tonight."

Crap. I sat straight in my chair, ready to intervene.

Madeline put her hand up to stop me. "Charlotte, what happened? You are clearly upset. Maybe we can help."

Ava, Staci and Hanna murmured in agreement.

"How many times have I complained about my ex? Or about John's bitchy friend?" Staci's arm swished in the air for emphasis and came dangerously close to her glass of wine on the table. "Come on, what's wrong?"

Seconds passed. All I could hear was the grandfather clock ticking in the foyer.

A moan escaped Charlotte's mouth as two tears rolled down her cheeks. "I… he… what the hell's the use?" She dissolved into tears, covering her face with her hands.

I began to rise, but Madeline gestured me back. Tenderly, she said, "It's okay to cry." Madeline touched Charlotte's shoulder. "Let it all out."

I wanted to get up and hug Charlotte, but I followed Madeline's lead, trusting that for once she'd be nurturing and not judgmental.

After several moments, Charlotte's tears lessened, and she tried to choke out a few words. "He's … helping…" She dabbed under both eyes with a cocktail napkin Ava handed her.

"It's okay, take a few minutes to calm down," Madeline told her. As the stress in the room diminished, I stood and went into the kitchen, returning with a box of tissues. I handed them to Charlotte. She took a few and mouthed, "Thank you." I placed the box in front of her on the table.

"Shit, sorry. That was embarrassing." Charlotte twisted a tissue in her fingers. "I feel lost, like I did after my divorce. I don't trust my gut. It had misled me once before."

"Why?" I asked. "What's going on?"

"Maxwell told me he's helping his ex-wife move into her new apartment on Saturday. We were out to dinner, and I just upped and left." Charlotte's eyes narrowed and her lips compressed. "Can you believe I did that? I feel ridiculous now. Instead of telling him how I felt, I had a hissy fit and walked out." She wrung her hands tightly together. "I was happy dating without strings, but he made me love him. And now his ex-wife, whom he loved dearly, is making a play for him. What the hell am I going to do?"

"Does Maxwell want to get back together with his ex-wife?" Madeline asked.

"I don't know." Charlotte wiped her nose. "But maybe she does know now that her other relationship is over. It's not so great being alone. So she's trying to jump back on the Maxwell train. Why else would she get transferred here? Plus, his kids are plotting for their parents to reconcile. How the hell can I compete with that?"

Charlotte had sworn off love forever after her divorce. But then Maxwell made her believe again. My gut said he loved her. I blurted out, "He is nothing like your ex-husband."

Ava added, "That's for damn sure. Grant was a sadistic prick. Maxwell is a prince compared to him."

Hanna and Staci nodded.

Madeline remained quiet, placing her hand on Charlotte's arm and listening intently. Normally, she'd be dictating everything we should say and do, but not this time. After a moment, she spoke up.

"I think you're still haunted by what Grant did. But you're not the same person you were then. You've grown and changed."

I tensed, not sure how Charlotte would react. I opened my mouth to say something but bit my lip instead.

Charlotte looked at her lap.

Undeterred, Madeline continued. "Do you remember when we discussed *A Farewell to Arms,* at book club? We talked about how the 'world breaks everyone and afterward many are strong at the broken places?'" She shook her head. "That's you."

Madeline's voice was soft and calm, a departure from her usual assertive tone.

"Do you also remember that night when we shared our own personal challenges and how we overcame them? How we grew stronger and more resilient?"

Charlotte sat still; her eyes scrunched tight. "Yeah. But…"

I held my breath, waiting for her to continue.

Charlotte took a deep breath, closing her eyes as she did so. "You don't understand. After Grant and I separated, I'd lay in bed, suffocated by the silence. The only thing that pierced it was the dark voice in my head. And it wasn't kind." She opened her eyes. "Hour after hour, day after day. A year. Maybe two. No more late-night kisses or loving warmth. Coldness crept in. Blankets didn't help. Hell, I even missed his snoring." Charlotte paused; her voice filled with pain. "The loneliness was unbearable."

Madeline nodded sympathetically. "I understand. But if Maxwell chooses to go back with his ex-wife, you'll get through it. You won't like it, but you won't hide from life in bed, either." She squeezed Charlotte's hand and whispered. "Trust me. I know what it feels like to be completely alone."

Charlotte's eyes widened in surprise. "No, you don't. How could you? You're still married."

Madeline's shoulders sagged. "Let's just say I had a lonely childhood."

Charlotte stared at her for a moment. Her tone softened as she said, "I'm terrified. I've fallen in love with Maxwell and can't bear the idea of losing him or feeling that isolated and alone again."

"No one wants to feel like that," Madeline said. "But you're stronger now than you were before. It will never be like that again."

Charlotte crumpled her cocktail napkin in her hands and put it on the coffee table. "Wish I had your faith."

Madeline raised an eyebrow. "Hey, I'm not saying Maxwell is bowing out, either. You both seem happy when you're together."

Charlotte shrugged. "Why couldn't this relationship just be easy? Haven't I been through enough?"

"*Que es fácil?*" Ava interjected. "Sorry. Nothing's friggin easy. You know that."

"I guess. But still." Charlotte slumped deeper into the chair. Her lips were red and swollen from being bitten.

"Don't give up on him yet. He may surprise you," I said.

Charlotte nodded.

I wanted to hug her and melt away her anxiety. She has been through a lot, and it pained me to see her like this.

"Alright, that's enough of my whining," Charlotte said. "Someone else take over. Please."

The group quieted for a minute, each lost in our thoughts.

That's my cue. A good time to bring in the food. I rose and carried out sandwiches, paper plates and napkins from the kitchen. Staci jumped up to help and knocked her leg on the kitchen table.

"Do you need ice for that? You slammed it hard." I asked her.

She rubbed her knee and laughed. "No. I bang my knees all the time. They're used to it."

We brought out the rest of the plates, including the cookies I had made that morning. There was just enough room on the coffee table for everything.

When Staci sat, she asked, "Madeline, how the hell did you

remember that passage? I barely remember Hemingway writing *A Farewell to Arms.*"

Everyone laughed.

Charlotte reached into her purse, pulled out a pastel pink gloss tube, and applied it to her swollen lips.

I exhaled. *That's better.*

"Since you've passed the baton, I'm not sure about my relationship with Neil, either." Ava began. Her dark hair had grown to her shoulders and the bangs that had driven her nuts had finally grown out and were neatly layered into the cut. "I built him up as the love of my life for so long and now, well... I spend too much time thinking up excuses not to see him. He's pushing so hard for a permanent commitment, but it rings hollow to me. I don't know. This isn't how I'd thought it would be."

"Is it because of that doctor you met in Puerto Rico?" I asked.

She shook her head. "No. I'm a one-man kinda girl. Not that Gabriel isn't on my mind, but I'm gonna figure this thing out with Neil first." Ava stood. "I'm getting another glass of wine. Anyone else?"

"I'll go with you," Hanna said.

Ava looked beautiful tonight. My three friends out in the world, dating after 50. *Ugh.* I couldn't even imagine.

"Well, being that we're in sharing mode tonight, I'm driving up to Vermont in a few days. I can't wait to see John." Staci almost popped off the couch with excitement.

Hanna returned with Ava from the kitchen. "How's he feeling?"

"Good. Back to normal. Some leftover headaches from the concussion."

Madeline smirked. "Don't forget, if you need any help with that Vermont vixen, call me."

Staci laughed out loud. "I sure will."

I heard a buzzing. Must be someone's cell. Madeline reached

into her sweater and pulled out her phone. "Excuse me. I have to take this." She rose and headed for the kitchen.

Dumbfounded, I looked at the others.

"Did Madeline just pick up a call at book club?" Ava asked.

"Hell, yes, she did," Hanna said.

"How many times did she torture me when I had a business call that I had to take? Buyers and sellers don't care about your plans or how late it is. But that didn't matter to her. No phone calls. And now she takes a call?"

Madeline returned a few minutes later. Stopping at the couch, she started to say, "I'm…

"I can't believe you were on the phone. After all these years of berating me, you broke your own damn rule," Ava interrupted her. "This better be good."

Madeline's steely gaze caught and held Ava's.

"Is there a problem?" I chimed in, trying to avoid a confrontation.

Madeline broke eye contact and turned toward me. "I don't think so. A misunderstanding between Stan and me."

"How could there ever be a misunderstanding between the two of you? Your rules are absolute – no one's allowed to break them." Ava sneered, using air quotes around the word "misunderstanding."

Madeline snapped her head toward Ava. "Your damn phone rings nonstop. Let them wait. You need to set boundaries with your clients. Calling you around the clock. Absurd."

Ava scrunched up her face. "And she's back. Just when I thought you grew a heart, bam, you come roaring back."

As Madeline squared off, I popped up. "All right, enough, you two. To her defense, I've never seen Madeline answer her phone before in one of our meetings. Is something wrong?"

Madeline deflated and collapsed into the closest chair. She took a few deep breaths, settling into the seat.

A few moments passed. "Madeline?"

Jaw clenched, she grabbed the armrests and pulled herself up. "I can't do this. I have to go."

"Wait. I'm sorry. I didn't realize you were upset about something. Sit down and tell us. Maybe we can help." Ava's voice was low and soothing.

Madeline hesitated, her body halfway out of the chair as she scanned the room with her eyes. She slowly sat back down. "There's nothing any of you can do. But thank you for asking," she said with a small smile.

"We're here to listen. Like you just did for me," Charlotte said. "We're not going to judge you. You helped me. Let me – let us – return the favor." She patted Madeline's hand.

Madeline cleared her throat. "The one thing I can't stand is pity. If I see that in anyone's eyes, even for a second, I'm out of here."

I remembered her telling me something similar when she talked about growing up in an alcoholic home. Did that have something to do with today?

"I'm going to tell you this once and no one is going to ask questions. Understood?"

Riveted, I put my glass on the table, inching closer.

"Stan thinks I'm being an overprotective parent with Sarah," she began.

Ava interrupted. "Just Sarah?"

Madeline glared at her.

"Shush. Don't interrupt. Why does Stan feel that way?" I asked.

Madeline turned toward me. "My mother and father were alcoholics. I see some of those tendencies in Sarah and Stan thinks I'm nuts. There, that's it in a nutshell."

For the second time tonight, all we could hear was the grandfather clock ticking.

"Hold on a second. Dropping that hefty parcel on us without delving into it? That's not how it works," Staci remarked. "In all the years of our book club gatherings, your childhood has never once surfaced. Not even during our ride home from Vermont, where I spilled about my tumultuous upbringing with my narcissistic mother. Take a look around. The expressions we wear aren't ones of pity, but of genuine concern. We want to help and support you."

I nodded. "Madeline, sharing is not a weakness. It makes you human."

Her face looked pensive as she proceeded. "The night of Bri's Christmas party, Sarah was arrested on a DUI."

It was so silent that I thought everyone could hear the beating of my heart. "Jesus, I'm so so sorry," I choked out. "Why didn't you call me?" Slowly, I grasped the magnitude of what she was saying.

Madeline sat in silence for a moment or two, her expression unreadable. "In the end, it all comes down to genetics." Madeline shook her head in disbelief. "I made sure to teach my two daughters about addiction at a young age, just in case. But, of course, Stan thought I was being ridiculous. I knew that I couldn't change their genetic makeup, but I could educate them and instill a healthy fear. My goal was for them to be afraid of experimenting with drugs and alcohol."

A hush fell over the room once more as we grappled with this new piece of information. It was shocking to learn that Madeline had been carrying such a weighty burden and hadn't shared it before. She always appeared so composed and in control.

"My Achilles heel," she admitted, taking a deep breath that seemed to catch in her throat. "My childhood was filled with years of abuse, neglect and total chaos. When I left for college, I never looked back. I wiped my hands clean of my parents. I've had nothing to do with people with addictive tendencies ever since. Not my problem," she paused, and her voice softened as she added, "but now, seeing one of my own daughters struggling… I just can't walk away."

The grandfather clock struck ten o'clock – each chime echoed through the still room.

Chapter 8

MADELINE

MY HEAD THROBBED as I lay in bed. I looked around for Stan, but he wasn't in the room. Jesus, it's so late in the morning. My head couldn't be throbbing this much from one glass of wine at book club last night. With a sigh, I swung my legs over the edge of the bed and inched my way toward the shower.

As the water beat down on me, I thought back to that night we picked Sarah up from the police station. Knowing how difficult this must be the desk sergeant was polite. We went into a room to talk, and I saw Sarah through a large, framed window. Shock overrode my normal demeanor, and I stood stoically, and quietly, absorbing.

She sat hunched at a table, rocking from side-to-side, wiping tears away. My beautiful, happy, honor student looked like hell. Fear and shock oozed out of my every one of my pores. I didn't hear anything the sergeant said. Just saw my baby framed in an image I knew I'd see every night when I closed my eyes. Lightheaded, I stepped back and supported myself against the wall. *Dear God in Heaven, not again.*

Noise from the bedroom snapped me back into the present and

I turned the water off. Stepping from the shower, I felt nauseated. A deep, dark fear lay in the pit of my stomach.

The damn mirror was fogged. I had forgotten to put on the fan. As I wiped the moisture with a towel, I thought back to my childhood home. We only had one bathroom and its mirror always fogged up. The fan never worked, ever. When things broke, they were never fixed. Even when the foundation cracked and started to buckle in the garage, nothing was done. My parents just parked their cars in the driveway.

What am I going to do? Sarah has no idea the danger she's in. I threw the moist towel in the hamper.

Maybe I should do what my grandmother did for me. She took me to an Alateen meeting. My grandma told me that it was a safe place for children of alcoholics to gather and talk, so they don't feel so alone.

That meeting was God-awful. I listened to teenagers say how their drunk parents beat them or abused them sexually. One young girl had been thrown out of the house at age eight and was in foster care. At the time, I didn't understand why my grandmother brought me to the meeting. But I did find some comfort in knowing that my life wasn't as messed up as others.

I was unbelievably naive when I was young. I thought my parents weren't that bad. But they were. I wish Sarah could see just how destructive alcohol could be on the families of alcoholics. She needs to see beyond the comfortable suburban bubble we created for her and face the harsh realities of the world outside. Addiction runs in families. Perhaps I should follow my grandmother's lead and bring her to an AA meeting because she is the one with the potential problem. I need her to see the absolute destruction alcohol can cause and the reality of addiction.

Stan was in the bedroom when I walked in. "I'm going to take Sarah to an AA meeting," I told him. I went into my walk-in closet and dressed in jeans and a sweater. The meeting gave me a place to start and a tangible thing to do rather than just ruminating.

Both of Stan's arms shot into the air. "What? She's not an alcoholic. She made a mistake. For Christ's sake!"

His harsh words shook me. Was I jumping to conclusions? Maybe it really was just a stupid mistake. But with every fiber of my being, I felt there was more to it.

"Stan, honey. There were times when Sarah was in high school that we should have paid more attention to. Like when she came home from spending the night at a friend's house and her dirty clothes reeked of beer. I chalked that up to normal teenage behavior." I walked to my dresser and put my watch on. "I even found her one morning sleeping in the family room on the floor. She smelled like vomit. Sarah told me she had eaten something with her friends that upset her stomach. She got physically sick and didn't want to wake us, so she slept downstairs and used the bathroom next to the family room. Again, I ignored the little voice in my head telling me something more might be going on."

Thinking back now, I could recall even more instances. *Did I just choose to ignore the warning signs?*

He just stared at me.

I took a deep breath. "You just don't understand." I pulled a pair of socks out of my dresser and turned toward Stan. "I know how this shit starts. Little party here, little party there and before you know it, it's a little party all the time. I need to protect her as best as I can. Otherwise, I'm not doing my job as her parent."

Stan plopped in a chair in our bedroom and dropped his head, running his hands through his hair. "So now, I'm not being a good parent?"

I shook my head. "No, that's not what I meant. You're a great parent. But you haven't had to deal with this. Addiction creeps up on you so gradually, festering and growing. Then, it's all you want.

It isolates and paralyzes you. And you're left battling it for the rest of your life."

"I simply can't fight you on this right now. I don't have it in me," Stan said.

He seemed to have shrunk in width and height since his partner and best friend had been arrested. His CPA business lay in shatters because of that betrayal. Stan couldn't handle anything else right now.

I picked up the picture of all four of us on my dresser. It was taken two years ago. My nagging mind just wouldn't let it go. I had to save her. "Honey, there's no need to fight. Everything will be okay. I'll take care of Sarah. She'll be home for two more weeks before she returns to college. I'll just make sure she understands what addiction is. That's all."

"I know you better than that." He leaned back in the chair. "You tend to overdo things."

"Nonsense," I said. "Trust me."

The furrow on Stan's brow said otherwise.

I went into the office and looked up AA meetings in our town. I found one in a nearby church and demanded Sarah attend it with me that night.

*

My heart pounded as we approached the door to the church, where the meeting was held. Why? I had promised myself I'd walk away from anyone in my life with an addiction problem – even my husband. But how do you walk away from your child? I took a deep breath and squared my shoulders, yanking the door open. I never thought I'd have to deal with this again.

"In you go, dear," I said to Sarah.

"Really?" She huffed past me.

We took seats in the back of the room. The format of the

meeting was similar to the one I'd attended with my grandmother thirty-plus years ago. Several people took the podium to talk about how alcohol had ruined their lives.

Sarah sat still for about forty minutes and two speakers, her face increasingly turning red. She whispered in my ear when a third speaker approached the podium. "Jesus, Mom. Look at these people. They're ancient. I'm not like them. For God's sake, I made a mistake. You're the one with the problem." She started to rise.

I put my hand around her arm, pulling back into her seat. "You will sit and listen until the meeting is over. Understood?"

She plunked down and slumped as far as she could in the chair. Her face was still crimson when the meeting ended, and she bolted out the door.

Neither of us spoke until I drove into our development. "Sarah, I'm trying to make you understand that addiction is a disease that runs in families. Those poor souls' lives in that meeting were turned upside down because of it. You heard their stories. I understand that it's hard to relate to older people, but I couldn't find a younger meeting. I will for the next one."

She reared straight up in the seat. "No way am I ever going to one of those again."

I took a deep breath. Maybe this is too much too soon. "All right. You don't have to go to another meeting as long as you and I see Dr. Mann before you go back to school."

"What?" Sarah turned her head and looked out the passenger window. "No, absolutely not."

I wanted to shake her. Couldn't she see I was trying to help? "You are going to Dr. Mann's. Or you're not going back to school."

"You're such a …

I held up my hand. "Careful."

"Ugh!" She kicked her feet under the dash.

When we got home, Sarah flew up the stairs and slammed her bedroom door.

Stan met me in the kitchen. "Looks like it went as well as I expected." He poured himself a glass of red wine from the bottle on the counter.

"Please pour one for me."

"Kind of ironic, don't you think?" he said as he handed me the glass.

"Yeah, it is." I exhaled. "Here I am coming home from an AA meeting and heading right for the wine."

Stan sat next to me, and we both lost ourselves in our thoughts.

"I'm not asking her not to drink. I want her to understand that she must be careful. That's all." I touched his arm.

Ah... my sweet Sarah. How do I reach you? You'd have been better off never touching the stuff. I'd been fortunate. The disease skipped me.

I held the stem of my wine glass. "She could have seen what the disease did to my parents had they lived longer. Sarah doesn't even remember them. She was four when they passed away." I took a long sip of wine. "Do you think I should tell her what Danny and I went through?"

Stan shrugged. "I don't know. But if you have that conversation with her, I'd like to sit in. I'm not sure I know everything."

"It's hard, Stan. Mortifying, in fact – to go back there and relive those times. The memories make me anxious. Afraid." I closed my eyes. "Here's a warm family recollection for you. I finally made chorus in seventh grade. I kept practicing and practicing until I made it. I was desperate to be with my friends. The practice was every Thursday night. We were rehearsing for a holiday concert. At the first practice, my mother picked me up on time. Shocker. After the second practice was over, I waited for one of my parents to pick me up. A few friends asked if they could bring me home, but I knew my parents would kill me if they came to pick me up and I wasn't there. So, I stood for an hour. I had to convince the choir teacher that my mother was definitely coming and watched as she finally left the parking lot. There I stood, freezing and all alone. It was December and damn cold."

"Jesus, honey. That's horrible. How late were they?"

"Those assholes never came. I walked five miles home in a pair of espadrilles with a short coat covering an even shorter dress. I had dressed up for practice. What an idiot I was back then."

"No. You weren't an idiot." Stan clasped my hand. "I'm so sorry."

I inhaled deeply. "The small country town I grew up in had no streetlights except at intersections, making the walk home very dark." My stomach ached as I retold this story. "I was walking along a section of street where the homes were close together. A man in a blue Camaro with long blonde hair pulled over to the sidewalk where I was and asked if he could bring me home. I was so cold. I thought about it. I'd be home in ten minutes if I went with him. But the hair on the back of my neck stood at attention. I didn't understand why I felt like that, because all my friends hitchhiked all over the place and no one thought about getting harmed or killed. But the feeling was so strong that I told the Camaro driver that I lived at the house I was standing in front of and walked down the driveway to the back of the house. The car drove away, and I waited another ten minutes in the cold. I was terrified and thought of knocking on the door of the house I was hiding behind and asking them to call my parents. But I knew they wouldn't come. I was on my own. The next two miles, I would get off the road if I saw headlines and hide behind a bush. I didn't want to see that blue Camaro again, especially on this part of the long, isolated and dark road."

"I can't believe your parents did that to you. What did they say when you walked in?"

"Where the hell had I been? I was late for dinner." I cleared my throat. "When I told them that they were supposed to pick me up after practice, they told me to quit or get my own damn ride home. Did I think they were my own private taxi service?"

"Oh, my God. Did you quit?"

"Hell, no. I worked so hard to make the choir. I figured it out."

I looked at my arms. Goosebumps spotted them, up and down the length of both arms.

Stan followed my gaze. He began to rub them. "Christ, you're cold."

"I told you. I relive this shit when I talk about it. That's why I'd rather not. Pour me another glass of wine. I'm getting a sweater."

When I returned to the kitchen, Stan said, "A student would never be left at a school alone today. The teacher would have to wait for a parent. I think that's a good rule."

"A lot of things are better today than in the seventies." The wine had a floral bouquet. I sipped it, inhaling deeply. "A young girl was found dead a day after my long walk home. I've always wondered if it had anything to do with the man in the blue Camaro."

"That's scary as shit."

"Yup." The wine turned sour in my mouth. I walked to the sink and poured it down the drain. "I don't think my childhood memories will move Sarah in a better direction. Maybe it's best to let Dr. Mann explain it. She might actually listen to her."

*

The next morning, I made Sarah's favorite blueberry pancakes for breakfast.

When she arrived at the table, she said, "What's this, an apology for dragging me to that awful meeting?"

"No, dear. I love you and I'm simply trying to do what's best." I handed her warm syrup from the microwave. "You need to see Dr. Mann."

She started to gripe, but I silenced her. "Yes, you are."

"Fine. Anything except those horrible AA meetings."

I called the doctor's office and was told they had an opening and could accommodate us at two.

"Ugh! Of course, anything Mama wants Mama gets, even a

last-minute appointment." Sarah barked and left the table, having taken only two bites from her pancakes.

We had both been patients before, so we didn't have to do that annoying assessment and were ushered right in. Sarah had struggled with friends in high school and Dr. Mann was able to help. Naturally, everything I said fell on deaf ears. I was hoping Dr. Mann could work her magic now on Sarah or on me. Maybe Stan's right and I was the one out in left field.

We managed to squeeze in two therapy sessions before her school break was over. Both seemed to go well, and Sarah stopped bitching at me for forcing her to go. After the first session, Dr. Mann pulled me aside and told me not to push too hard.

*

"You know, Mom, I don't have a problem. I don't wake up in the morning and look for the vodka." Sarah hauled her suitcase into the back of my SUV.

"Good," I said. "Let's get going. I'd like to be back before midnight."

I drove her to Lehigh University because we took her car away as part of her punishment for DUI. While I had taken Dr. Mann's advice and stopped pounding on her about addiction, it was a perfect opportunity to talk while I had her undivided attention on the drive.

"I swore I'd never drink when I was a child. I hated the smell of liquor."

Immediately, Sarah groaned. "God, Mom. Not again."

Ignoring her, I pushed on. "Instead, it's coffee I don't drink. It still surprises me. The two smells that dominated my childhood home were booze and coffee and I shun coffee."

Sarah edged closer to the passenger side window, turning her face away.

"It's hard not to drink when you're young with all eyes on you. I get it. I drank. But I knew what booze could do."

She bent forward, rummaging around in her purse on the floor, pulling out her constant companion – her earphones.

"Wait, before you put those in. I want to tell you one thing that happened when I was young. It has nothing to do with your grandparents."

Slamming the earphones into her lap, she sighed loudly. "Fine."

"I've talked a lot about addiction, but you don't have to be addicted to die from alcohol."

"Oh, for God's sake, Mom. Alcohol poisoning is all over the news. I know." She put her eyephones in and turned her head toward the window again.

I pulled the left bud out of her ear. "You said you'd listen to my story." I drove into a strip mall parking lot and turned off the engine.

"Why are you stopping? Let's go. I need to get to school."

"Because this story is hard for me to tell, and I don't want to drive while I tell it."

Sarah stared straight out of the windshield.

"When I was in my freshman year of college, your uncle Danny was a senior in high school and still home with our alcoholic parents. I spoke to him every day and he basically stayed as far away from our parents as possible, crashing at friends' homes most of the year," I began.

"I'm sorry Uncle Danny had a hard time. I truly am. Can we get going now?" Sarah's leg began bouncing.

"Listen, damnit." I shut my eyes, remembering the day Danny called me, hysterical.

"Mads. Pam's dead. I can't believe it. And it's all my fault. Oh, dear God," Danny had screamed into the phone.

Chapter 9

BRI

RUSHING OUT OF the house for my meeting with the web designer, I tripped over Eric's tennis bag. "Damn it," I yelled. Picking up the bag, I dropped it on the bench by the back door. I had an urge to kick it, but with my luck, these pointed boots would poke a hole in one of his tennis rackets. And God forbid anything happened to his precious sporting equipment. You'd think if it was so damn important, he'd learn how to take care of it. *Men*.

Slamming the door to the garage, my phone rang. Once in the car, I heard a ding indicating a voicemail. Looking at it, I didn't recognize the number and tapped the icon to listen.

"Hi Bri. I'm Cindy Rowan. Hanna gave me your number. Emily, a young girl in our neighborhood, has leukemia and needs a bone marrow transplant. The mother is a match, but their medical bills are mounting. The neighbors want to help and have started an online page to donate money. We thought a small event would generate local awareness – neighbor helping neighbor. That sort of thing. We haven't a clue where to begin. Hanna thought you could help. Any advice you could give us would be great. Call me anytime on his number. Thank you."

I called her immediately.

*

Two weeks later, boxes were brought into my kitchen by a couple of volunteers. I tore one of them open and pulled out a custom T-shirt we'd designed to raise money through a drive at the local schools for Emily. I was honored to be helping this beleaguered family and their precious daughter. No one should go through this alone.

"Cindy, come look at these," I called.

She put a box of mediums next to me as I held up the T-shirt. "They look great. I like the *We can do this together* slogan on the back." Cindy flipped the T-shirt around. "Emily's so precious," she said, her voice breaking as she looked at the young girl's picture on the front.

I laid out the remaining shirts according to size on my dining room table. I had no plans to charge any fees for my services and even placed the order on my credit card so that I could be reimbursed when the shirts sold. I wondered if Nicole, my ex-boss, ever did anything pro bono. I doubted it.

Emily's family was the first official client of my new company, A Perfect Event. And what a great cause as my launch pad. Thanks to my friends, who have been giving my business card to their connections, I already had two other small events to plan.

Cindy took the small tees and put them into a box marked S. "I'll bring the shirts to the schools. Our volunteers will sell them during lunch periods and at after-school activities."

"Perfect. I'm putting together a box of multiple sizes for The Busy Bean coffee shop. The owner offered to sell them."

"Wonderful. That place is always busy, and people come from neighboring towns," Cindy said.

"Come on. I'll help load the boxes for the schools into your cars." I picked one up and headed for the door. The volunteers followed.

After everyone left, I thought back to when I was eight years old, like Emily. I had been living with my mother's parents for two years by then. My mother died in a car accident when I was six and soon after, my father dropped me off at my grandparents. I haven't seen him since. No cards, no calls – no communication at all. I don't even know if he's alive. Vanished without a trace.

God, if I had needed a bone marrow donor back then, I would have died. My seventy-year-old grandparents were too old, and I have no siblings or cousins.

How the hell do you abandon a child? Ever? On our last day together, we went for a fall walk on a tree-lined path. It was just a month after my mother had died.

I can still hear his voice. "Brianna, honey. Daddy's going away. You are going to stay with Nana and Papa. Won't that be fun? You can swim in their pool all the time and not have to wait to visit."

I remembered leaves twirling around my feet when the cold breeze picked up. He straightened my hat and buttoned my coat. He told me Nana and Papa were excited to have me stay with them.

A day later, I stood at their front door, tears streaming down my cheeks as my father drove away. I waved good-bye, trying to be strong, even though I had just lost my mother, my father, my home, and everything familiar to me. *But children are resilient. Right?*

A chill coursed through me. Okay, enough of all that. It's long past and I had a job to do.

That's right. I have a job. And one I love. Being fired a few months ago seemed like the best thing that could have happened to me. I was making a difference – helping a family at the worst point in their lives. It gave me a sense of community, but more than that, it was a worthwhile purpose. A reason to spring out of bed every morning.

*

The Busy Bean buzzed with afternoon pick-me-uppers, who needed a caffeine jolt late in the day. Juggling the large, heavy box at the front counter, I asked, "Is Tara here?"

"In the back, making fresh scones," the counterperson said. Tara must have heard me and poked her head out from the back room. "Hi Bri."

"Here are the T-shirts for Emily." I looked around the shop. "Where would you like them?"

She wiped her hands on her apron and gestured for me to follow. Tara walked to the far-left side of the store. "Let's empty these two shelves," she said, grabbing some decorative plates and bowls.

I laid the box on the floor and removed some bags of coffee and tea for sale on the upper shelf. I followed Tara as we dodged patrons on our way to the back of the shop. "I brought a small poster with Emily's story and the price of the shirts."

"Great. That makes it much easier for us to sell them."

"This place is hopping. I usually come in the morning rush."

"I'm blessed. It's always busy." She placed the plates and bowls on the counter. "The locals come here rather than the chain coffeehouse down the street." Tara clasped her hands together as if in prayer.

"Well, that's because your coffee is phenomenal." The aroma of the shop tickled my nose, and I could almost taste my favorite blend. "I'll put the shirts on the shelves."

Tara nodded and went back to making scones.

I placed the neatly folded tees on the shelves. I brought a small easel that fit nicely between some of the shirts. I placed the poster there. Stepping back to get a better view of the display, I heard a familiar screech.

"Well, well. Look who we have here. Miss PTO. How quaintly provincial this is," Nicole uttered behind me.

My shoulders instantly rose, and a shiver slivered down my spine. I closed my eyes, hoping it was just a bad daydream.

"Well, hello, Bri. Looks like you're keeping busy," she sniggered.

I turned toward her. "Hello, Nicole."

"This display looks like your standard PTO design. Fits you, not much originality." She shook her head, laughing. "Good luck with it."

I wilted. My happy mood had disappeared. *God, how I hate her.* I bowed my head. Damnit. Someday, Nicole, I'm going to wipe that smile off your face.

*

I couldn't get that bitch, Nicole, out of my head. She humiliated me yesterday. My doorbell rang. Taking a deep breath, I rose from the kitchen table, trying to push the incident out of my mind.

"Hey, Bri." I heard Ava's sing-song voice as I opened the front door.

She was helping me sell the T-shirts and had come over to pick up some boxes. All my friends had offered to pinch in. I didn't know where I'd be without them.

Ava and I walked into the kitchen. I pointed to the boxes by the chair. "There are two of every size. Whatever you don't sell, just return to me."

"Tell me how much both boxes of shirts are?" Ava pulled out her checkbook. "And who do I make the check payable to?"

"I thought you were going to sell them. Not make a donation."

"No. I decided to give them to clients and friends and tell them all about Emily and her family. My clients tend to be local. They'd welcome helping a neighbor, especially someone in crisis."

"That would be awesome."

Ava handed me the check, grinning.

"You're especially cheery today," I said, placing the check in my wallet.

"I am. I just came from Aiding the Children. They're going to honor Sister Mary Joseph for her fifty years of service at their annual gala this year."

"It's about time somebody honored her. She's a living saint. How long have you been helping her?" I asked.

"About fifteen years," Ava said. "I can't tell you how many children I've transported with their families to and from the hospital and to checkups."

"You should be recognized, too."

Ava shook her head. "No. I don't do all that much. It's all Sister. She's worthy of every accolade she gets. She does everything for those families and makes it look easy. It isn't. She has to find a hospital and doctor who will perform the surgery for free, then organize a place to stay for the child and the family and provide transportation. It's a lot of balls in the air. And she does it smoothly and efficiently."

"That's a demanding job, especially since she does it for free," I said.

"Can you imagine serving others your entire life? With no thought of yourself. I'll tell you; Sister Mary Joseph inspired me from the moment we met. I don't think I realized how much until recently," Ava said.

"Sister is one of those truly special people. Do you want us all to buy tickets to the gala? When is it?" Bri asked.

"Yes, I do. But – and this is the important thing – Aiding the Children needs an event planner and I think you should apply."

I was staggered at the idea. "What?"

"My friend Joselyn is on the board, and she told me that the event coordinator's favorite planner is ill, so they need a replacement immediately," Ava said.

"I don't know. I mean, you're right; this is a great opportunity. But I'm not sure I'm up to the task." I told Ava about my run-in with Nicole yesterday.

"Don't you dare let her make you feel inferior. I hope I run into her someday. I'll give her a tongue lashing she'll never get over." Ava's voice rose as she spoke.

"Thanks. But I'll deal with her," I said, despite not feeling that confident.

Ava rummaged in her tote. "Forget her. Let's get back to the gala. Here is the program from their last event. I thought it might help you come up with something amazing."

I took the program from her. "When is the gala? Do they want a proposal?"

"In about six weeks. And yes, by Friday."

I sank into my chair. "Impossible. No way I can do that."

"Hey, don't give up. You can do this. How much harder can it be than the Build-A-Home event you did last summer with Madeline?"

"A lot. For one thing, it was a local event and Madeline did half the work. This is so much bigger. It's the New Jersey chapter of a national non-profit."

"So? What's the worst thing that can happen? You don't get the job."

*

Four days later, exhausted from lack of sleep but totally keyed up, I sat before the charity coordinator of Aiding the Children and Mother Superior Catherine Marie at the Sisters of Charitable Care. The convent itself had been a gilded aged mansion once, with stables and other buildings set high on Bernardsville Mountain. At the clifftop sat the remnants of a brick building, weathered and worn, resembling the ancient ruins scattered across Europe. Beyond the peak, an expansive view unfolded, revealing miles of gently sloping, undulating hills. I had been to other fundraisers here and knew the property well. I drew up plans to hold the event by the ruin. I thought it was the perfect place, with one of their own being honored.

"Thank you both for this opportunity," I said, deciding to keep it short. My hands shook as I opened the portfolio.

The rendering I held up was a mockup of the venue titled Angels in our Midst Gala.

Mother Superior stood and walked over to the poster. "This is here?" She pointed out the window to the ruin.

"Yes. I thought it was the perfect place."

Evelyn Woodall, the charity coordinator, said, "What a good idea."

They stared at the poster for a while and then began asking questions about the costs and logistics involved.

"The area can be transformed fairly inexpensively, so more money will go to the cause. We will, of course, need to rent a tent in case of rain." I reviewed additional posters, showing what the various event areas would look like. "I thought we'd put the silent auction here on the border of the parking lot under a tent."

Mother Superior looked out the window and back at the area suggested for a dining space. "Yes, it's big enough to handle three-hundred guests."

I slid out the final poster. "Plus, there's tons of parking already here."

"Is that fabric?" Evelyn asked, pointing to the initial poster.

"It's tulle. I'll drape it high over the dinner tables and other areas with tiny twinkling lights."

"There's an ethereal romanticism about the way it looks. I love it," said Evelyn.

As I concluded my proposal, a bit out of breath, I realized how much I wanted this.

"Lovely, just lovely," Mother Superior said to me as I packed my posters.

"Indeed," Evelyn said. "We'll be in touch in a couple of days."

With a grateful smile, I exited the office, relieved and proud that I had successfully planned the event. I hoped it would meet their expectations. As I stepped into the reception area, I was grinning ear to ear.

I stopped short. *Holy shit!* I tried to regain my composure, but my face felt hot.

"You've got to be kidding. You? This isn't some T-shirt sale.

You don't have the skills for an event this big. What a joke!" Nicole sneered.

Stung, I inhaled deeply. Nicole's worker bees buzzed around, holding files, large posters and color boards. I willed my legs forward, but they wouldn't move.

Nicole approached. "Did you tell them you tried to seduce a client?" She snickered. "No? It's okay, I'll tell them."

I dropped my portfolio. I quickly bent down to retrieve the scattered pages, flashing back through how badly she'd always treated me. Every time she was bitchy spooled out before me in slow motion. Every damn criticism cut me. My civility evaporated. Taking a step toward her, staring into those beady eyes, I itched to slam her into the wall.

No! I dug down deep. No, I won't let her see me upset. Outbursts never win. And I need to act professionally, even if she doesn't. Inhaling, I squashed my anger as I walked to the exit. Turning back, I faced her. "You're wrong. I do have the skills for an event of this size. Good luck. You're gonna need it."

As I walked down the steps, I heard Nicole tell the receptionist in a loud, agitated voice, "Make sure you tell your Mother Superior that that woman is totally inexperienced. I actually had to fire her. I don't want to speak ill of people, so you just let them know."

Her frantic voice betrayed her. I prayed she was as worried as she sounded.

*

Half an hour later, I met Ava for lunch. My hands had stopped shaking by the time I entered Redwoods. She waved to me from a table by the window.

Patting the chair for me to sit, she asked, "Well, did you knock'em out? I totally loved your proposal. Come on, tell me all about it."

"Ahhh…" I relayed what had happened.

"You have to be shitting me." She slammed her hand on the table. "That's it. I don't care what you say, I'm going to call my friend on the board. This is wrong on so many levels. I'm speechless."

Holding up both hands, I stopped her. "Absolutely not! I get this job on my own merits or I don't. I mean it, Ava. No favors."

She started sputtering in Spanish and I looked at the menu, realizing I hadn't eaten much for the past few days. And no breakfast today, either.

I stared out the window until Ava calmed down and returned to English. I remembered some shrink somewhere or other telling me that we are doomed to repeat our mistakes until we learn from them. But what the hell was I supposed to learn from this?

Chapter 10

HANNA

"Hanna, I'm in the foyer with the dogs ready to go," Mark yelled upstairs.

I sprang down the back staircase trying to put on my coat at the same time. "Coming." I flew through the kitchen and picked up the house keys because I knew he'd forgotten. Mark's elbow was balanced on the newel post, calmly swiping through his emails on his phone when I popped into the foyer. The dogs' tails were wagging furiously. They loved going for walks.

He looked up. "Which critter do you want today?" Mark held out both leashes. His cheeks were still flushed from an earlier work-out in the basement.

"Rusty, I guess. He pulls the least." I grabbed the Saint Bernard's harness. Lucky, our Labrador, was smaller, but he yanked me all over the place.

"Chop. Chop. I have to be at work in an hour." He dashed out the door and down our front steps while I struggled to zip my coat on the landing.

Rusty, caught up in Mark's swiftness, spun around and bolted after him, nearly pulling me off the landing and down the stairs. I yanked hard on his harness, holding tight to the handrail at the same time. "Jesus. Wait."

Mark stopped and started jogging in place until I caught up.

"What, are you trying out for the Olympics?" I asked.

He laughed and spread his arms wide. "Are you having a bad morning? Do you need a hug?"

I curled into his arms, but the dogs weren't having it. They started pulling hard on their leashes. "Ok. Ok. Let's go," I said, annoyed.

Both dogs snorted and bounded forward. For the next half hour, we walked around the neighborhood. Mark talked nonstop about his latest project at work. I tried to be fully in the moment, but my mind drifted to my guilt about Jim. My sister was right. If I told him now, he'd be enraged. *Damn. I should have told him then.*

"Hey, Hanna. What's up? Did you hear me?"

Startled, I stopped. "Yes, of course. I was… I was just looking at their deck." I pointed. "Isn't that nice?" Not sure that was even slightly believable.

He turned to look at the deck. "It's okay, I guess. Is something bothering you? You don't seem yourself today."

"I'm fine." I shook my head at his concern. "Really."

He glanced at me and then at his watch. "We've got to hurry or I'll be late."

*

I watched Mark drive away from the house before collapsing into a family room chair. Sarah's warning had stopped me from telling Mark about Jim. I should have told Mark when he came home from his trip and confessed that a naked woman had been left as a gift in his hotel room as some sort of archaic business custom. I remembered him pacing saying, *honestly, honey, nothing happened. I asked her to leave and left the room.*

I should have confessed then. When he was sorry about being away all the time, letting work consume him. Not now, eight months later. I stood and rummaged through the bookcase until I found the picture of Jim and me that Staci took at Katie's soccer match. I marched to my office and put the picture through the shredder.

But the shredder couldn't destroy what had happened. Mark and I were in a good place. I didn't want to upset that.

My cell rang. It was my mother. I pushed my anxiety away and answered.

*

"Hanna. Help me," Mark whined from the office.

Leaving the dinner dishes to dry in the drainer, I walked to his desk, wiping my hands on a towel. "Yes, dear."

"You use Facebook, right?"

"Yup," I replied.

"How the hell do you set this up?" He threw his hands in the air. "My buddies are always badgering me to post my ski pictures so I don't have to send them in texts."

I laughed. "You can't be serious. Children can set up a Facebook account in less than five minutes. And yet you, Mr. Technical, need my help."

"Yeah. Well. You can do this with your eyes shut. Come on. Just do it for me." He turned back to the computer.

I took my towel, twirled it, and flicked it at his back. I spun the towel again, but Mark turned around quickly and caught one end.

"Come on. Please." He drew the towel into him and I followed, laughing, until I was sitting on his lap and he was kissing my neck.

"All right. But I want some more of those kisses later." I stood, letting him stand before I took his chair. "Did you want to use your name or a nickname?"

"My name is fine. I'm getting another glass of wine. Do you want one?"

"No," I answered, already typing the keys.

By the time he returned to the office, the account was set up. "Done," I said.

"Wow. That was fast."

I gave him a five-minute tutorial about Facebook and how to post images. "Have fun. I'm going to finish cleaning the kitchen. I'll meet you upstairs." I wrapped my arms around his neck. "Don't forget you promised me more kisses."

An hour later, I stopped in the office.

"Which picture of me do you like better?" he asked.

I came up and stood behind him at the computer. "What, for your profile?"

"Yes." He brought up seven pictures, one after the other. "Maybe one of these?"

"Don't be a prima donna. Just pick one." I laughed and said I was going to bed.

I brought my iPad with me as I crawled under the covers to check out my Facebook page. My love/hate relationship with the app means I stay dormant for months at a time. Then I'll get a call from a distant friend or relative asking if I'm okay. The conversation always turns to *you can tell me – happy people always post and you haven't.* This hollow wisdom makes me cringe. Of course, the key for me is distance. The fringe people in my life don't need a daily, weekly, or even monthly update.

Redirecting myself, I clicked on notifications. Yikes. There must be a thousand here dating back to the summer. Scrolling through the multitudes, I like some and ignore others until I came to a few posts from September. There were a series of pictures I was tagged in. The first picture was of Ginny and Greg, a married couple who had been practicing for the marathon with me that day at the shore.

Shit. I don't remember anyone taking pictures. My heart pounded. My finger hovered over the arrow for the next image.

Then I clicked fast, hoping I was overreacting. I recognized Jim and his daughter making a sandcastle. *Crap. I don't remember that.* Several of the next pictures showed our training team running the 10K that Jim had planned out for us. But as I clicked the next arrow, I gasped. There was Jim and me from a distance. I'm standing slightly to one side, facing him with my back to the camera. He's looking into my eyes with his arm around my shoulder. *Oh, dear God.* The next minute, Jim would lean in and kiss me. I clicked through the rest of the pictures, my body shaking. To my slight relief, there was no picture of us kissing. But whoever took that picture must have seen us kiss.

Underneath the picture, someone put "Hey Jimbo, who's the babe?"

I ran to the bathroom. Bile rising.

Later that evening, I felt Mark slip into bed. I prayed he thought I was sound asleep. I could barely breathe, much less talk.

*

Mark strolled into the kitchen the next morning after the kids were done with their breakfast and scrambled outside to play. It was a crisp Saturday morning.

Avoiding eye contact, I asked, "Did you finally decide on a profile picture?" I decided in the wee hours of the morning to act as normal as possible this morning until I had a chance to process what I saw.

"You'll never guess who reached out to me on Facebook." He picked up a cup and poured some coffee.

"No, probably not." I closed the utensil drawer trying to sound uninterested, but I was scared shitless.

"Melissa."

"Who?" I turned to face him.

"You remember her. My old girlfriend. Can you believe that? Like – what was I on, an hour? And she found me. Unbelievable."

I walked over to the sink and picked up the sponge. I didn't want him to see my face. Hiding any telltale signs of my anxiety. Wiping the counter again, relaxing my cheeks and forehead with each swipe, I breathed in and out. How easily he tells me his ex-girlfriend contacted him. Cockiness aside, he spit it right out. No coverup. Nothing like his lying wife.

"Hanna. I think that spot on the counter is clean," he teased me. I stopped wiping. Shame oozed into my mouth with its bitter, chalk-like taste, making it hard to talk. "Ah." I cleared my throat. "Yeah. I think so too." I quickly moved to the stove. "Did you have fun catching up?" I still couldn't look at him.

"I only answered her direct message and told her I was happily married with kids. She mentioned her ongoing divorce, which made me feel sightly uncomfortable. I excused myself, claiming that I needed to put my kids to bed." He turned the screen of his phone towards me, showing me his updated profile picture. "See, I changed it to one of us together. That way anyone looking knows I'm off the market."

Now. Right now. I'm gonna tell him. Working up the courage, I turned to face him. "Mark." Both kids bolted through the kitchen door, Katie chasing Brandon, screaming she was going to murder him.

"Hey. Stop it. No running in the house." Mark put his coffee on the table. "Hold that thought. I better see what's going on."

He left the kitchen and I let out a deep, long breath. I couldn't believe I almost blurted it out. I needed to think this through. As I put the sponge into the drainer, I decided to do one thing. Unfriend Mark's ex-girlfriend. If things go south with us, I don't want him turning to her for comfort.

*

Three days later, I stood in Madeline's home alongside Bri and Ava, helping our friend figure out what was worth saving and what needed to be thrown out before she downsized.

"Ava, I must say that the three-bedroom townhouse in Bedminster is perfect. Thank you for finding that for us," Madeline said as she led us into her basement. "But as you can see, I simply can't take all of this with me." She pointed to the walls of cabinets and neatly stacked shelves of decorations for every occasion, along with multiple sets of china, clothing, and photo albums.

"Whoa, Madeline. This looks like Home Goods on steroids." I walked to the closest cabinet, not believing my eyes. "You actually typed up labels for all these?"

"Well, how else would you know what's in them?" she replied, raising her eyebrows.

Madeline looked impeccable in a crisp white shirt tucked into her pants, cinched with a silver and black belt. The creases in her black trousers ran sharp lines down the legs, neatly laying over her low-heeled, black boots. Her precision bob was her trademark, and she never had a hair out of place. I, on the other hand, had thrown on a faded sweatshirt and my ripped jeans, complemented by sneakers featuring a gash on one side. I completed my sorry-ass look with no makeup, my hair in a sloppy pony.

Turning my attention away from her, I looked around. "It's huge down here. I can't believe I've never seen your basement before."

"We never finished it, so we use it just for storage. Unless someone helps me put away decorations or glassware, there's no reason to come down to this dark, dusty place." Madeline gestured with her hand like she was trying to push away the dust in the air.

Ava, armed with a clipboard uttered, "I'll be right back." She went upstairs.

"Dusty? There are no dust balls anywhere." Bri picked up a box marked First Grade and ran her hand over it. "Look, nothing. And knowing you, you filled this box years ago."

Madeline walked over to Bri and pulled out a folder with Sarah's name on it. "She made this dinosaur picture with sponges and paint." She stared at it, her cheeks flushed.

Her eyes held a glazed-over stare, distant, almost sad. I wanted to know what was going on inside her head, but probably the issue was related to Sarah and her recent DUI. So I decided not to probe and took a box marked Third Grade, popping open the top. "I just loved it when the kids came home with pictures they drew for us," I said.

"Me too," Bri agreed. "Although I ran out of room on the refrigerator by the first week of school."

Madeline took the box from Bri. "Please put the school stuff on this table. I'll go through them later."

I heard Ava in the foyer above us. Her heels on the tile floor click-clacking, a crisp, echoing sound that set my nerves on edge. Though maybe my nerves were already on edge, having nothing to do with Ava and her high heels. Placing one of the school boxes on the table, I told myself to stop focusing on my guilt.

Ava came downstairs, talking rapidly before she rounded the corner of the staircase. "Madeline, I made a list of things we need to discuss." She held out her clipboard. "I'll go over them with you when we're done organizing down here."

She took off her red blazer and draped it over a chair. Ava also wore a white shirt. Hers was silk. Who wears white to organize a basement? At least Bri had on a pair of jeans and a black turtleneck. Much more appropriate for basement clearing.

"What day is the estate sale?" Bri asked.

Madeline suddenly looked tired. "Too soon. That's when."

"Two weeks from Saturday," Ava said. "The Velvet Glove is organizing and running the sale. They're super careful." She nodded at Madeline.

We all shared a collective look of understanding. Whomever Ava hired was going to have to be the best of the best when it came to Madeline's possessions.

Picking up a game of Monopoly to pack in one of the boxes, I instantly thought about game night at my house this coming Saturday. My brother-in-law Josh would be there. Had Sarah told him about the kiss? About Jim? He's like a brother to my husband. Did she tell him? She said she wouldn't. But most spouses tell each other everything, no matter what they promise. Would he look at me differently? Is that how I'd know?

My stomach tightened. I wasn't sure I could deal with that. I didn't think I could spend much time with Josh if he knew. How could I even look at him?

"What did you say? Speak up." Madeline stood beside me, her arms full.

"Nothing. Just muttering to myself." I lugged the box filled with games over to the designated spot for items to be taken to the new house. I wondered if Madeline suspected that I was worried. Trying to change the subject, I blurted out, "Bri, what's the book we're supposed to read this month?"

"Seriously, don't you read her emails? Ever?" Madeline asked, her voice filled with weariness and frustration.

I wracked my brain, trying to remember. "Oh, wait. It's that World War II story with the sister's book. Right?"

Madeline sighed and dropped the heavy box she was carrying with a thud. She stood a moment catching her breath. "I just don't have the energy for this right now."

My body tensed. I knew she was talking about me. That she didn't have the energy for my inability to remember book titles or dates. But she had a point. I'd been so distracted since last summer, rambling on about nonsense most of the time. My fear of confessing to my husband had made me an anxious mess.

Bri came over and put her hand on Madeline's back. "Why don't you take a break? Why don't we all? I could use some water."

Madeline nodded. "Where are my manners? Come on. I have some sandwiches and drinks upstairs."

When we finished our lunch and started tidying the kitchen, Bri asked, "I know this is an overwhelming time, but are you sad about selling?"

"No. I don't think so. We don't want to stretch ourselves too thin financially since James got us into this mess," she said.

Madeline glided through her kitchen with ease, knowing every inch and curve. Who would have suspected James Shepard, Stan's long-time pal and partner, was a criminal? He and Stan ran parallel CPA companies and saved on overhead by sharing resources, such as office rent. They even went on family vacations together. When the police took James away in handcuffs, the huge scandal resulted in Stan losing many of his clients. He was – they were starting over.

Ava put a plate into the dishwasher. "The townhouse they're purchasing is incredible. They'll be very happy there."

Madeline agreed and we all followed her back into the basement. "Ok, let's finish for the day with this cabinet of glassware. I have bubble wrap over there." She pointed.

We each took a shelf. Bubble wrap popped as we twisted it around the glasses.

"I'm astonished that you finished next month's book in less than a week with everything on your plate," Bri said, continuing our conversation from lunch. Madeline had told us exactly what she thought of the book at lunch. "You don't have to come to every meeting, you know."

"Why be part of a book club and not go? That doesn't make sense to me." Madeline paused. "Well, unless I'm on vacation." She carefully placed a wrapped glass in a box. "I don't always like the books we've read, though."

When Madeline disliked a book, she expressed her opinion quite succinctly. I wished I'd taped her when we read *Fifty Shades of Grey*, and she'd spent about an hour deriding Charlotte for picking it.

In a light-hearted tone, I said, "Well, maybe you'd like *Madam Bovary*. You're always trying to get us to read a classic."

Madeline stopped packing and her sheet of bubble wrap floated to the floor. Staring. Silent.

I turned away; afraid she could read my mind. Cold stabbed at me. *What a blunder. Say something, you idiot.* I turned and faced Ava. "Hey, how is Neil doing?"

Madeline tugged my arm, frowning. "Not again. No deflection this time. You're always bringing up books about adultery. Why?"

I shuddered. "What are you talking about?" Shaking my head, I turned away.

Madeline stepped forward and raised her index finger. "First, there was *Anna Karenina* on our tenth anniversary of book club." Second finger. "Then, *The Girl on the Train*, last November." Third finger. "At Bri's Christmas party, you suggested *Heartburn*. There may have been another one. Oh. Yes. At last month's book club, you wanted to read *The Great Gatsby*." She paused. "And now, *Madame Bovary*. I mean, it couldn't be more obvious."

My heart pounded in my ears. She'd never let this go. *Damn it.* Speechless, I stood in silence for ten seconds, though it felt like twenty minutes.

Ava and Bri stopped packing and turned toward me. I wanted to bolt upstairs and fly home. But knowing them, they'd follow.

Clearing my throat, I said, "I have no idea what you're talking about."

Madeline's face relaxed. "Come on. Something's up."

"Hanna. Is something wrong?" Bri interrupted walking toward me. "We're your friends. Anything you say will stay in this room. You're safe here. Maybe we can help."

I gulped, then dropped into a chair by the table, burying my face in my hands. "I'm in a real mess and don't know what to do."

They all moved close to me. I told them about Jim and that kiss on the beach and the pictures I found on Facebook.

When I finished, they all started talking at once. I closed my eyes. My head ached.

"This is eating me up," I whispered. "Now you know, and my sister knows, and she probably told her husband Josh. And you'll all tell your husbands and pretty soon I won't have to tell Mark because he'll hear it everywhere he goes."

Bri bent and hugged me.

"My sister told me not to tell Mark. If he found out, it could be the end." A tear traveled down my cheek as I imagined my children living in two separate homes. My heart broke, thinking of it.

"What? It was just a stupid-ass kiss. I agree with your sister. No need to say anything," Ava stated. "If you tell him, Mark could get angry, especially since you didn't tell him for so long. Just leave it alone. It didn't mean anything."

My shoulders dropped in relief as I exhaled deeply for the first time all day.

"Are you nuts, Ava? I think it did mean something. Remember that picture Staci took of Hanna, Katie and him at that soccer game. It was definitely more than just a kiss and relationships are based on honesty. She must tell Mark." Madeline picked up the fallen piece of bubble wrap. "And now with that picture on Facebook, she has no choice."

My mouth opened and closed. "I was lonely and angry at Mark for never being around. I did like Jim and I thought about him a lot back then. But as soon as he kissed me it was like an electric shock snapping me out of my fantasy and back to reality." I stood.

"You have to tell him. It's the right thing to do." Madeline's voice raised several octaves as she drew out the final words.

Ava interrupted, asking, "Do you still have feelings for Jim?"

I tried to keep my composure, but it was difficult. My voice shook as I replied, "No. I mean, I appreciate him and all, but I'm not in love with him. I haven't seen him in months." Please, let's change the subject. He stopped coaching Katie in soccer and me in the running club."

"So, you don't see him at all?" Madeline persisted. "It's over? Whatever 'it' was?"

My jaw clenched. "Yes, it's over. If it was ever anything at all."

Turning toward Bri, my words quiet but urgent, I asked, "Do you think I should tell him?" My hands shook as I pushed my hair back from my face.

Bri squeezed me tight, her gentle demeanor radiating reassurance. "It will be less painful if you tell him yourself then if he finds out from someone else."

Chapter 11

CHARLOTTE

ISTRACTED BY MY never-ending thoughts these last four days about Maxwell getting back with his ex-wife, and mortified by my behavior at the restaurant, I almost slammed right into a couple exiting Tatianna's Café.

"Jesus. Watch out."

Shocked, I looked left. The voice was altogether too familiar – and not in a good way.

"Well, well. Look who's in my neck of the woods." My ex-husband, Grant, stood there with a smug expression that made me want to hit him. "You already heard the news and came to see for yourself."

Oh God. Not him. Not now. Shaking my head, I asked, "What are you talking about? I just came…"

Not letting me finish, he said, "Misty, this is my ex-wife." He pointed at me with his free hand. "Charlotte, this is my fiancée, Misty."

What? Shocked, I started to tell him I was at my doctor for my annual checkup but stopped.

Misty wrapped her arm snugly around Grant's.

Like that will keep him tethered. My ex-husband slithers into other women's arms faster than a cheetah chases prey.

"So, you just happened to be here? Right." He looked at his fiancée with a smirk, insinuating that I had come here solely to run into him.

I opened my mouth and closed it. I opened it again, then shut it. I must have looked like a dying fish gasping for air. Floored by his announcement, I couldn't make my body or mind work. I just stood there like a fence post.

The doctor had told me earlier that my blood pressure was high. It must be in the stratosphere now. *Damn it.* All I wanted was a tuna sandwich from Lorelai's down the street. Not his shit. It's 11:30 am on a Wednesday. It never occurred to me that I'd run into him at this hour. Grant had moved to Summit after our divorce. Except for my doctor, I never come here. Initially, I didn't want to see him out dating other women. Now, I just don't want anything to do with him.

"Well? Are you going to congratulate us or not?" he said in his usual mocking tone.

The day closed in on me. "Congratulations." It was all I could come up with – wanting desperately to extradite myself and continue to Lorelai's. Not that I was hungry anymore.

Misty watched our exchange with an unreadable expression, then said, "Oh, Grant is such a romantic, as I'm sure you know." She stared up at him adoringly with large blue eyes.

I could hear Madeline in my head. They're not large; they're bug eyes. I suppressed a smile.

"Thank you, darling." He kissed the top of her head as he noticed a group of women cross the street. Two of them looked back, checking him out. I'm sure they loved his thick, disheveled chestnut hair or his broad shoulders too tightly wrapped in his t-shirt. He gave them his typical haughty grin, then winked. The expression that says call me. Cocksure. Obnoxious. He hadn't changed at all.

In a moment of sisterhood solidarity, I wanted to tell Misty to run. Get out now. But she'd never believe a word I said.

She squeezed his captured arm tighter, showing off what looked like a three-carat diamond ring. Her ring finger wiggled, catching the sun's rays. She's sly making me notice it without talking about it. "Such a romantic," she repeated. "The night he proposed —what a magical night!" She pressed her body against his. *Christ.* She had to be twenty years younger than me, with long blonde hair and a body honed by fitness trainers.

"Yes, it was," Grant purred, nestling into her. "I rented out the rooftop section of our favorite restaurant in New York City and serenaded her through dinner with a three-piece jazz ensemble."

I wanted to puke. They're both insufferable. Misty continued to babble on about the type of wedding she wanted. Ignoring her, I dug my nails into my right palm. *Just walk away. Why was I still standing here?* I tried to speak but could only clear my throat.

"Don't tell the boys. I'll call them tonight and let them know the good news," Grant instructed me.

Finally, I pushed out, "I hope you'll be very happy."

"Oh, we will be." Misty beamed at me. Confident.

Sure. Time will tell.

Grant took a step. "Let's get home."

"It's fun having a day off in the middle of the week." Misty, still clutching his arm, walked past me. "I'm sure we can think of something to occupy ourselves with this afternoon."

Poor thing doesn't know what she's in for. We were both headed in the same direction, so I waited to let them go ahead.

At the crosswalk, I heard him say, "I can't believe she found out so fast. See how possessive she is? That's why I'm not with her anymore. Couldn't breathe," Grant said loud enough for everyone around to hear.

Possessive? Maybe I was. But I didn't like sharing my husband with other women. Lots of other women. Good luck to her. I don't need that in my life anymore.

"She's so much older than I thought she'd be." Misty giggled. "Definitely too old for you, my handsome man."

Grant turned around and looked at me.

Pivoting, I crossed the street. I didn't need to listen to his shit anymore. I slipped into a store and waited, looking at cards and watching the time. *Why was I upset?* About that asshole?

I inhaled a couple of deep breaths. My engagement to Grant had been nothing like theirs. We didn't have money for fancy rings and restaurants back then. He made me dinner at his apartment one night. A nice bottle of champagne chilled in the refrigerator, and after dinner he uncorked it and poured it into wine glasses. Grant got down on one knee and asked me to marry him. Simple. But to me it had been incredible that this amazing man wanted to spend the rest of his life with me. I sighed now as a tear slid down my cheek and disappeared under my chin. Not for him but for that moment in my life when I thought I had met the man of my dreams. How naïve was I? Was I still?

"Charlotte?"

Startled out of my reverie, I looked up and saw Hanna. "Hi."

"Fancy running into you here. Are you shopping?" She looked at the card in my hand.

"No." I blurted, "Grant is engaged."

"What?"

"I just ran into him, and he couldn't wait to tell me. Thinks I heard about it somehow and came to Summit to see if it were true."

"Are you kidding? What a miserable excuse for a human being." Hanna paused. "Are you okay?"

"There's no reason why it should, but it bothers me."

"Of course, it does. You loved him."

"It must be seven years now since we divorced. I don't want him back. I still shudder when I think of how wrong I was about him." I bit my lower lip. "By the way, the ring he bought her must be three carats."

"You should have asked for more alimony," Hanna said. "Clearly, he can afford it."

"Back then, I just wanted him out of my life. The quicker, the better. She can have her big ring. She's got to deal with him, and I don't think he's changed at all."

"I'm so sorry. Come on let's grab lunch and talk about it." Hanna said.

"Yeah, okay. Want to go to Lorelai's?" I pointed down the street. She looped her arm in mine. "Sure. Love the place. I've been going there for years."

"That's right. You grew up here in Summit," I said. We left the card store and walked to the restaurant.

"Let's sit here by the window." Hanna pulled out a chair and sat.

It was early in the restaurant, so Lorelai's wasn't full, and we were able to sit right in front of the main window. I sat down opposite Hanna. "I used to think I was the luckiest woman in the world to be married to Grant. What an idiot."

"You weren't an idiot. You loved and trusted him. He betrayed you by lying and cheating. Don't take the blame for any of it," Hanna said.

"I know he's a total shit," I said.

The waitress came over, and I ordered my eagerly awaited tuna sandwich and an iced tea.

Hanna ordered and handed her the menu.

As we waited for our food to arrive, Hanna told me about the yoga class she had just come from in Summit with some of her high school friends. "We try to get together once a month or so and go for a walk or take a class."

"That's a good way to stay in touch," I said. Our food arrived quickly because we were so early.

Hanna turned the subject back to me and said, "Love is a hard thing to turn off."

"What? No. I don't love him. He's such an ass. If anything, he repels me. It's Maxwell. Not Grant. That's bothering me. I can't stand the fact that his ex-wife is back in town and he's helping her move."

"I get it. That would probably bother me too."

Lunch arrived, and the sandwiches were as large as I remembered them.

Hanna took a big bite of her sandwich. "Sorry. I'm starving."

I laughed. "I can see that." My stomach growled and I picked up my own sandwich.

"Maxwell looked smitten with you at Bri's party." Hanna spoke around her mouth full.

"Yes. Everyone keeps telling me that. But… it's… I don't know. It's something I sense more than anything. And it makes me doubt." I shook my head. "Do you know that when Maxwell told me he was helping his ex-wife move, I jumped up and left the restaurant? Christ, I'm acting like one of those silly housewives on that cable show."

Hanna swallowed and giggled. "Well, maybe you should audition."

I grimaced. "No thanks."

"I'd never tell anyone to ignore a feeling. But if Maxwell's been honest with you, then maybe cut him some slack. He could genuinely just be assisting her." Hanna bit into her sandwich once again, taking a slightly smaller bite this time.

"I don't know. Doesn't everyone fantasize about getting back together with their ex?" I felt a crumb on my mouth and wiped it away. "Even when the breakup is sheer hell."

Hanna shrugged. "Did you fantasize about getting back with Grant?"

"I did the first year. Can you believe it – even after what he put me through? But he was my last place of warmth. The man I loved. I missed being in a relationship. Loneliness sucks."

How pathetic. I pushed my sandwich away – not feeling hungry anymore.

Hanna stopped midbite and put her sandwich on the plate. "Hey, it's okay. Don't worry so much. Look how far you've come since your divorce. This ex-wife thing will resolve itself. You'll see."

"Maybe." I smiled and watched as Hanna picked up her sandwich, stuffing a full quarter in her mouth.

"How you aren't choking is beyond me," I told her.

"It's a talent," she mumbled. A piece of crust fell to the table.

Chuckling, I pulled my plate back. Lorelei's tuna sandwich was as delicious as I remembered.

"You know, blended families are hard to navigate. At least, that's what the parents at school tell me all the time. Try talking with him. He might set your mind at ease," she said.

Nodding, I said, "You're right, of course."

Hanna swallowed the final crumb of her sandwich. "I should take my own advice sometime."

"Is something wrong?"

"No, not really. It's just that I should talk more things out with Mark than I do."

"Do you mean what happened with Jim? Bri mentioned what you told the group at Madeline's."

"Oh, for God's sake. Is nothing sacred?" Hanna stood abruptly. "That isn't a conversation I want spread all over town."

"Hey, come down. I won't say anything. Sit."

Hanna plopped back in the chair. Her mood had definitely changed.

"Don't be mad. Bri is just concerned. Your confession will stay within the confines of our book club. And you know we are all there for you. Whatever you need – you call anytime. You hear me?"

She nodded glumly.

I grabbed the check from the waiter and paid for both of us. "I'm glad we ran into each other."

Hanna protested, reaching for her wallet.

"Let me, please. It's the least I can do after you listening to me all through lunch."

Once in my car, I slid down in the driver's seat, closing my eyes. Grant's scent seemed different. I wondered if he'd changed his cologne. Funny, I can't seem to recall the original scent exactly. But I remembered the way he'd look at me before we embraced. His large brown eyes slightly turned up at the ends. Intense. Smoldering. Enhancing his good looks. *Damn, he was still handsome.* I opened my eyes and remembered how much he loved my lasagna and garlic bread. He acted like a kid whenever I made that for dinner. We had our moments. After Chad's birth, he lay in the hospital bed with me, stroking my arm and whispering in my ear how much he loved me.

But those treasured memories of Grant fade more and more every year. Even the ones I still remember were dimming without the vibrancy of love. I never thought I'd love another man as intensely as I had Grant. But I do. All I want is to make vivid colored memories with Maxwell now.

*

It had been eight days watching the clock. This weekend Maxwell was helping his ex-wife move into her new apartment. His kids had flown in from college on their spring break to help. I guess they really wanted their parents back together to give up having fun in the sun.

When we spoke on Friday, I told him I was sorry I'd stormed out of the restaurant and that I wanted to talk. I suggested Sunday late afternoon or night. He told me he'd call. He wasn't sure how long it would take. *Jesus, how much damn stuff does she have?*

By one o'clock on Sunday afternoon, I still hadn't heard from him. How could he not understand how upset I was? Or was my own jealousy making me crazy?

Yesterday, I kept busy helping Bri with the Aiding the Children event. She can calm me down when I get all worked up.

"Talk to him and let him know how you feel," Bri said. "And you have to accept that they have children together, so the ex will always be around."

I knew this, at least rationally, but my emotions still made me nuts.

Tucker whimpered. I looked at him on the floor curled up sleeping next to my chair. I had worn him out with a five-mile walk this morning. "Too bad you couldn't have a little caffeine. It would help." I raised my coffee mug to him then took a satisfying sip. Righting myself in the seat, I watched the digital clock on the microwave tick minute after minute.

Ugh. After ten clicks, I couldn't stand it anymore. I took a fast shower, ushered Tucker into his crate, and grabbed my purse and car keys. Time to find a dress for Bri's event.

I called Hanna from the car. "Thanks again for the other day. How are you feeling?"

"I don't know what to do. I can't stop thinking about it. Sometimes, I think I'm being absolutely ridiculous and should just forget about it. But then I... oh, I just don't know. You sound like you're in the car. Where are you off too?" she asked.

"Dress shopping. I'm trying to take my mind off of Maxwell being with his family. So, I'm distracting myself by looking for something to wear to Bri's event. Do you know what you're wearing?" I asked. "It's an outside event. Even with those patio heaters it could be chilly."

"Yeah. I will definitely bring a shawl or coat. Once I figure out what I'm wearing. Bri thinks she might wear her silk pants suit. But she's not sure yet," Hanna said.

"I'm sure whatever she decides, she'll be stunning in it." Clicking off, I turned up the car radio and eased onto the road.

*

Well, stress might not be good for my high blood pressure, but it seemed to be good for my weight. Everything I tried on looked decent. That's a first. I bought three different outfits. One long, sleeky black dress with ruching around the waist and hips and one sleeveless, bandage-style black dress with fringe at the knee. Perfect for dancing. I also bought a black halter-style jumpsuit piped with lace trim. I'll have to get an evening jacket or wrap after I decide which outfit I'm going to wear.

Excited by my purchases, I wanted Maxwell to help me choose which one to keep. As I left the mall, I checked the time. It was six o'clock on Sunday night. Moving time had to be over by now. They had all day yesterday and today. That's more than enough time.

I turned my car around and headed for Maxwell's home. I couldn't wait to model these new clothes for him. Who knows where we might go from there? My friends were right. He loves me. Shaking off any lingering doubts about us, I accelerated, eager to see him.

A few cars were parked in his driveway. Maybe they're the kids. I parked on the street. Once outside, I heard laugher coming from behind the home and decided not to bring in my purchases just yet. Maxwell is probably cooking the kids' dinner. I rang the doorbell, but no one answered. I walked around the house.

And froze.

Maxwell, his children, and his ex-wife were down at the dock. I stood motionless, hidden by the big hedge that abuts the side fence. What was she doing here? Empty plates and leftover food were scattered on the table. They must have finished dinner.

I couldn't move. Just like the other day with Grant. *Walk away. Now.* This was not the moment I wanted with Maxwell. *No. No. No.* They looked so happy. He stood, looking down at her face with his hand on his hip. His hair disheveled from a day of moving. So comfortable. So familiar. Why the hell did he come into my life if he was going to break my heart? I don't need this shit.

I yanked myself away and back into my car. I used every bit of self-control not to peel away from the house. I didn't want him to see me.

Once I was out of sight, I released my anger and started pounding the steering wheel. "Shit. Shit. Shit."

A car horn blared. I had slipped into the oncoming lane. Pulling on the wheel, I slid back where I belonged. Shocked back into sense, I inhaled shallow breaths to calm myself, recalling my yoga teacher counting as she instructed us to breathe in and breathe out.

My hands finally unclenched the steering wheel. With each breath in, I heard Maxwell's warm, melodic voice telling me how much he loved me. The sounds of the cars and the noise of the street diminished. Only his sensuous voice played over and over in my ears. *Does he still love her? What about me?*

Twilight loomed, casting deeper and deeper oranges and reds across the sky. Feeling numb and sad and angry all at once, I couldn't believe this was happening.

Wrapped in my thoughts and memories, I followed the setting sun home.

Chapter 12

AVA

IT'S BEEN A week since Neil left my house in a huff over that stupid ferret. But it didn't take long for him to call, leaving voicemails that he was sorry. Apparently, the deal he had bragged about earlier that week had fallen through and affected his mood. *What a horseshit excuse that was.* I ignored him. Then the flowers started coming. By Thursday, the floral scent in my office was so thick it was hard to breathe, like standing in the fragrance section of a department store after zealous sales associates spray their samples on passing customers.

The scent and clutter of so many flowers overwhelmed me, and I started handing arrangements to clients when they stopped by.

"Oh my," Theresa Sadler said when she came to drop off the seller's disclosures for her home. "Somebody sure loves you."

Not sure love has anything to do with it. I took the newest arrangement of roses that had been delivered an hour earlier and handed it to her. "Please enjoy these. I have no more room."

"Aren't you worried that your boyfriend will be mad at you for giving away his flowers?" Theresa giggled.

I glanced around the room. "I don't think he'll notice."

As my eyes wandered around the office, I remembered the first bouquet Neil ever gave me. He had shown up unannounced at my family's small basement apartment when we first dated. He was twenty-four and I barely twenty. My sister answered the door and ushered him into our tiny, crammed living room. Dinner was almost on the table. He carried a large bouquet of long-stem red roses, the largest I had ever seen. I rushed over to him, shocked that he had just shown up. I tried to convince him to leave. We always met away from home. When he'd asked to meet my parents months earlier, I found excuse after excuse. And I tried to prevent him knowing where I lived.

"What... How did you find my home?" I asked, grabbing his arm to move him to the door.

He handed me the roses. "These are eternity roses for our..."

My father, sprawling on the couch just a few feet away, rose and interrupted Neil. "Well, we finally get to meet you." He held out his hand and Neil shook it. "You must stay for dinner."

I stood, holding two dozen roses, looking from my father to Neil. *Oh my God.* Mortified. What will Neil think about the apartment? About my family?

I turned on my heel and escaped into the kitchen. "Mami, what am I supposed to do with these?"

She pointed to the top of the refrigerator. "Take those two plastic juice pitchers and divide the roses. Put one dozen in each container."

I shook my head. "Are you kidding? I can't do that. Can I just put them in the refrigerator until Neil leaves?"

"No. That's rude," she said, stirring the spicy pollo guisado. "Put one on the table and one on the hutch behind it."

I just couldn't do it. He'd see we were so poor that we didn't even have proper vases! I went into my room and grabbed some foiled wrapping paper I'd brought for a friend's birthday gift, twisting the paper around both pitchers. I heard him and my father laughing from the living room. Then I heard my father burp loudly. *Dear God. Could this get any worse?*

"Ava. Call everyone to dinner," Mami said. "And take this." She handed me a large salad bowl.

I didn't want to go out there. I clutched the bowl, digging my fingers into the ridges around it. "Dinner," I quietly said, placing the salad by my father's chair.

"What's that? I can't hear you. Since when are you quiet about anything?" Dad stood. "Ava's my outspoken child," he said to Neil. "Has an opinion about everything and makes sure everyone knows it."

Neil looked at me, not sure where to sit.

Before I had a chance, my dad smacked the tabletop and told Neil to sit next to him. "Ava. Get us two beers."

Gritting my teeth, I took two beers from the fridge, poured one in a glass for Neil and brought my father the can. I remembered Neil drinking a beer once, maybe twice. It was an expensive brand, not this whizz water my father drank.

Slumping in my chair, and cradling my head in my left hand, I pushed my food around my plate. I thought about last week's dinner with Neil where the sommelier paired our red wine with different courses.

Praying the dinner would be over quickly, I kept my eyes on my plate. My cheeks burned. When it was finally over, I was certain I'd never see him again. My hand shook when he held it as we walked to the door. He gave me a big kiss and headed off into the night.

Helping my mother clean the dinner dishes, she said, "He's a nice young man."

Dad came in to get another beer. "Hey, he's a stand-up guy." He slapped me on the back.

My stomach ached.

Two weeks later, it was over. Just like that. No more Neil and me. He asked to meet me for coffee one morning. *Coffee?* Not our usual date.

"I'm leaving for California in two days," he began.

I stared at him. "For how long?"

He paused. "Years. Maybe."

"What?" The air left my lungs. "No."

Neil reached across the table and took my hand. "I'm sorry."

I held back tears. "Why are you going?"

"I have to go. I'll inherit this company one day, but right now, I have to do what the boss wants."

It sounded hollow to me. A total lie. So many things ran through my mind, but I said nothing.

"Honey, I'm so sorry. I'm gonna miss you," he said, releasing my hand and picking up his coffee mug.

How could he be so indifferent? "Couldn't we have a long-distance relationship?" But as soon as I said it, I wished I hadn't. I already knew the answer.

Neil put down the mug. "Long-distance never works... Besides, you're so young and beautiful that you'll have a new boyfriend in a week." He tried to smile but just one side of his lips rose. "Believe me. This is as hard on me as it is on you. I'll miss you terribly."

"Then why?" I could scarcely contain my emotions.

"I don't have a choice." He stood, throwing some singles on the table. "Come on. I'll walk you home."

I didn't get out of bed for days. Mami brought me food but never asked me what was wrong. I think she knew. I replayed every word Neil had said in that final conversation. I couldn't remember a time when he'd been dismissive or condescending to me during the year we'd dated. He knew my heritage. This was definitely more than his relocation to California. I had a feeling – no, I was certain – that when he saw the stark contrast between our lifestyles, he just couldn't handle it.

Shattered at being so easily discarded, I vowed to make something of myself and never feel inferior again.

A loud, explosive sneeze came from the depths of my head, knocking me back to the present and almost out of my chair. *Damn these flowers.*

I picked up my cell and called Neil. "Thank you for the flowers. You've got my attention now so stop sending them. I can barely breathe. A simple apology would have been enough."

"My dear. Sorry, I was so cranky," he began. "But I have…"

Interrupting his apology, I said, "Being cranky is one thing; telling me how to raise my children is another."

He hesitated. "Of course, you're right. What do I know about raising children?" Neil cleared his throat. "Now that we've cleared that up. I have fabulous news."

I walked outside for some fresh air and took a deep breath. "Did you resurrect your deal?"

"What deal? Oh, that. No." He waited for a beat. "No. I have a surprise for you."

I knew he was beaming from ear to ear. I could hear it in his voice.

But I hate surprises. Especially from Neil. "Remember the last time you wanted to surprise me? It didn't go so well. Just tell me." Seven months ago, Neil had shown up at my house to see me after I returned from Puerto Rico with my mother and her best friend, Lola. He came with two beautiful bouquets and champagne. He also had a small, blue box with a silver bow. Mami and Lola started rambling in Spanish and fluttering around the kitchen when they saw the box. I ushered Neil outside onto the deck away from their prying eyes and asked what he was doing. My hands shook as I untied the bow, thinking of what I would say if it was an engagement ring. Thank God it wasn't. But then he asked me to move in with him. I was furious because we'd just had a lengthy discussion about my needing more time. His controlling nature had started to wear on me then.

"Yes. Yes. I remember. But that was months ago," he said. "Just meet me in Morristown at Romano's Bistro on Saturday around one. Yes?"

Shit. "This is the first weekend I don't have any open houses or meetings scheduled, and I just wanted to relax. Can we do something next week?"

But Neil would not be deterred. "Nope. Has to be Saturday, and I'm not saying another word. You'll have to wait and see."

"Neil."

"Not another word. Gotta go. See you Saturday."

*

By the end of the day, the flowers stopped coming. *Thank God.* I put some arrangements in my car to take home. Remembering that dinner so long ago made me sad. How stupid I'd been to be embarrassed by my family. I would give anything to have a watered-down beer with my dad right now. Who gives a crap about pairing swanky wine with your meal? Half the time I got acid reflux and ended up eating half a bottle of Tums afterward. Young, naïve and vulnerable, I deluded myself into thinking money would make me special. Give me a life of dignity. It hadn't. Dignity is earned, not purchased.

I had a full-blown headache when I arrived home, probably from the flowers. I ate some crackers and swallowed an aspirin, then sat in a long, steamy bath with a warm wet washcloth over my eyes. An hour later, I emerged feeling better.

I poured myself a glass of wine, went into the family room, and called my mother. "Mami, how are you?"

"*Buena. Sabes que?*"

"No. What's up?" I slid back onto the couch. "Speak English or slow down. It's hard to hear you."

"Did you get the invitation?" she asked.

I could hear her excitement. "No. What…"

"So thrilling. Miguel is getting married to Sophia, and we're all invited."

"Wow. That was fast. Has the ink even dried on his divorce papers?" I smirked as I said it. But I should talk.

"Don't you like Sophia?" she asked.

People were talking in the background. "Mami, where are you?"

She laughed. "I'm at Lola's drinking a glass of champagne to the couple."

Miguel was Mami's best friend's oldest son. Lola never liked Miguel's first wife. It seemed she did care for Sophia, though.

Ava, promise me you won't bring that boyfriend of yours to the wedding," Mami added. "Gabriel will be there."

*

I arrived late at Romano's. Neil sat by the window, and there were champagne glasses on the table. The sight of them made me anxious. Just what the hell were we celebrating?

Neil bounded toward me when he noticed me standing in the doorway. He threw his arms around me, kissed my cheek, and directed me to my chair. He nodded at the waiter, who brought a bottle of champagne to the table.

"What's this all about?" I asked. I hoped I didn't sound as irritated as I felt.

"You remember me telling you that I wanted a place outside the city?"

I unfolded my napkin slowly, placing it on my lap. "Neil, your father has a mansion in the Hamptons that you use all the time."

"But it's not mine."

I looked at him, noticing the grin that stretched across his face. The sight made me even more uneasy.

"I found the perfect home." He was so excited, practically giddy. "I spoke with the listing realtor, and we're all set to see the house at three. Thought we'd eat lunch first. I want you to make the buyer's commission on the house if I purchase it, so I told the agent about you."

"Well, that's nice of you. Wait. You found a house in New Jersey?" My breath caught. I could only get a commission if the house was in New Jersey. I'd given up my New York license when we sold the management business during the divorce.

"I know how busy you are, so I've been looking for months. And I finally found the perfect home." He bounced with excitement like a little boy. He handed me the home brochure and the MLS listing. I sunk back into the chair.

His eyes gleamed. "Isn't it amazing?"

I picked up the documents and looked through them. "It's huge." I tried to sound enthusiastic, but my heart wasn't in it.

"What's wrong?" he asked, his voice curt. Had he finally sensed my hesitation?

My palms were sweating. "I thought we agreed to take things slow. Buying a mansion near me is not taking things slow."

Neil's smile faltered. "I know, but I thought..."

"You thought what?"

"Well, this house is perfect for me," he said. "You have all the time you need to decide whether you want to move in with me or not. I won't pressure you."

If only I believed that.

"Come on, let's order. I can't wait to see the house."

I stared at him. Why was he moving so close to me? I liked the distance between us – it gave me a sense of freedom. Now I'll see him everywhere. At the grocery store, the cleaners, and the post office. It felt like he was closing in on me. Did I want to break free? I had to figure out what I wanted from this relationship. I didn't remember him being this controlling when we were younger. But back then, I had placed him on a pedestal.

After lunch, we walked outside, and Neil told me he had taken a car service here from the city.

"Oh, you did? Then how are you getting back to the city?" I asked.

He wrapped his arm around my shoulders. "I thought we'd have a romantic evening tonight at your home."

That pissed me off. "You're assuming a lot of things where I'm concerned. I happen to have plans tonight!" I stormed off to my car.

He came up behind me and wrapped me in a hug. "Ava. Come on. Let's make this a fun day. Don't be like this. I'm not asking you to marry me."

His touch still moved me.

"All right. Get in." I reversed too fast and had to abruptly stop, lunging both of us forward.

"Easy, girl," he said, sounding amused.

As we drove to the house, Neil talked, and I listened. We wound down a long driveway with landscaping. Out in the country, these perfectly manicured acres didn't always look right. But Neil glowed, impressed by it all.

The mansion lived up to the brochure with all the bells and whistles of an opulent, obnoxious hotel-like home meant just to impress guests.

I hated it.

I looked at the listing again. "Don't you think that twenty thousand square feet is a little big for one person?"

He shook his head. "Wait until you see the back. There's a pool and a large guesthouse where your kids can stay when they visit."

I spun toward him. "My children will stay where I do. What the hell are you talking about, they'll stay in the pool house?" The way I felt right now, none of my family would ever stay here.

Neil shrugged. "Sure. Whatever you want. I just thought they would like it better."

I turned away and walked back into the house. Normally, I would speak with the listing agent, but right now, I couldn't care less. Neil had some questions. I watched him and wondered if he was the same man, I had pined for so many years. More and more he seemed like my ex-husband rather than my memories of the perfect man. Had he always been like this? Or was it me who changed?

When we reached my car, Neil started asking me a million questions about the home.

"Write down all your questions, and I'll send the listing agent an email," I said. "But first, I want to know why you want to live here."

"Because it's close to you."

Exasperated, I sighed. "Neil, I've told you a million times that I'm not ready for a big commitment right now. I may never be."

His phone rang. "I have to take this." Neil moved away from the car.

I heard the easy cadence of his voice and thought it must be someone he liked – a friend or a family member. It wasn't the curt tone he used for business.

Neil ended the call. "That was my father. He wants us to have dinner with him next Saturday. I told him yes." He slid into the passenger side of the car.

That set me off. "God damn it." I hit the steering wheel. "You need to ask me and not make plans for me. Why can't you do that?"

His face turned red but he said nothing.

I started the car and accelerated down the winding driveway. I turned left onto Route 24.

"Where are we going?" he asked.

"I'm dropping you off at the train station. I have plans tonight with my friends." I didn't have any plans but I was not in the mood for Neil.

He averted his gaze, staring out the window, his mouth pulled tightly to one side.

Chapter 13

STACI

DRIVING UP THIS undulating road put me in a state of harmony, lulling me into a peaceful feeling. Traveling up and over the scenic hills on Rt. 22A in Vermont always had this effect on me. My mother's harsh words slid away as I glanced at the passing scenery. The majestic snow-covered mountains urged me forward with the promise of renewal. Just as my father taught me: nature heals. He'd say, "Go outside, witness the beauty all around you, and relax." It never failed. It always soothed me

But I anticipated something even better than nature on this trip – my sweet John. I hadn't seen him for weeks. My elation grew with every mile. I've respected his desire to slow our relationship down, but not because I wanted to. What did that mean anyway – slow things down? I ached for a little charity – what exactly did he mean by slow? His grief was still raw from the death of his wife nearly five years ago. His prolonged sorrow baffled me. To try and understand him, I searched dozens of websites about mourning. Most explain that it is complicated and that everyone reacts differently. *Five years, though?*

I passed a building under construction, which made me think

about my new home. Several boxes still littered the townhouse, but most of my belongings are now in place. I love my new home's warmth, with lots of wood and texture and how there is nothing contemporary about it. Oh, how my ex loved shiny surfaces. He was always staring into them. Pulling into a gas station to fuel up, I squelched my sudden negative vibe about George. No sense wasting time thinking about him.

I texted John with my ETA and called Bri to find out how the meeting went with Aiding the Children and the Sisters of Charitable Care.

"I think it went well," Bri declared.

"That's great."

"But after I finished my proposal and was leaving, Nicole came in with her staff and their proposal. She told the receptionist that she fired me, that I had tried to seduce a client. Can you believe that?"

"What? No way. That's crap. What a bitch that ex-boss of yours is," I said. "You know why she said that, of course. She's afraid that you'll get the event instead of her, so she's lashing out like a teenager. So unprofessional!"

Bri then described her vision for the event.

"That sounds beautiful. I'm sure you'll get it. The hell with Nicole," I said. "I'll be back in a week. Let's get together then."

Driving up another hill on this bucolic route, I couldn't help but think about Maryanne, John's best friend's wife. I was bewildered by her with that inscrutable smile when we first met, but her real nature – not a good one – surfaced quickly. My good mood deflated as I tried to understand why she loathed me. When I wasn't with her, I could come up with ways to deal with her. But faced by her sneering presence, in the heat of the moment, I never seemed to counter her torrent of blistering epithets with a quick retort of my own. I've kept John out of it in the past, but now, considering how serious I wanted our relationship to become, maybe I should mention it to him.

*

Pulling down John's long tree-lined driveway, I spotted him on his horse by the barn. *Oh, please no riding today. I'm still sore from the last time we went horseback riding.* I parked by the garage and walked over. He smiled and waved, and I sensed he'd mostly recovered from his tractor accident.

"How are you feeling?" I stretched my neck to speak with him. He looked like a god perched on that enormous horse.

"Good, back to normal." He climbed down and handed the reins to someone who must work there.

I wrapped my arms around him and we kissed. It was everything I'd been longing for. "How can you ride in all this snow?"

"You really are a city woman, aren't you?"

I laughed. "You betcha."

He draped his arm around my shoulders and led me inside his home. A big fire was roaring in the family room. No gas here, but a crackling wood fire popping with intensity. So reassuring and cozy. I wanted to throw a blanket on the floor and lie down right in front of the fire with John. I shivered. Was I cold or just nervous? Or both?

"Give me your coat and go sit." He pointed to two leather chairs close to the fireplace. "I'll get us a drink." He disappeared into the kitchen and came back with a wine for me and a beer for him.

"Thanks." I closed my eyes for a moment and took a deep breath, breathing in the aroma of the room. The fire, the chair, the wood paneling, all mixing and complementing one other. This is what a home should smell like. Not the Clorox of my childhood or the beach-scented candles that George insisted we burn daily. No, this had a baked bread aroma mixed with cedar wood and a hint of floral.

John sat in the chair next to me. "How was the drive? Where the roads clear from snow?"

"Yes. I've always loved the drive up here. It's relaxing." I sipped my wine. "Are you still getting headaches?"

John shook his head. "No. I feel as good as new."

I smiled, not sure what to say next. I hated this awkward feeling I sometimes get around him.

"I thought we'd have dinner here tonight if you're okay with that." John stood and stoked the fire.

"Sounds wonderful."

He sat down, leaning toward me. "It's good to see you. I've missed you."

I felt the flush on my neck and cheeks. "I've missed you too," I murmured, wanting to jump up and pull him into an embrace. *Slow. Go slow.* My anticipation simmered.

He cleared his throat. "I have a chicken in the oven, and dinner should be ready in about 30 minutes. I imagine you're tired and hungry from the long drive."

I was definitely hungry, but not for some damn chicken. "I'd like to freshen up before dinner. If that's…"

John stood and held out his hand. "Sorry, I should have asked when you first came in."

Taking his hand, I said, "Sit. Let's finish our drinks first." A lightheadedness came over me. Must be wine on an empty stomach.

Instead, John knelt down next to me. "You look beautiful."

Oh, his smell, so close. My nerves tingled all over my body. I managed to inhale deeply before his lips met mine. A surge of warmth spread over me as his tongue slipped inside.

He pulled me to my feet. Our lips locked, and we entwined in one other's arms. John's mouth grew hungry and intense, and my need rose to meet it. His fingers slipped under my shirt. Longing overtook me, and I pressed into him.

In a quick move, John threw a blanket on the floor and we lay down, pulling at each other's clothes and tossing them aside. We made urgent, rhythmic love. Pausing for breath, I stared at him and wondered: why me? He could have anyone. But then his lips touched mine again and sensation rippled through me, frantically sending shivers up and down my spine.

Afterward, I leaned back, closed my eyes, and tried to steady my breathing. *Slow, my ass.* I haven't even been here for an hour yet and look what happened.

"Oh shit! The chicken." John jumped up and flew into the kitchen. Naked.

Laughing, joyous, I could do this kind of slow all day long.

*

Watching snowflakes gently kiss the frosted windowpane, I wished John were still next to me in bed. His side of the bed still warm, he rose early to tackle the morning chores. In the shower, I replayed what happened in minute detail. Ecstatic thoughts filled my mind and I pushed away any cautionary warnings. Maybe the pace John needed had finally enabled him to move on.

I meandered into the kitchen as John walked through the back door.

"I'm famished," he said and fried some sunny-side-up eggs and bacon.

My triumphant smile may have been premature, but I couldn't help it. Here I was, watching the man I loved cook me breakfast. *Wow. Did I just think the L word?*

His face still pink from the cold outside, he slid a plate brimming with food before me.

"One of my horses is about to give birth," John said. "The vet will be here sometime today to check on her."

"How exciting!" What my dad wouldn't give to see a foal come into the world. He would have loved working on the farm with John. I wished they could have met. "Can I see her too?"

"Of course."

After we finished breakfast, John picked up my plate and brought it to the sink.

"Hey, I'll do the dishes. You made breakfast," I said.

He kissed the top of my head. "I've got some things to do before the vet gets here. Get dressed and I'll take you to see the mare."

I threw on some clothes and went out with John to the barn.

"Look at that belly! I thought mine was big when I was pregnant," I laughed. "How long is the gestation period?"

"Somewhere from 315 days to a year sometimes." He gave the mare a couple of apple slices as he talked softly to her. "Lucy, this is Staci."

Watching how gentle he was with Lucy confirmed everything I thought about him. When he turned and smiled – words escaped me. My eyes misted. How in the world did I find someone like him?

He rubbed his hands together. "It's a cold one today. Let's get you back inside."

Despite not feeling cold, I trailed after him. Entering the house, John said, "Will you be okay here? Or…"

I put my hand up to stop him. "I'm fine. Don't worry about me. I've got some writing to do."

"Great. Oh, by the way, we have dinner with Carl and Kevin and their wives tonight in Burlington. Dress casually." He left.

My perfect day shattered. Those lovely, happy thoughts I was having stopped like a screeching semi-tractor trailer right before impact. *Oh, dear God, no. Not her.* Maryanne has been my nemesis, causing me many sleepless nights. She likes to ambush me in the bathroom or a hallway and tell me that I'm not good enough for John. When he was in the hospital right after his accident, she'd been vicious. Madeline had wanted to deal with her, but I knew it was up to me. Or she would never leave me alone. I hoped she heeded what I had said. If not, tonight probably wouldn't go so well.

*

Throughout the day, John came back and forth to check on me at the house. His work never seems to stop. "The vet thinks Lucy will give birth any day now," he told me during one visit.

"That's wonderful." I smiled. What I should tell him is how uncomfortable his best friend's wife makes me.

"Communication is the key to all good marriages." I remembered the marriage counselor saying that to George and me years ago. Shouldn't I tell John about Maryanne's verbal assaults?

Anxiety hijacked my entire day, and I couldn't concentrate. Sometime in the afternoon I gave up pretending to write and ventured into the bedroom to go through my clothes. Nothing seemed right. I spent about an hour trying to decide on the perfect casual outfit. Such a stupid waste of time. Who cares what I wear? I wasn't a teenager trying to fit in. Or was I?

Pondering that question, I finally picked something out and went into the family room to read. But I still couldn't concentrate on anything, except tonight.

"Hey," John came through the backdoor. "I hope you're writing about Vermont again. I liked the article you wrote on Burlington's Jazz Festival last summer. You really got the vibe of the event." He took off his gloves, hat and boots.

"No, sorry," I said.

Touching my arm, he said, "I'm gonna grab a shower."

"Okay." I would have jumped in with him. But right now, all I could think about was seeing Maryanne again.

I tried to hide how I felt before we left for dinner. But the dread dragged down my smile. I wasn't sure our fledgling relationship could handle stress. Not yet. Not like this. And that irritated me.

*

I watched the mile signs going by on the highway – Burlington ten miles, Burlington five miles. Each mile made my stomach cramp more. By the time we were close, I wanted to jump from the car, rush into the restaurant, and just get this over with. I couldn't take the anxiety a minute longer.

Everyone was there when we arrived. I hadn't had anything to drink for hours. No bathroom visits for me tonight. Maryanne wouldn't ambush me in the ladies' room again.

John and I sat directly across the table from her and her husband. Kevin and Sally were at either end of the table.

Everyone had a beer, and John also ordered one. I hesitated for a minute but then requested a Cosmo. Yes, it would confirm Maryanne's vision of me as a pretentious city woman. But she'd find fault no matter what I ordered, so I got what I wanted.

John asked how Carl and Maryanne's daughter and her new husband were doing.

"They had a great time on their honeymoon. The skiing in British Columbia was phenomenal." Maryanne paused. "They bought a home in Shelburne when they returned and are busy fixing it up."

"Wonderful. If they need help, let me know. I can wield a paintbrush with the best of them." John winked at me.

We ordered dinner and a light banter arose regarding the best quarterback that season. I half listened, sneaking peeks at Maryanne. She didn't seem fazed sitting across from me. She was engrossed in the football conversation, insisting that Drew Brees was the best, backing up her opinion with statistics.

Blah, blah, blah. Just listening to her gave me a headache. It didn't surprise me that she liked contact sports – she loves to land hard shots, then run away.

Carl must have noticed the faraway look in my eyes and asked, "Staci, what do you do in New Jersey?"

His face showed none of the malevolence of his wife's. "I write articles for local papers."

John put his hand over mine. "She wrote that nice piece about the Jazz Festival last summer."

Anticipating a snide comment from Maryanne, my leg wiggled under the table. The waiter came over with our dinner. Saved by the meal.

I picked at my dinner and remained quiet unless asked a question. The minutes dragged on, and all I wanted was to be back in front of the big fireplace at John's house.

Toward the end of dinner, my phone vibrated in my cardigan pocket. I ignored it. Then I heard the ding of a text, then another. I pulled the phone out of my pocket and looked at it. It was from my older son, Chris.

Dad had a heart attack. He's in Morristown Medical Center. Jeff and Grandma are with me. Call.

Oh, no. The color must have drained from my face because John asked if everything was okay.

I whispered, "I have to go home now. George had a heart attack and is in the hospital."

"Absolutely," John said, rising. "Guys, we have to leave. Staci's ex-husband is in the hospital." He threw a hundred-dollar bill on the table. "Carl, let me know if I owe you anything."

John left to get our coats, and I rose from the table, apologizing for the disruption. I walked to the door.

Loud enough for me to hear, Maryanne said, "Why does she have to go see her ex-husband? I guess she still loves him."

I whipped around and walked back to the table. "What is wrong with you?" My eyes bore into hers, seething. "Why are you always saying things about me?" My jaw clenched, and through gritted teeth, I said, "My sons need me. What damn business is it of yours?"

Maryanne began to rise but Carl put a hand on hers, shaking his head.

I turned, gut tight, looking for John. We met at the door. I grabbed my coat and left. Ushering me into his car, he asked me questions that I vaguely heard and never answered. I called Chris but the call went to voicemail. I left a message telling him I was leaving Vermont now and to call me when he could. I called a couple more times, also trying to reach Jeff, my younger son.

"Staci, it's a minimum of six hours to get back to New Jersey. Are you sure you want to make that trek tonight? You could fly home tomorrow. That might be safer," John said.

I exhaled, collecting my thoughts. It wasn't that I had any love for George, but he was my sons' father. Wait. I paused in mid-thought. *He isn't coming with me.* But I didn't have time for this now.

Pushing aside my disappointment, I ran into the house as soon as we arrived and threw my clothes and toiletries into the suitcase. It was eight thirty at night and I should be able to get to the hospital by two thirty.

John had insisted on making me coffee while I packed my things and came out to the car holding a traveling mug, a thermos with refills, and a paper bag.

"There are chocolates in the bag to help keep you awake. I wish you'd fly out in the morning."

"Thanks." I stepped into the car, placing the mug in the cup slot and the thermos on the passenger's seat with the sweets.

John hovered by the car door, looking like he was going to say something. I didn't have time for his guilt or whatever he might be feeling.

"Ok. I'll call when I get to the hospital."

"Please drive safe." He closed the driver's door.

Adrenaline kicked in and I drove up and over the hills with an alert precision that didn't diminish until I got on the Thruway. The tightness in my arms subsided, and I took some deep breaths. My mind relaxed and I remembered the first time I met George. We both worked in New York City and saw one other on the Hoboken platform. He'd smile at me every day, but he never came over to introduce himself. So, I did. When the boys were born, he held them so tenderly and talked softly, imitating their babbling. I loved that George. The one at the beginning of our marriage before he started making money. Other memories flooded back of those good years. Tears rolled down my cheeks. I hoped I'd get there in time.

My fear turned to anger as my mind kept racing though today's events. Maryanne's snide comment tonight made my skin crawl.

Then my attention went to John. Why hadn't he offered to drive me home or come with me? Of course, he did have a mare giving birth. Was I expecting too much? I would have offered if the situation were reversed. Didn't I want someone who would be there for me?

I called Chris several times on my way back to New Jersey, but he didn't pick up. I texted him when I'd arrive at the hospital. I asked him to call me when he could.

Finally, four hours into the drive, he called. "Mom, where are you?"

"I'm about two hours away." Hearing the stress in my son's voice concerned me. "How is he?"

"Doctor said if he makes it through the night that's a good sign."

"What happened?"

Chris coughed. "He was at his office in the middle of deal negotiations that grew heated. At least, that's what his secretary told me. And he collapsed on the floor clutching his chest. She called 911."

"Ok. I'll be there soon. How is Jeff holding up?"

"All right, I guess. It's the not knowing that's getting to us. I better get back in there. I'll see you soon." Chris hung up.

Pressing my foot on the accelerator, I prayed.

*

The Emergency Room corridor was dimly lit and quiet except for an intermittent beeping noise. A woman at the entrance asked if she could help me.

"Yes, I'm here to see George Hughes. I'm his wife... I mean ex-wife. My sons and mother are here with him."

"He's down the hall. Come with me," she said.

"Thank you." I followed her.

George's doctor was reviewing his chart before entering the room.

"Doctor, this is Mrs. Hughes," the nurse said.

"Come in. I'll tell you and the boys the test results together," he said. "We'll move him to the cardiac unit shortly."

The doctor took me to George. He was hooked up to various machines and tubes. His gray face alarmed me. Both boys jumped up and hugged me. I nodded at my mother.

The doctor referred to his iPad. "I have the blood test and the ECG results. George had a non-ST-elevated myocardial infarction. That's means that one of his arteries was partially blocked and reduced his blood flow. The good news is that he is stable and will survive. His vitals are strong."

"Oh, thank God," I uttered. I looked at my sons, who were smiling.

My mother glared at me.

"Tomorrow he'll be given tests to figure out his Grace score. The score will determine whether he needs medication or, if the number is on the higher side, a bypass. Don't worry about that tonight. Go home and get some sleep. He's stable."

Relieved, I stood and thanked the doctor. I went to George's bed. "Everything's going to be all right." Patting his arm, I asked, "Does anyone need a ride home?"

My sons shook their heads. "We came with Grandma." Chris said.

My mother ignored me and left the room.

We made our way to the elevator. When the doors closed my mother turned on me. "This is all your fault! You gave George that heart attack. Taking up with that hobo of yours and shoving it in his face. Spending all his money on your lavish lifestyle. You should be ashamed of yourself."

The elevator door opened, and she raced out. "Let's go, boys. Your mother needs to think about what she's done."

The boys stared at me.

"Gram, honestly." Chris called after her, walking out the door. "Why say something like that?"

Jeff stepped out from behind his brother. "Jesus." He looked at me with his tear-dampened face, not sure what to do.

I tried to smile. "Go, honey. I'll be fine."

Overwhelmed, I watched as my family left me at the entrance to the hospital. I braced myself on a column, feeling the air whooshed out of my lungs. In the glare of the strong florescent lights, I stood exposed, abandoned, and all alone.

Chapter 14

MADELINE

"Is a storm coming?" I asked Stan as we made our way to Ava's office. The air felt heavy and humid, and the sun disappeared behind a thick blanket of grey clouds. The change had happened so suddenly it felt ominous.

Stan didn't answer. He seemed to struggle under the weight of the file he held, even though it was only two inches thick.

Ava met us as we walked in. "The buyer's agent notified me this morning that all the inspections on your house are done. Everything is fine."

"Did you expect anything different?" I pecked her cheek. "We took great care of our home."

Stan muttered a weak, "Hello."

"Come into my office and we can go over the by-laws and the remaining closing paperwork for your new townhouse." Ava pointed toward her office.

Stan set the file he carried on the desk. His eyes focused just on it. "Wow. This is really happening."

I touched his arm and smiled at him warmly. Turning to Ava, I said, "Thanks for reducing your commission."

"What are friends for?" Ava said. "Selling a home and buying another at the same time can be difficult. You've been lucky. This transaction came together nicely."

Stan slouched in his chair. "I don't think luck has had anything to do with this deal."

His face showed a lifetime of worry and anxiety that broke my heart.

Ava shifted in her chair. "Can I take you both to lunch?"

"Thank you for the offer, but I have to start packing in earnest now," I replied.

Ava stood behind her desk, reaching for a Rolodex on top of her back cabinet. "I have a great mover. Never had a complaint yet."

Grabbing Stan's arm, I pulled him up from the chair. "Ava, come one, it's me – I'll find lots of issues."

She laughed.

As we left the office, I paused. "You know, I'll take that number anyway. If they're as good as you say, I'll use them."

Stan and I had brought both cars to Ava's office. He left for work, and I went home to continue packing. Hours passed quickly, and I was surprised to look up and see that it was dark outside.

I had just finished with the crystal in the dining room. I stretched my aching muscles just as Stan came in. I hadn't heard him arrive home. He leaned against the door frame, looking at the ground. "I'm so, so sorry." His voice was choked with emotion.

Our eyes locked, his filled with misery and guilt. "Honey, this wasn't your fault. You don't need to apologize. I don't care about this house. You're my home. Not this box." I cupped his face in my hands. "You make me feel safe and secure. You're all that matters. You are my life."

And I knew then that I really didn't give a crap about the house.

*

Moving day went smoothly. My friends from book club left a beautiful basket with champagne and a nice selection of food at our new townhouse. They'd all volunteered to come and help. But I wanted to do this myself. Put everything where I wanted it.

By the end of that first day, most of the kitchen and our bedroom were unpacked and in good functioning order. Around eight at night, exhaustion claimed us both. We collapsed on the stools in the kitchen and peeled back the cellophane around the gift basket. Thank God I didn't have to make dinner. I was too tired to even order something.

We opened the champagne, and I pulled two glasses from the cabinet. I handed one to Stan and raised mine. "To our new life. I know it will be a great one."

He shrugged but we clinked glasses. I rummaged in the basket for something to eat.

"Stan, this is filled with things we like. Look, your favorite crackers are here." I pulled them from underneath a large chunk of cheese. Six different types of cheese, salami, crackers and bread were carefully packed in the basket. A perfect dinner for tonight. By the time we cleaned up, I wasn't sure I could even walk to the bedroom. I was beyond tired and don't even remember my head touching the pillow.

My phone vibrated on the nightstand. *No. No. I don't want to wake up. So tired. Go away.* Another vibration forced my eyes open. Groggy, blinking. I reached for my phone and glanced at the clock – 3:45 a.m. A bolt of electricity ran through my body. I heaved myself out of bed while pushing the call button, missing it twice. "Hello?" I shouted into the phone. The number unrecognizable, but it was a 610 exchange – Bethlehem, Lehigh University.

"Mrs. Miller?"

"Yes, who else? Who is this? Is Sarah, okay? Why are you calling at this hour?" I barked into the phone. Pacing.

"What's going on?" Stan threw the covers back and got out of bed.

"This is Dr. Katcha at St. Joseph's Hospital in Bethlehem. Your daughter was admitted about two hours ago, unconscious with a high level of alcohol in her bloodstream. We gave her IV fluids, and she came around quickly. She was lucky we didn't have to pump her stomach. That's not a pleasant experience. But she's fine now."

"Oh, my God!" I shot daggers at Stan. "I knew it."

"What, Mrs. Miller? You knew what?" Dr. Katcha asked.

"Nothing. I'll be there in two hours to pick her up."

"She should stay until this afternoon for observation, so take your time. She's okay. Sleep and come in the morning." He clicked off.

"And just how the hell am I supposed to sleep now? What an ass."

Stan had moved near me to listen to the call. "He must get a lot of anxious and angry parents and doesn't want to engage." He rubbed my back.

Irritated, I moved away from his hand. "Well, I'll engage when I get there. Get dressed. Now."

I drove. Arms straight at ten and two. Body rigid. Stan stared out the window and was silent for most of the trip.

"Honey," he finally said, his voice low. "Maybe you should talk to her calmly and not go batshit on her the moment you walk into the hospital room. Even I occasionally overdrank in college."

I slammed on the brakes and pulled off the road into the dimly lit parking lot of a closed furniture store. I wanted to slap him. Why didn't he understand? I took two deep breaths to settle down. "She could have died," I said through gritted teeth.

Stan choked back his next words and stared out the window.

I couldn't hold back my fury. "It's un-fucking believable that she drank so much after the story I told her about Danny when I dropped her off at college after her DUI."

Stan rubbed his face in his hands. "What story?"

Pins and needles pulsed through both hands still wrapped tightly around the steering wheel. I released the wheel and shook them. "Jesus. She even told me she knew all about alcohol poisoning when I took her back to school. She said they all knew from media coverage how dangerous it is."

"That's the point. A few drinks in and no one is in their right mind," Stan said. "Let's not assume anything until we speak to her."

The sky was still dark, even though it was almost dawn. Where was the sunrise? My mind clouded with tension, and I didn't fully hear Stan's next words. "What?" I snapped.

"What story about Danny?" he asked.

"Never mind that. You need to understand me. It's not some random fear. You keep dismissing it. You both do." I slapped the steering wheel. "Damn it." I slapped it again. "Fuck." The car closed in on me. My breath came in short spurts. I threw open the door and stepped out. Breathing hard. Christ. *Am I having a panic attack?*

I heard Stan. Close. "Madeline?" He pulled me into him. "I do hear you. I just don't want it to be true." His embrace was gentle. His words, soft.

Instead of pushing him away, I remained there until the sun finally peeked through the greenish tinge of night. My arms wrapped around Stan's neck. Neither of us spoke.

My mind calmed as my strength returned.

Stan kissed the top of my head and stepped back. "Let's get our daughter."

I agreed.

"I'll drive the rest of the way." He slipped into the driver's seat.

We pulled into a parking spot at the hospital at 7:43 a.m. I opened my door.

Stan grabbed my arm. "Wait. We have hours before the hospital will release Sarah. Why don't you tell me the story about Danny?" He handed me the car keys.

I paused, half out of the car. Turning awkwardly to face him, I noticed that the corners of his mouth were drawn down. Sadness had crept into his eyes. I slid back into the car. The thought of pacing by Sarah's bed for hours didn't thrill me either but – "I have to see her and make sure she's all right. I can't just sit here."

He nodded but clearly didn't agree with me.

We made our way to Sarah's room. Her face was bloated and tinged with green. When I approached her bed, she turned away from me. I pushed a wayward strand of hair off her forehead.

"Hi, sweetheart. How are you feeling?" I asked. Gently. Calmly.

She swung her head around, face scrunched, ready for a fight, but just then the doctor pulled the curtain back and introduced himself.

"How is she?" I asked.

"She's fine. Vitals are good." He picked up the chart at the end of her bed. "I need to speak with Sarah alone for a minute. There's a waiting room at the end of the hall. I'll stop by when I'm done."

"Whatever you have to say, you can say it in front of us. We're her parents," I snored.

"Sarah is of legal age, and if she is okay with you being here then…"

"No, they don't need to stay," Sarah pointed and said, "Leave."

I yanked the curtain away and marched down the hall to the waiting room. My anger slowly wilted as I tuned out the hospital noises and found myself transported back to Harrow's Funeral Home thirty years earlier, holding my brother's hand tightly. We chose to skip the receiving line and remain inconspicuous at the rear of the room. Even there, you could see Danny's beautiful friend, Pam, in a bed of pink taffeta, surrounded by flowers, forever frozen in her youth.

A tear slid down my cheek. Pam's parents' ravaged faces were forever etched into my mind. Their utter sorrow still made me shudder.

I buried my head in my hands. *Dear God. That could have been Sarah.*

"Madeline." Stan roused me.

"What?" I asked. Then I noticed the doctor standing beside him. I rose.

"Sarah is feeling better now that we flushed her system with fluids." He motioned for us both to sit down. "I talked to her about the risks of heavy drinking. She confessed to getting a DUI recently and mentioned that you were constantly calling her an alcoholic."

His eyes shifted to me, and a wave of guilt filled me. Had I gone too far?

The doctor continued, "We discussed addiction in general, how it runs in families, and what risks she's facing. I think it's best if she gets some therapy."

I nodded.

He asked us if we had any more questions. We shook our heads no. He gave us his contact information should we need him in the future.

Stan and I watched him leave and stood in silence for a moment before Stan put his hand on my shoulder. He pulled me into an embrace. All the emotion I had been holding back escaped like a flood. Tears streamed down my face as I buried my head in his chest. He held me tight until both our tears were gone. Then we walked down the hall to Sarah's room.

*

Two days later, we packed Sarah's dorm room into our SUV. Stan and I decided she would spend a semester at home and go to community college. As Sarah said goodbye to some friends, I received both a text and an email from the college stating that she had been placed on academic probation. Sarah had gotten drunk in a dorm room against college regulations. I showed her the notification on our way home.

She stared at it, her eyes widening. "No way…" she whispered. "I can't believe it… I just… Everybody was drinking!" Teardrops trickled down her cheeks.

"There are always consequences," I said. "You got so badly drunk you had to be hospitalized. The doctor told us you were the only student admitted."

Once we were home and had unpacked the car, Sarah went to her room. I walked outside so I could think without interruption.

I sat on the porch steps, breathing in the cool fresh air and letting it calm my nerves. Sarah's situation had shocked us, but I prayed we'd get through this together. *God.* Help me find a way to reach her.

Sarah emerged a few minutes later and quietly settled down beside me. We watched as the sun slowly set. It cast a warm glow over everything. For what felt like hours, no words passed between us. But somehow, in the silence, I sensed a willingness in her to listen for the first time.

Finally, Sarah broke the silence. "I know what I did was wrong and that I have to take responsibility for my actions," she said softly. "But I never meant to do something so stupid."

I placed my arm around her shoulders and pulled her into a hug. "I know, " I murmured reassuringly. "It can be very dangerous." I stopped myself from saying anything further. No lectures. No fore-warnings. I just hugged her tightly.

She leaned against my chest and let out a deep sigh before continuing. "What happens now?" Her voice was muffled against my shirt.

"Now we take it one step at a time," I replied gently. "We'll figure out some way to get you back on track with your studies and come up with a therapy schedule with Dr. Mann. This can't happen again."

We sat snuggled into one another a few moments longer. Sarah pulled away from the embrace. "Thank you, Mom. I mean it. "

We both walked into the kitchen and looked around for something to eat. She grabbed a yogurt and offered me one. I wasn't hungry but realized I hadn't eaten anything all day, so I took the yogurt.

Stan joined us. "That's not enough to eat. Let me whip up some scrambled eggs and toast."

Sarah and I, still eating our yogurts, thanked him with smiles.

"Thanks, Dad. Your scrambled eggs are the best," Sarah said.

Watching Stan prepare the food and Sarah set the table brought back a feeling of normality. It felt good. A pleasant departure from the chaos that had filled the air all year. Tonight, the world didn't press down on me so heavily. Everything was light and cheery, filled with love. Even though I knew it wouldn't last, it gave me strength.

*

Sarah and Stan tidied the kitchen, and I went upstairs. I ran a bath and sank low in the tub, soaking the muscles in my back and shoulders until the tension slowly ebbed away.

Toweling off, I heard the bedroom door open, and Stan walked in. "You, okay?"

I nodded. "Sarah finally accepted that she did something wrong and stopped accusing me of being a crazy, controlling parent." We sat at the edge of our bed, me still wrapped in my towel.

Stan grasped my hand then stroked my fingers. It seemed like he was searching for the right words. "I know that your parents were alcoholics. But why do you think Sarah has the disease?" He released my hand, sitting back.

All I wanted to do was crawl under the blankets and sleep, but he deserved to know. "I saw some telltale signs that could indicate trouble ahead. You didn't grow up in a house of alcoholics so you don't know how insidious this disease can be," I said, louder than I meant.

"No, I don't know." Stan shrugged. "Which means I need you to help me understand why you're so afraid for Sarah. To me, your parents made that choice. Sarah's smarter than that."

I grumbled and rubbed my temples. "You know nothing, then."

Stan bowed his head. "You're probably right. But would it help me better understand if you started with what happened to your brother, Danny? Why have you never told me the story?"

"All these years we've been together, and you never asked why Danny didn't drink. I wasn't sure if you just didn't notice or didn't want to know."

He shrugged. "Fair enough. I did notice but I just assumed he decided never to touch the stuff after what your parents went through."

I shot him a look. "All right, you want to know what happened to Danny. I'll tell you." I noticed my car keys on the dresser. Standing, I picked them up. On the keychain was a silver four-leaf clover my grandmother had given me. The charm was a token meant to bring me comfort and solace. A gift she presented to me the day she dragged me to the Alateen meeting some thirty years before. She thought I needed some good luck – something she had never had, living with my alcoholic grandfather.

I rolled the clover between my fingertips and breathed deeply, trying to calm my nerves before sinking back to the bed. I dreaded having to relive this moment again with Stan. But he had every right to know. So, I closed my eyes tightly. Within seconds, that awful morning rushed back to me, and I could practically hear the loud knocking on my dorm door. *Bang. Bang. Bang.*

"I was in my dorm room. The damn banging was so loud it woke up the entire floor. Someone screamed, 'Phone!' I stumbled out into the hallway, exhausted from studying the night before and totally unaware it was six-thirty in the morning 'What?' I shouted into the receiver.

A tingle ran up my spine as I recalled Danny's panicked, hysterical voice that morning and how it cut through my grogginess like a knife. "Mads. Pam's dead. I told her to drink, said it would be fun. I even helped her on the slide. Oh, dear God."

Stan interrupted me. "What? Wait a minute. Danny's friend died? I don't get it."

Staring at my sweet husband who simply wanted to understand and support me, I took another deep breath. The genuine worry etched across his face filled me with warmth. He believed some rational explanation would make everything better. What he didn't understand is that addiction isn't logical. It's cruel and harsh to anyone unfortunate enough to suffer from it.

I cleared my throat. "Back in the 1980s, parents let their kids drink."

"Mads, I know. I was there too. Remember?"

"Well, liquor flowed like a river at our house. My parents might not have the money to buy food, but they always had lots of booze. During my weekly calls with Danny, I noticed that he spoke about partying and booze all the time. He bragged about all the bottles of booze he stole from our parents and shared with his friends. He'd drink at night at home after they passed out and then water down the bottles so they couldn't tell anything was missing. He boasted about all the crazy stunts he and his friends pulled when they were drunk. They'd climb onto one of their roofs to howl at the moon or skate on a pond that had *No Skating* signs. He was out there partying every weekend, and each week his group of friends grew more reckless. My warnings fell on deaf ears. I was angry that he was being so foolish. Why was he drinking so much when he knew what it could do?"

Stan cocked his head. "Sarah's not like that."

"How the hell do you know what she's doing when she's not home? Don't interrupt. Just let me get through this." Closing my eyes, I returned to my dorm and that six-thirty phone call with my frantic brother.

"I remember Danny jabbering nonsense on the phone to me. Nothing made any sense. He was hysterical. I told him I'd be on the next train home. He told me to hurry."

I paused for a second, my back aching. "I had finals in two weeks, and it couldn't have happened at a worse time. I threw my notebooks with some clothes into a bag and ran to the train station."

Rubbing the charm, I remembered how anxious I'd been on that train ride. I prayed the whole way. Pleading for guidance. Danny just had me. Our parents were useless and self-destructive. I decided not to share how wretched and helpless I felt on the train with Stan. What was the use? It was ages ago.

I glanced at him and admitted, "I hadn't the faintest idea who Pam was. I thought maybe she was a new girlfriend. I realized there was a lot I didn't know about my brother. And I felt so guilty for leaving him behind. He needed me and I left to go to college. I was desperate to escape that house. But I should have been there for him. I never would have allowed his excessive drinking to continue but... "My thoughts trailed off.

Stan interrupted. "Jesus. It's not your fault. None of this is your fault."

"Would you let me finish. Please."

His face fell. "You're right. I'm sorry."

I reluctantly shut my eyes again to conjure up the scene. "I opened the front door and that damn smell hit me first. Stale tobacco smoke so strong you could almost see a haze in the air. I gagged. Yellow stains climbed up the walls and gathered at the ceiling, creating strange curly creatures. Nothing had changed. Both parents were out. I knocked on Danny's bedroom door and he threw his arms around me, sobbing – loud, heavy cries."

I felt a lump in my throat. "You can't imagine how bad Danny looked. He reeked of booze. His hair was plastered to his head. His clothes were filthy. Shocked, I just stood there."

Stan leaned in closer, touching my arm.

"Danny grabbed my hand and we left the house so we wouldn't have to face our parents. We found our way to the diner and our usual booth. How many times have we sought shelter there? I insisted we order some food. He looked like he hadn't eaten in a week. But when his food arrived, Danny just sat there sipping coffee.

"I asked him what the hell happened. His hands shook badly when he brought the cup to his lips. "I took her to a party. My buddy Tom - his parents were away for the weekend.""

"'Okay. Then what?' I had to pull every detail from him." I paused, took a shaky breath.

"He told me, 'I got her a beer, but she didn't like it, so I gave her a vodka and cranberry, which she did. We joined my friends in the basement. Pam seemed to get along with everyone and started to relax.'"

"'Then, what?' I asked."

"'Well, I poured her a couple of drinks and then we set up a luge slide for vodka. I convinced her to try it and held her in place while she took a big gulp. I got drunk after that and don't remember all the details.'"

"Tapping my foot under the table, I was trying to keep calm. But I was furious. He'd put himself and this poor girl in danger. But you know me. Eventually I cracked and said, 'Jesus, Danny. Weren't you tipsy enough without doing the luge? Straight vodka. And what the hell's up with all the partying? Week after week. Do you want to be like our parents? You should know better.'"

"Jesus," Stan interjected.

"You had to see the look on Danny's face after I admonished him. I knew I had to calm down. I watched him push food around his plate for a minute. Then I asked again, 'What happened next?'

"He dropped his fork on his plate. 'Everyone was having fun at the party, and Pam seemed fine.' He looked around the diner, as if waiting for someone to accuse him of a crime. I had to ask him again.

I closed my eyes, remembering.

"Tears streamed down his face. He told me he didn't remember much after the slide shots. He thinks he passed out. When he woke up, the police and paramedics were trying to wake Pam. She had vomit all over her, and they had started CPR. Voices were booming and he couldn't quite make out what was happening."

"Christ Almighty," Stan interrupted, bringing me back.

Annoyance pulsed through me. "Would you stop interrupting and let me finish? This is hard for me."

Stan furrowed his brow but remained quiet.

"The police took Danny to the station and questioned him for hours. Dad, of course, refused to pick him up. One of the cops took pity on him and drove him home."

I looked at my cramping hand. An imprint of one of the leaves of the clover keyring was imprinted on my palm. Releasing my grip, I rubbed the area. "Danny didn't remember much more."

"Jesus. What a mess." Stan interrupted again.

Shooting him a scathing look, "I spoke with the cop who took him home. He told me this was the third time Danny had been brought to the police station for underage drinking and disruptive behavior. I couldn't believe what I was hearing. He never told me he had gotten in trouble. I felt so guilty for leaving him to go to college. But in the end, no one was charged. It was deemed a tragic accident.

"I still remember how badly Danny's hands shook. He couldn't drink or eat anything. Was it shock? Was it alcohol withdrawal? I hoped he'd be scared straight."

Exhaustion overwhelmed me, and I opened my eyes. Stan pulled me close to him in a comforting embrace.

"That's a terrible story, but how exactly does it relate to Sarah?" he asked, stroking my hair.

"Are you kidding me?" I pulled away. "Didn't you listen to what I said? There are parallels in Danny's story to what Sarah is going through now. First, both got in trouble with the police – Danny was brought in three times, and Sarah got a DUI. Second, they both drank excessively to the point of blacking out. Sarah was hospitalized for God's sake."

Stan sat up again. "But Sarah doesn't live in a dysfunctional home, honey. We're here to guide her."

My head was pounding. "Did she listen when we talked to her after the DUI? No. Danny ignored my protests about his drinking until Pam died. They both have a genetic predisposition to alcoholism, and their heavy drinking only increases that chance."

Stan looked down but said nothing.

His denial started to aggravate me. "Look it up. Talk to Dr. Mann. I'll make you an appointment. But I'm not backing down." I stood. "I helped Danny, and I'll do the same for my daughter."

"How did you help Danny?" he asked.

I put my hand on my hip. "When he graduated from high school, he came to live with me. I watched him like a hawk. He stopped drinking and joined AA."

Stan nodded.

"I've been through this before. I'm not letting history repeat itself. Not with my daughter."

Chapter 15

BRI

"How is George feeling?" I asked Staci, who had called just as I entered the supermarket.

"He's his usual pain-in-the-ass self. The boys are taking turns staying at his house, and a visiting nurse stops by every few days. I just dropped off some supplies. I wanted to thank you for the delicious dinner you sent over to him. That was kind of you. Even his churlish ass-self appreciated it."

Smiling, I replied, "It's the least I could do."

"Have you heard anything about the Aiding the Children event yet?" Staci asked.

Looking at my grocery list, I said, "No. Any minute, I'm told. It's just a month away."

"Good luck. And don't worry. You know we'll all help."

After hanging up, I remembered that Eric wanted me to get a low calorie/organic cranberry juice. He wants to cut down on his sugar intake. I'd countered that if he wanted to cut down, he should skip the freaking vodka with the cranberry. Turning my shopping cart around, I made my way to the juice aisle.

As I was comparing two brands of low-sugar and sugar-free

cranberry, my cell rang. *Now what?* Placing one of the juices down, I rummaged around in my purse with my free hand for my phone. *Damn it.* Nothing's easy. I couldn't find it with the voluminous amount of stuff in the bag. Finally, on the fourth ring, I snatched it up. "Hello," I screeched into the phone and slid the other juice bottle on the shelf.

"Brianna, this is Evelyn Woodall from Aiding the Children."

I lowered my voice. "Hi, Evelyn."

"I wanted to let you know that we have picked your proposal for our annual meeting."

I jumped up and knocked a large plastic bottle of apple juice off the shelf and onto my foot. *Jesus Mary and Joseph.* "Thank you so much," I said through gritted teeth.

"Did I catch you at a bad time?" she asked.

I cleared my throat. "No, not at all."

"I have a couple of things I'd like to go over with you if now is convenient?"

I should have said I'd call her back and race home. But instead, I said, "Now is fine."

"Great. We need you to adjust some of the figures. Should I just list these? Do you have a pen and paper?"

Crap. My hand went back in my bag to look for a pen. I knew I didn't have any paper. I scanned the shelves, saw some stationary items at the top of the aisle, and ran there. I yanked a ream of paper off the shelf, ripping it open. I couldn't find a pen and tore open a package of pens. "All set. Go ahead," I said as calmly as I could.

Evelyn began to spit out figures and terms and spaces and guests in rapid succession. I did my best to keep up in the middle of a grocery aisle, holding my cell between my shoulder and head. I didn't want her to hear any background noises like *cleanup in aisle 7,* so I kept it off speakerphone. After twenty minutes, my neck ached and sweat was trinkling down my back, but I kept writing and clarifying with her.

"Let's meet at the beginning of next week at my office," Evelyn said. "Is that enough time for you to readjust the proposal and begin work?"

"Yes, of course." *How the hell am I going to get all this done by then?* "How about Tuesday, at 11:00 am?"

I must have looked like a frantic adult with an obsession for stationary items as I limped to the register with my torn packages of paper and pens. At least I wasn't covered in chocolate and cookie crumbs like the child at the next checkout. But the look from the teenager checking out my items made me laugh.

Throwing the bag into the front seat of my car, I dialed Eric. "I got it!" I shouted into the phone.

"That's great, honey. I'm so proud of you."

"I can't believe I beat out my old boss for this event. I'm so excited." Then it hit me, and I felt my heart race. "Jesus. I hope I can handle it."

"Come on. It's a big party. You can do this in your sleep," Eric said. "I'll be home around six. What's for dinner?"

"About that. You're on your own. Sorry."

"Great. This isn't gonna be like working for that lunatic again – is it?" he asked.

"Time-wise – maybe worse. But this time I'm the boss," I said. "See you tonight."

*

I barely slept over the weekend and when I did figures danced in my mind. Evelyn had set the date for the event before I was hired, and her staff had started posting on social media weeks ago. They'd handle the ticket sales and sponsors, freeing up my time. Evelyn also sent me the names of college students majoring in marketing who were looking for internships. I don't know how I would have handled all this in such a short timetable without her.

Two of the college students met me at my meeting with Evelyn. By the end of the discussion, their eyes were wide with excitement. "The last thing I have on today's list is the silent auction. Do you have a list of past participants?" I asked.

"Yes, I'll email it to you," Evelyn said.

The girls had arrived separately, so I told them to come to my house tomorrow. I needed the time to organize everything. When I got in the car, I checked my messages. Nothing. I called Ava.

"I'm just leaving a meeting with Evelyn. We were talking about the silent auction, and I was wondering if you'd head that up." I heard her groan.

"Madeline's great at that. Why not ask her?"

"Nice try. But you got me into this. Remember?"

"Ugh. All right," Ava grumbled.

"I'll send you a list of past participants," I said.

"We can talk about it over dinner. Your treat. How about tomorrow? I want to try Hanks, that new restaurant in Morristown. Pick me up at seven," she said.

*

Searching the dining room table for the notes I had taken at my meeting with Evelyn, I heard Eric talking to our son on his cell in the kitchen.

"Logan, I don't think that's a good idea," he said.

I moved close to the door to eavesdrop, but the conversation was over. Entering the kitchen, I asked, "What's not a good idea?"

"I forget you hear like an owl." Eric slid his phone into his back pocket. "Nothing, just his usual nonsense."

Shaking my head, I said, "Out with it."

He looked out the sliders leading to our deck.

"Well?" I persisted.

"It's about a girl, and he asked me not to say anything. You'll have to ask him." He picked up his tennis bag. "I've gotta go. I'm late."

Hmmm. That's odd. Well, I had too much to do tonight, but maybe tomorrow I'd give Logan a call.

*

I called my son several times, but he could never talk more than a minute or two. Something was clearly on his mind. I guessed that when he was ready, he'd tell me. It didn't seem to be anything important.

Ava brought over some of the items for the silent auction. The gold bangle bracelet from Dream Jewelers was my favorite. She had dinners at local restaurants, spa treatments, two vacation homes, a trip to a local winery, and a white-gold necklace with a coin pendant.

"You're amazing," I said, looking over the items.

"More to come," Ava said. "Come on and help me write up the descriptions for the program and publicity." When we finished, we then handed the items and descriptions off to the college students to put into the program they were preparing.

"How are you doing since your fight with Neil?" I asked Ava when we were done.

She paused. "Okay. I told him I'm busy this week and won't be able to speak with him until the weekend. It's been peaceful. No one telling me what to do. I can't believe he's the same man I went goo-goo over when I was young. What the hell was I thinking?"

I laughed. "People change. He just didn't change for the better."

Ava grabbed her purse. "Ugh, I have to go to Neil's father's place in the city for dinner this weekend. Why the hell I agreed to that, I just don't know. But I'm not that shy, insecure young girl anymore, and I'm not going to put up with any of their shit."

The college students bounded into the dining room, talking excitedly. One said, "Aiding the Children emailed us the current guest list. I made a copy for you." Mary put a file in front of me.

"How many tickets have been sold so far?" I asked.

Mary answered, "Three hundred and ten."

"Wow. Everything over 150 tickets is profit."

"Anybody we know on the list?" Ava took the file from me. "Crap. Shit. Damnit to hell."

"What?" I grabbed the file back. "What's got you so riled up... oh, dear." Neil had bought a table for ten.

Ava asked, "When did he buy that table?"

I looked at the column titled Date of Purchase. "Yesterday."

Ava's eyes narrowed. "So that asshole bought those tickets without even telling me."

"He's not the only one who bought tickets," I said pointing to the list. My shoulders slumped.

"Shelby always comes to this event. That's how I met her. I thought you knew that."

"She bought a table for eight. Does that mean Nicole will be there too?"

Ava shrugged. "No idea. Probably. Do you want me to call Shelby?"

"God. No." Everything I did would be scrutinized down to the last detail. Suddenly exhausted, I just wanted to take a nap.

*

After I finished preparing dinner, I picked up the recyclables and trash to throw out. I heard Eric's voice through the door to the garage. I paused, listening.

"Logan, this is not a good time. Your mom has that event in two weeks and is super stressed. I told you not to do this to begin with."

Eric's voice grew low, and the rest of the conversation was muffled.

What the hell are these two up to? I left the garbage by the door and hurried back into the kitchen.

Two minutes later, Eric walked in.

I stood with my arms across my chest. "What is going on?"

Eric's face flushed. "I told you before, it's just Logan's usual nonsense."

"About a girl?"

"And that."

"Bullshit! What does Logan's dating life have to do with me being stressed out? And it's not a good time for what exactly?"

"You're eavesdropping?"

Throwing up both arms, I said, "What do you expect me to do when you won't tell me what's going on?"

Shaking his head, he said, "It's nothing you need to be bothered with right now. Honestly, just leave it alone. Trust me." Eric walked to the sink and reached into the cabinet for a glass. He sipped some water and switched into lawyer mode. Channeled into Mr. Rational, ready to persuade me to let this go or offer some other sort of diversion.

Oh no, you don't. I know your tricks. Squeezing my lips into a tight line, trying to clamp down on my fury, I asked, "Why are you being so secretive? Just tell me."

Eric walked over to me, placed both hands on my shoulders, and looked directly into my eyes. "Look, you've got a lot on your plate." His voice was soothing. "You're not sleeping or eating well." He pushed a piece of hair behind my ear. "This can wait a couple of weeks. It's not a big deal. It's waited this long."

I backed away from him. "What the hell does that mean? What waited this long?"

His lips pursed and his face flushed. His voice rose. "Just forget about it. Let it go."

I grabbed my purse off the counter. "Don't you dare get mad at me. I'm not the one keeping secrets. I need some air." I got into the car, slamming the door. Flooring the gas in reverse, I ran over the curb. *Shit. Calm down.* I steadied myself and drove into town.

Not sure where to go, I pulled into the grocery store's parking lot. I turned the car off and just sat there.

What in the name of God could these two be up to?

I picked up my cell and called Logan.

"Hey, Mom. What's up?"

"Are you in some kind of trouble?"

He laughed. "No, Mom. Why would you say that?"

"Well, I keep catching your dad whispering on the phone when he's talking to you. He says it's nothing. But I think it is. Come on – out with it."

"Um… I'm… studying for a test tomorrow. How about I swing by on Friday night before I crash at Kevin's?"

This was going nowhere. I couldn't seem to get a straight answer out of either of them. "You expect me to believe you're actually studying for an exam?"

"Mom, it's college. Not as easy as high school. I'll talk to you on Friday. Bye." He clicked off.

Logan was expected at his best friend, Kevin's, home for his 19th birthday. His mom had called and asked me to chaperone. With only a few weeks before the event, I had no time for an all-night party with college-aged kids. The boys had been inseparable since grammar school, so I told his mom that Eric and I would stop by to wish him well.

A light went out in the grocery store. Then another until the store was dimly lit. I stayed parked there thinking about how angry I'd become earlier with Eric. We tell each other everything, or at least I thought we did. What's with all the secrecy? What if they're planning a little something special for me and I'm acting like a raging maniac because I'm so anxious about this damn event and having that bitch Nicole there judging me? Wouldn't I look foolish if that was the case? Shaking my head, I started the car again and headed home.

*

For the next two days, every time I tried to address the issue, Eric walked away and refused to engage. By Friday, we weren't talking to one another. Thoughts good and bad popped into my mind as I tried to figure it out.

"What time is Logan coming home?" he asked on Friday morning.

"Around 5 pm. Why?"

"Why? Because I'd like to see my son." He grabbed his bag for work and opened the garage door to leave.

I wanted to stamp my feet like a child. Instead, I called after him, "You're hiding something from me and I'm angry as hell with you."

He turned back toward me. "I'm damn angry, too. You should trust me and let this go." He slammed the door.

Every 20 minutes or so, I checked the time. I hoped I wasn't making a big deal out of nothing. I've been known to do that before. Like the time the kids and Eric planned a surprise birthday party for me. I kept noticing them whispering and laughing, and when I asked what was funny or what they were talking about, they clammed up. It drove me nuts. I'd figured Logan was the weakest link and pestered him until he finally cracked and told me. Then, of course, I felt terrible. I ruined my own surprise, and Logan made sure the whole family knew. Both Eric and Julianna never let me forget it. Am I ruining another surprise?

Eric was home before 5 pm. Logan, of course, was late. He was always late. Just born that way. The kitchen door opened around 6 pm. Logan hustled in with his bag open and a couple of shirts hanging out.

"Hey, Mom."

"Hi, honey." I kissed him. "You know your shirts are hanging out of your bag.? I picked up one that had fallen halfway out.

He put the bag on the countertop.

"Off. Not on the countertop. Go put that in your room."

"Mom, I need some of this washed. Can you do that for me?"

"You know where the washing machine is and you can put in a load. I'm not your maid."

"Come on, Mom. No one does laundry like you."

His wide smile moved me just like it did when he was my sweet little boy with flyaway hair running around the house with a chocolate chip cookie in his hand.

"Nice try. Get your bag off the kitchen counter and put it in the laundry room."

Logan lumbered off, and I heard the bag clang down on the top of the washing machine.

A minute later, he returned with his car keys in his hand.

"I didn't hear the washing machine start," I said.

"I have to get to Kevin's. I'm late."

"You're always late." I grabbed his car keys. "Sit down. Let's talk. What's going on?" I pointed to the counter stool.

"Did you talk to Dad?" He began squirming in the seat. "You remember what happened with your surprise birthday party. You don't want that again, do you?

Eric walked into the kitchen and patted his son on the back. "How was the drive?"

Enough small talk. "Is all this secrecy about a girl?" I paced around the counter. Getting my nerve up, I blurted out, "Is she pregnant?"

He turned pink. "What? What girl? Pregnant?" He looked at his father, who shrugged.

I'd had enough of this. "Out with it."

Logan popped up out of his seat. "Mom, this will blow your mind." He spread his arms out wide, grinning.

Putting my hands on my hips, I said. "What's gonna blow my mind? This better be good."

Eric moved next to me. "This is not the time for this conversation."

Pointing at him, I said, "Not another word from you."

A huge smile crossed Logan's face. "Mom. I found him. Your dad. And you have two half-sisters and two half-brothers. I have a bunch of new aunts, uncles, and cousins. Isn't that great?"

Air left my lungs. I began to fall. Eric caught me and helped me onto a chair. "Logan, I told you this was a bad idea. Especially springing it on her like this," he said.

They bickered back and forth, but I didn't hear anything else. A memory swam up from the depths of a leaf-strewn path. I closed my eyes and blocked everything else out.

Chapter 16

HANNA

THE SUN WAS slowly descending in the horizon, illuminating the kitchen with its golden rays. I paused to take in the beautiful view, trying to hold onto the moment's serenity. I heard Mark walking around upstairs. A sudden weight fell on my shoulders, and I leaned onto the counter for support. With every shuffling step he took, my anxiety grew as I prepared for game night with my sister and her husband, Josh. Had she told him?

Just as the thought crossed my mind, Ashley and Josh burst through our kitchen door. She had a heaping platter of sandwiches and he carried a case of beer.

"That's enough to feed an army; there's just six of us tonight," I said.

She chuckled. "It looks like more than it is. I put lots of garnish on the platter to make it look pretty." Ashley lifted the tray onto the countertop.

I helped her take off the plastic wrap. "It's artistic, that's for sure." The tiered sandwiches sat on an arrangement of salad greens peppered with olives, radishes cut into flowers and cherry tomatoes.

Josh gave me a quick peck on the cheek before Mark bounded

into the room with a big smile on his face. He slapped Josh on the back and helped him put the beer in the refrigerator.

Feeling awkward, I gathered plates, utensils, and napkins, setting them on the counter. "Joan and Rob will be here in about ten minutes. Something about the babysitter."

"I'm getting a beer," Mark declared. "Josh?"

"Sure," he replied.

I glanced at Josh to see if he'd look away. But he didn't. I wondered if he had a Facebook account.

Just as we were ready to dig into Ashley's delicious-looking sandwiches, the doorbell rang and Rob and Joan walked in. After a flurry of hugs, we took our places around the kitchen table and dug into Ashley's three-tiered sandwiches and then Joan's triple chocolate brownies. After dinner, we made our way to the family room to play a game.

"Your kids are at sleepovers? Right?" Josh asked.

"Yup. We can be as loud as we want." Mark opened another can of beer.

It was Josh's turn to pick the game for tonight. He walked over to our bookcase where we keep the games and pulled the worn box of Truth and Dare off the shelf.

I groaned. "Not that game, Josh. That's for teenagers." Why hadn't I thrown that damn game out? My stomach soured. Why'd he pick that game? Did my sister tell him? Did he see that picture on Facebook? Was he trying to get me to slip up in front of everyone? No. He'd never do that. I glanced at Ashley, but she avoided my gaze.

Mark and Josh grabbed some chairs and placed them by the couch. I stood, unable to move.

Josh declared that if someone didn't answer a question or complete a challenge, they had to take a shot. He grabbed a bottle of tequila and six shot glasses, giving one to each person. He began the game by asking Joan, "Truth or Dare?" She chose truth, and the game commenced.

"Have you ever stolen anything from work?" he asked.

"No," Joan answered confidently as she grabbed the next card on the stack. "Mark, truth or dare?"

"Truth."

Joan took a card from the pile. "What is the one thing about your partner that you find least attractive?"

Mark threw up his hands. "What? Are you trying to get me into trouble?"

Everyone laughed.

He shook his head. "What's the dare?"

Joan took a card from the dare pile. "Take a selfie on the toilet and post it on your social media."

"What? Oh, wait. I don't have any social media. Ha," Mark replied.

Ashley smirked. "Oh, yes, you do. Hanna helped you open a Facebook account."

Mark dropped his head and groaned in defeat. "Shit. That's right. But there's no way I'm gonna do that. What if my bosses see it?" He pointed at me and continued in a mocking tone. "Hanna, darling, your most unattractive thing is that mole on your back with the hairs growing out of it."

The group burst into laughter but then quickly reminded Mark that he couldn't decide to answer the dare question once he'd picked truth – so two shots for him!

"No way. Why didn't you tell me when I asked for the dare card? Are you just making up rules as we play?" Mark protested.

It was my turn. Ashley asked me, "Truth or Dare?" She picked up a card from both piles.

That was odd. Why take a card from both piles? I was about to say something when I noticed a look of anxiety on her face. Trying to figure out what it meant, I didn't say anything. No one else seemed to notice. They were all watching Mark down the second shot. Then I saw her place one card beneath the sofa cushion. What the hell?

"Hey, whose turn is it anyway?" Josh asked.

My mind raced through the scenarios. *Jesus. Which card is safest to pick?* "Dare," I blurted. No damn way am I taking a chance on answering anything.

Josh grinned and clapped his hands together. "Yes! Hanna is daring it up. Who doesn't love a good dare?" He scooted closer to the edge of the couch.

Josh's enthusiasm seemed genuine. Maybe Ashley didn't tell him about Jim.

"Are you ready?" my sister asked.

Turning toward her, I thought: how bad could a dare be? I nodded.

"Peel a banana with just your toes." Ashley read in a mischievous tone.

My eyes widened. "You've got to be kidding me. Wait. We don't have bananas. You'll have to pick another dare."

"No. I think we do. I'll look." Mark bounced up and was back in less than a minute with a black banana.

"That's nasty. It was in the garbage, for heaven's sake. I'm not peeling that rotten thing." I protested.

Ashley smirked. "It's your dare."

Glancing around the room, I noticed that the guys were all staring me down with mischievous glints in their eyes, so excited to see me make a fool of myself. With a sigh, I kicked off my shoes. "Fine. If you guys are so damn eager to see this, I'll do it."

Mark grabbed a large towel from the bathroom and put it on the rug for me to sit on. I dropped on top of it.

The overly ripe banana made the dare easier, but what a damn mess! The stem was so loose I tucked it under my big toe. I used the other foot to hold it down as I peeled it while banana guts squeezed out between my toes. "Yuck."

The guys were in hysterics by the time I wiped off my feet with a wet washcloth that Mark lovingly handed me.

"You know you could've said no, right?" Ashley said.

"I know. But I hate tequila." I shrugged.

After that, I relaxed. I could do the dares all night long. But Ashley's hidden card loomed in my mind.

I was still trying to get off all the banana gunk when Mark said, "Hanna, it's your turn to ask."

"Right." I stood and sat back on the couch, keeping the towel under my feet. "Rob, truth or dare?" I asked.

"Truth. I don't want any food on me."

I cleared my throat and asked, "What's your biggest fantasy?"

Rob hesitated for a moment, then his eyes widened and a huge smile spread across his face.

"From that expression, it looks like you thought of something," I snickered.

Rob flashed his notorious grin again. "My biggest fantasy," he began slowly, drawing out the words, "involves two women."

Joan leaped in quickly. "Ok. That's enough." Her cheeks coloring, she added, "He answered the question. Next."

Rob tossed back the rest of his beer. "Oh, come on, Joan. It's just us. Don't be such a prude."

Joan dropped her head into her hands. "Shut up. Rob."

He swiveled to face Joan. "Seriously. You're constantly carrying on about some neighbor or coach or teacher you think is hot."

Joan's cheeks burned red.

"Don't play coy," Rob said. "How many times have you told me you'd love to have a round in the hay with that Jim fellow? What's his name... the soccer coach... Synder."

What? "Wait, what did you say about Jim Synder?" My voice trembled as I tried to compose myself.

Rob shot me a quizzical look. I needed to be careful.

I hesitated for a moment, trying to think. "He was Katie's soccer coach," I managed to say, my stomach churning and threatening to expel its contents.

"Well, my wife fantasizes about him all the time." Rob picked up the tequila and filled Joan's shot glass. "Here, drink this."

She refused, shaking her head, then looked around the room. "All right, whose turn is it? Someone pick a card."

Jim's name echoed in my mind, bringing back memories of last summer and that damn picture on Facebook. If Joan thinks Jim is hot, maybe she's stalked him on social media. Oh God! Joan and Rob are good friends. This whole thing is creeping too close. I'll have to tell Mark tomorrow. I tried to shake off a feeling of nausea, but it was no use. The room spun around me, and my mouth felt as dry as if I had just swallowed sand.

"I'll be right back," I muttered, my voice barely above a whisper. Without waiting for a response, I went to the bathroom and sat on the toilet with my head in my hands. When the nausea subsided, I ventured back into the family room.

Rob, Josh, and Mark were having a hell of a time picking up a card and doing a shot. Not even bothering to read it out loud, much less answer a question. Ashley and Joan had gone into the kitchen, clearly not wanting to be part of the drunk fest.

The men drank for another hour, growing more boisterous with each round of shots. Ashley, Joan, and I stayed in the kitchen. Joan felt compelled to try to explain her husband's comments about her desire for other men.

"I don't know what Rob's talking about," Joan began. "Once in a blue moon, I might say that some man is handsome. But I'm not pining for anyone else."

"He's just teasing you," Ashley said.

"Do either of you want coffee or tea?" I asked, not wanting to continue this conversation, especially if either of them brought Jim back up. Both said tea and I busied myself with that while Joan talked nonstop for about an hour. I nodded every so often but my mind was elsewhere.

The men stumbled into the kitchen just as Joan was finally talked out. Ashley helped me pick up the glasses and snacks from the family room. I noticed she put something way down on the side of the garbage bag. I realized it must be the card she had hidden in the couch cushions. I was tempted to ask her about it but thought better of it with the men around. Especially Mark.

Joan, still miffed at Rob, decided to leave early, which prompted everyone else to go.

I told Mark to go to bed and I'd clean up. I rushed into the kitchen, searching through the garbage for the card my sister had thrown away. It read. "Had you ever done something to gain someone's attention that you later regretted?"

Letting out a heavy sigh, anxiety bubbled up inside me. Jesus. That question would have made me stumble and pause. Heaven knew what answer I'd come up with without stirring suspicion. Ashley was trying to protect me, and I loved her for it. But it wasn't her problem; there was already enough on her plate. Bri was right; I needed to come clean before this became any worse.

*

I smelled the bacon as I made my way downstairs to the kitchen. Mark had woken up early and was making breakfast when I hobbled in, still bleary-eyed from lack of sleep. I knew I had to tell him now. Katie and Brandon were at sleepovers, and we were alone.

"Good choice for breakfast," I said, nudging him in the arm. I poured some coffee and watched him move easily from the stove to the toaster to the refrigerator. He looked refreshed despite all those tequila shots. His hair was still wet from the shower. You'd never know how much he'd drunk. I, on the other hand, had a fraction of the alcohol that he did and was dehydrated with a pounding headache. I didn't bother to shower. I barely brushed my teeth. I hoped my hair wasn't sticking straight up in the back.

"Hope you're hungry," he said, cracking the eggs into the frying pan.

I plastered a smile on my face. "Yes." I lied. Acid burned from my stomach up into my mouth. The thought of food made me sick.

"I'm always parched after drinking," he said, pouring me a large glass of orange juice and handing it to me.

"Thanks." Just the sight of the OJ made my insides burn, but I forced myself to take a sip anyway.

"Just another minute. Waiting on the eggs. Everything else is done." He put a stack of buttered toast on the table. "Hand me those plates."

Mark put a heaping helping of bacon, eggs, and cantaloupe in front of me. "Are we picking the kids up early or meeting them at their basketball games today?" He sat down at the table with his plate.

My stomach churned at the sight of so much food. "We'll meet them at the middle school. Both games are there today." I bit into a piece of toast while listening to Mark's lecture on the proper way to fry eggs.

Forcing down a bite of eggs, I hated myself. Look how happy he was. And I had to shatter his good mood.

"Didn't you like how I made your eggs?" he asked, looking at my plate.

"I guess my stomach is still a little queasy from drinking."

"That's too bad. Can I have one of your eggs? I'm still hungry."

Pushing my plate toward him, I said, "Sure. It'll just go to waste otherwise."

I took a deep breath and mustered up the courage to speak. "Mark, I need to tell you something." My voice was barely audible, and my hands trembled as I reached for my coffee.

He paused mid-bite, frowning. "What?"

Inhaling deeply again, I said, "Last summer... hmmm... a... when you were away all the time... ... I... uh... there was an incident." My heart thumped against my ribs.

Mark cocked his head. His eyes on me. "What kind of incident?"

I took another sip of coffee, trying to steady my nerves. "Ah…"
His fork hit the plate with a clang. "Oh, for God's sake, just say
it."

The words tumbled out quickly. "Remember how we were
talking about Katies's soccer coach last night? Well, he kissed me
and…"

"What?" Mark's voice squeaked. "Like on the cheek?"

"No… on my lips…" I stammered. "You know like…"

Mark's jaw tightened. "Just what the hell are you telling me?"
His voice was eerily calm. "Are you saying some guy kissed you –
kissed you?"

I nodded, quivering. "It just happened. I've felt guilty ever
since… I…" My words faded out before I could finish. I had planned
this entire conversation all night long as I tossed and turned. But the
words just wouldn't come out right.

Mark sat silently.

"I'm so sorry." I shivered. "It was just a kiss. I've regretted it
every day since… I…" My voice faded off.

Tight lines hardened around Mark's mouth. "What are you
trying to tell me? Did you have an affair?"

"No. I…" A nagging, gnawing pain began behind my temples.

He stood, interrupting me, pacing around the kitchen. "This
guy… is it the one in the picture that Staci took of you and Katie?"

"Yes. But I threw that picture out."

"I knew something was up. You two looked like star-crossed
lovers for Christ's sake. I asked you about that at Bri's party. You lied
to me. Are you still lying to me?" Then he screamed, "Fuck."

The kitchen fell silent, the air heavy with tension. I slowly
walked toward Mark and put my arms out. "There's absolutely nothing going on. I swear. It was just a kiss."

His gaze burned into me. "I can't get that picture out of my
mind. Don't tell me it was some random kiss. There's more to it
than that."

My stomach churned. "He liked me, " I muttered, barely audible.

Mark frowned and turned away from me as if he couldn't bear to look at me a moment longer. He sighed heavily before swinging back to me. "Jesus, Hanna. Do you have feelings for this guy?" He sounded accusing, almost as if he knew the answer before asking the question.

I shook my head slowly. "No," I whispered.

But it wasn't enough; he didn't believe me and continued pacing around the kitchen.

I wanted to say something to make him feel better, but all my words seemed inadequate at that moment. After all, what could I possibly say that would make up for what had happened? All I could do was stand there helplessly while Mark stalked around the kitchen like a caged animal looking for a way out.

Finally, after a few more moments of uncomfortable silence, he rubbed his hand over his face and let out a deep sigh. "I don't know what to say, Hanna. I don't believe that it was only a kiss. This is a lot to process."

I nodded, tears streaming down my face. "I love you, honey. It was just a stupid thing that happened."

He whirled around, eyes wide and nostrils flared. He stalked out of the kitchen without a word, his boots clomping on the stairs as he went.

I sat alone at the kitchen table. The silence was punctuated by a growing sense of dread.

*

Ashley had warned me to keep quiet about Jim. I might have, but that damn Facebook post made that impossible. For months I'd told myself it had just been a kiss. But the truth was that it felt like so much more. A moment of emotion and confusion, a moment of my missing Mark, and a moment that Jim had stepped into the space his absence had left. But I didn't want to admit it. I constantly told myself it was nothing, that it didn't mean anything.

Mark's footsteps echoed from the upper story of the house, and I was tempted to head upstairs and talk to him. But he needed space. So, I turned my attention to the breakfast dishes, hoping that it would give us both time to think. Mark was a great cook but a sloppy one. Once the kitchen was spotless, I climbed the stairs to speak with him. That's when I heard it – the sound of the back door slamming shut. *Shit. Why can't we just talk about this?*

Exasperated, I sat on the edge of our bed. Now what? Am I supposed to go to our kids' games and pretend everything was okay? Will Mark be there? What will I tell the kids if he doesn't show up? I grabbed my cell off the dresser. Should I call Bri? Ashley? No. I just couldn't bear the thought of talking right now. I put the phone down and headed into the shower.

"Stop feeling so damn guilty," I shouted at my reflection in the fogged-up bathroom mirror. Anger flared. *Really, Mark?* I believed you unquestionably when you came home from your assignment in Asia and told me about the prostitute in your bed last summer. A gift of gratitude your client gave you to celebrate the deal's success. *Maybe I'm an idiot. Who would believe that story?* You came home so contrite and affectionate, and I bought it all. Well… because I do believe you. I know you. Why can't you do the same for me? You swore up and down that things would be different. And they have been.

Crap. This would've all been over if I had told him then.

I dressed and headed to the middle school to watch the basketball games. Anxious, sad, and amped up on caffeine, I felt edgy as I entered the school. Look at all the happy parents hoping that their child does well in the game. Pausing before I walked into the gym, I forced myself to smile, acting as if everything was okay. As I walked to the bleachers, I noticed Mark with his friend Jack in the top row.

Diane walked into the gym as soon as I sat on the bottom

bleacher. "The girls had a blast," she said, sitting next to me. "Though they stayed up way past their bedtime."

"Thanks for having Katie over," I replied. "We'll return the favor soon."

The first game featured Katie's team, followed by Brandon's—a total of two hours of idle chitchat. My stomach churned.

As the final buzzer sounded at the end of Brandon's game, Mark stood and made his way down the bleachers, nodding at his friend and muttering something to him. I followed him from the gym, but he didn't look back. We usually meet up at the games so we have both cars. Brandon goes with his father to get pizza on Saturdays and Katie comes with me.

My daughter talked the entire way home and then bolted into the house to let the dogs out. I sat in the car for a minute. Mark and I had stuck to our usual routine. Thank God. The kids don't need to be involved in this mess.

I could smell the pizza before they walked through the door. Mark unpacked the steaming pizza boxes onto the kitchen table. He didn't glance my way or say anything. His silence made me uneasy. I quietly dished out slices for everyone.

As we ate, the silence thickened between us. Brandon was texting friends, and Katie talked nonstop about her game.

Around nine o'clock, both kids were exhausted and went to bed. When I came back downstairs, Mark was outside with the dogs.

I threw on my coat and stepped outside. "Mark, let's talk about this. About us. I messed up, and I know that, but I want to make it right again."

He stared at his shoes. "I don't know if there's anything we can say that will change what happened. You kissed someone else, and that's it."

His dismissive tone grated on my nerves. "It takes two people to make a relationship work, Mark. You weren't around at all. You were consumed with your job and…"

He cut me off. "That was last summer, and I have changed. Haven't you noticed the difference, for Christ's sake?"

Inhaling sharply, I locked eyes with Mark, my heart racing. "I know what I did was wrong. I'm not trying to excuse it."

"It's not just about what happened, Hanna. It's about the fact that you didn't tell me. You broke my trust, and that hurts more than anything else."

My temper began to rise. "Yes, you've been great since returning from Asia. But the kiss happened months ago when you were gone. I didn't react this severely when you told me there was a woman in your hotel room. That's sure as shit different from one kiss."

His head snapped up, and his eyes met mine. "I told you nothing happened. You believed me then."

"I believe you now. Why don't you believe me?" I zipped up my coat. "When you were away, I felt so alone. I missed you, and I was angry that you weren't there for our family."

Mark snorted. "So, it's my fault? That's classic."

"That's not what I'm saying," I argued. "I'm trying to explain what happened and why."

Mark sighed heavily and ran a hand through his hair. "Fine. Talk. If all this happened over the summer, why did it take so long to tell me?"

"You were so apologetic and upset when you returned from Asia. Then Ashley got sick. There just never seemed to be the right time. I guess I was scared." No need to tell him about the picture on Facebook; it could make things worse. I hid that tagged photo, at least from my friends and family.

Mark started to say something then stopped. The air between us vibrated with anticipation, and all I could do was hope that I hadn't ruined our entire life together.

He let out a visible puff of air. "What you did hurts."

At that moment, all I wanted was to hug him. Would he turn away if I tried? "It hurts me too," I said in a quiet voice.

Mark looked at me finally, his gaze softening. "You look cold. Would you like to go inside?"

I nodded gratefully, not trusting myself to speak. I led him inside to the family room. We sat down on the couch facing each other.

"We need to talk about what happened," Mark said. He seemed calmer now but still wary.

I took a deep breath and nodded. "Yes. Let's start with why I didn't tell you earlier. I guess it felt like if I didn't say anything, then nothing happened and I wouldn't have to deal with hurting you. "

Mark was quiet for a moment before he spoke again. "So why did you kiss him? Did you have feelings for him?"

The question hung in the air between us like a weight waiting for an answer that would lighten it or make it heavier still.

Shaking my head slowly from side to side, I said, "No. I liked him as a person," I said softly but firmly. "It was just … loneliness."

He studied me carefully, his face composed. He extended his arm and softly caressed my hand.

"I'm sorry," I said sincerely.

"I wish you had told me sooner."

With a nod, I finally released the guilt and shame that had been burdening me since that summer day on the beach. Jim's kiss wasn't the only thing that distressed me. I was still upset by the feelings of weakness and desperation that had driven me to that point. It might all seem so foolish and trivial now, but the weight of my emotions over the past months had been real.

Mark and I talked for a while, and eventually our conversation veered toward lighter topics, including our upcoming trip to Hawaii. As we reminisced about our past travels, we both began to feel more at ease.

My fingers intertwined with his. "We'll work on this together." I meant more than our vacation.

Mark leaned in and our lips met in a soft and gentle kiss. As the intensity grew, I released all the anger and anxiety that had been weighing me down. I ran my fingers through his hair, pulling him closer to me. The warmth of Mark's body against mine brought waves of comfort and desire. As we continued to kiss, his hands roamed over my back, fueling the fire within me.

My heart raced as Mark's kisses traveled from my lips to my neck and down to my collarbone. The heat between us grew with each touch and caress. I let out a soft moan as he traced his fingers along my curves, sending shivers down my spine. His touch was both gentle and urgent. Our bodies intertwined as our need overcame us.

Afterward, we lay there for a while, catching our breath. Mark brushed a strand of hair away from my face. When we finally pulled away, our eyes met, and I saw a complex mix of emotions in his. Hurt, anger, desire, and most of all, love. Despite the complicated mess of feelings between us, I knew at that moment that we would be all right.

Chapter 17

CHARLOTTE

RAIN ASSAULTED MY car on my way home from work. The chaotic spring weather always makes me nuts. One minute it's pouring, the next sunny and humid. Why does everyone gush so when spring comes around? Damn season makes my hair fizz, my nose run, and my head throb. And it certainly isn't a season of romance. At least – not for me.

Stopping at the end of my driveway, I dragged myself from the car. My new dresses still lay on the backseat from the weekend. Who cares about what I look like at Bri's event? Not me anymore. I opened the mailbox, grabbing whatever was there. A raindrop splashed on my cheek. I brushed it away, hurrying back into the car.

I plopped the mail on the kitchen counter. Too early for dinner, and I wasn't hungry anyway. Couldn't run since it was pouring outside. My phone pinged. It was Maxwell again. He had called last night and left a lovely message. His sensuous tone of voice always got to me. I hadn't talked to him since I spied his family enjoying themselves together last weekend. Texted him a couple of excuses about being busy. I couldn't wrap my head around seeing him with his family, especially with that ex-wife of his. All of them having such a good time. Was I jealous? A green-eyed monster? Yeah, probably. Bri told me to talk to him. *What the hell?* Can't this just be simple? Instead, I'm left in limbo – can't forget it, can't address it.

My phone pinged again. I reached for it. Daisy, my college roommate, sent me a text.

How are things going with Mr. Handsome? Janice called me on Saturday, left a voice mail.
I haven't responded. Score one for me. Let her worry for once.
Got time this weekend. Come up and see me. I want to celebrate.
Please come. Please.

I started texting.

Celebrate?

Before pushing send, I realized she was taking control of her life by not running back to Janice the minute her former lover called. I was thrilled for her. Daisy deserved better.

I reread her text. Maybe a weekend away would be good for me. Take my mind off *him.* Tapping my finger on the counter, I texted Daisy, "Okay." It's got to be better than sitting here feeling sorry for myself.

She called me immediately. "Yay," she screamed into the phone.

We chatted about what we'd do while in Vermont. Finally, I told her I had to go and call the kennel to arrange for Tucker to spend the weekend. I knew Daisy wouldn't mind if I brought him, but closed in a car with that hairy beast for four hours all the way to Vermont would ignite my allergies to DEFCON 3. I'd sneeze with watery eyes the entire trip.

*

Daisy hugged me so hard that I couldn't breathe. "Easy girl," I squeaked out.

Chuckling, she backed away. "I'm so glad you came."

Her home hadn't changed in all these years. An eclectic mix of shabby bohemian chic, with a touch of traditional. A bit crazy overall. Just like my sweet friend. Two cats came out from hiding and purred around my ankles. I was glad I left Tucker home. Not sure what he would make of the cats.

Daisy took my overnight bag and brought it to the guest room. "Sit. Would you like a drink?"

"Just some water for now," I answered and remembered I hadn't eaten all day. I noticed her dining alcove was set with seven place settings. I guess we're having a dinner celebration.

Daisy handed me a glass. "Tell me what's going on with Maxwell?"

I told her everything.

*

Helping Daisy make dinner for seven was no small task. Everything was fresh, organic, and some of the herbs unpronounceable. I never thought Daisy could multitask with such precision and passion. But here she was, whisking up a storm.

"Who's coming tonight?" I asked. "Do I know anyone? And what are we celebrating?"

Daisy pushed a section of hair off her face with the arm. "We're celebrating friendship. I don't think you know my friends. But wait. Do you remember Sharon Caruso?"

I stopped chopping the carrots. "Oh, God no. You're kidding, right?"

She looked over at me. "No. What's wrong with Sharon?"

"She's a controlling pain-in-the-ass. You know that stupid club we joined our freshman year? The one we barely went to? Well, she nagged me to death every time I ran into her at college about never showing up. We were in some classes together during my sophomore and senior years. Annoyed me every chance she got with her expert advice on everything." I shivered involuntarily; Sharon made my skin crawl.

"Oh, come on. She's nice. Besides, that was thirty years ago." Daisy nudged my arm with her elbow. "Sharon's different now."

Sure she is. My mood darkened. Maybe I should start drinking. I chomped on a carrot instead.

*

The doorbell rang at precisely seven just as I finished applying lip gloss. Let me guess. I opened the door. Yup. Sharon. Figures. Who else comes exactly on time?

"Charlotte. It's nice to see you again. I can't believe you came," she said.

"A…" I began but saw Daisy come up behind me. I choked down the barbed remark I'd suddenly thought of and just smiled widely. "Time for a drink." Walking into the kitchen, I made myself a strong one.

The rest of the guests filtered in. Sharon held court with three of the women by the fireplace, so I stayed in the kitchen. I watched from the doorway as Daisy handed her a small bowl.

Maybe Daisy's right and Sharon isn't the same controlling, annoying pest she used to be. Maybe I'm the ass for standing here by myself in the kitchen. *Come on. Go make nice. It's for Daisy.*

Sharon held a small bowl out to me as I approached. "Here, have one."

Looking into the bowl, I saw candy pieces. "What are they?" I asked.

"What do they look like? Gummies, of course." Sharon popped one into her mouth.

Daisy hesitated, then grabbed one and did the same.

"Are they marijuana gummies?" My voice rose on the word gummies. "I prefer to drink my high on."

"That's not the woman I remember," Sharon said. Was that a sneer in her voice? "They're harmless. Just takes the edge off. I take one every night to sleep."

"I do too," Daisy said. "Every night. It helps with my anxiety."

Hmmm. Going to sleep sounded good. I had laid awake for the past string of nights, thinking about Maxwell. I grabbed a gummy and popped it into my mouth. I hadn't smoked marijuana in thirty years.

"I didn't think marijuana was legal for recreational use?" I asked.

"We all have a script from our doctor. It's totally safe," Sharon answered.

A memory crept into my mind of another party that Daisy and I attended during college where I smoked pot. What a disaster! I sure don't want a repeat of that.

Sharon went to every person, and they all grabbed a gummy. Surprising how many people use pot products now.

Some women were clustered around the fireplace, taking turns speaking loudly to a friend on a cell. I wasn't sure if it was a live call or if the person holding the phone was making a video to send to someone later. I didn't know anyone, so I didn't have to say anything. I returned to the kitchen to make another drink.

My edginess dissolved. I finished my second drink and poured myself a wine for dinner. As I put the bottle down, I saw the dish with the gummies on the table. I took another one, then another. I wanted a good night's sleep. I wandered around talking with Daisy's guests and started to relax.

"Time for dinner," someone said.

I don't know why, but I started to laugh.

"What's so funny?" Daisy asked, coming up behind me. "Didn't I tell you this would be fun?" She pulled me along to the table. "Sit here."

Excusing myself instead, I went into the bathroom. The two drinks went right through me. Washing my hands, I looked into the mirror. My hair looked askew. How could that be? Could the lighting in the bathroom be this terrible? It cast shadows. Opening my purse, I tugged out my brush and lip gloss. I smoothed on the gloss but couldn't see my mouth in this dreadful mirror, so I continued applying it. I put the gloss away and wondered why my brush was on the counter.

Swaying as I walked to the table, I kept my palm on the wall as a guide. Sitting down, I banged my knee on the table's leg. *Ouch.* I screamed in my head. Rubbing it, I looked around for Daisy who was putting food on the counter in the kitchen.

"Ladies, come and get it," she said.

I tried to get up, but my feet wouldn't obey me. *What the hell's going on?* Bending down to look under the table made me dizzy, so I sat up. The woman across from me pointed. I didn't remember her name. Had I met her? Why wasn't my mind making sense of things?

Daisy must have noticed that I was struggling to get up and offered to bring me food.

Good, I don't have to get up. As the guests returned with their plates, I tried to follow their conversations but couldn't. Instead, I heard plates, silverware, glasses clanking, and drawers sliding open. *How odd.*

"Here you go," Daisy said and put a plate heaped with food in front of me.

She and Sharon took seats on either side of me. Sharon raised her glass.

I held up my glass too. A toast, I thought, but her words all jumbled together, and when I tried to say *cheers,* I couldn't. My lips seemed stuck.

Daisy turned at my gibberish and said, "What's all over your mouth?" She grabbed her napkin and wiped away the sticky stuff. "Are you okay?"

I looked up at her and said, "… anks."

"You don't look so good? Are you sure you're, okay?"

"F… ine." I picked up my fork and stabbed a piece of chicken. I tried to plop it into my mouth but missed and poked it into my cheek. "Ohhhh." I used my other hand to guide the fork and chicken into my mouth. I rubbed my cheek as I chewed.

"How much THC is in those gummies?" I heard Daisy ask Sharon.

"I don't know. They're totally safe. I take them every night. My doctor prescribed them, and I get it from the medical dispensary downtown just like you do," she said. "All they do is take the edge off. Nothing else."

"Charlotte doesn't look good," Daisy said.

Damn, this chicken is really chewy. I couldn't seem to swallow it. Just kept chewing and chewing.

Daisy stood. "Where is the bottle they came in?"

"Seriously?" Sharon threw her napkin on the table, rose and found her purse on the couch. She rummaged in it, handing the bottle to Daisy. "Charlotte does seem a little green."

Still chewing. What's up with this frigging chicken?

"Sharon, these are 10 mg. How many did she have?" Daisy shouted. "She hasn't smoked pot since college. She has zero tolerance. And she had at least two strong drinks and nothing to eat before dinner. After a long drive up here, too."

"How was I supposed to know that? They're harmless." Sharon scowled. "Stop worrying so much."

I kept trying to swallow that damn piece of chicken. Muffled talking on my right and left irritated me. Ignoring it, I picked up my fork for another piece. *Hmmm…* My fork's not working right, food's tumbling off the side of the plate. Maybe if I come down straight and hard, I'll spear it. That'll do it. I heard a loud scraping noise and looked down. *Oops.* The piece of chicken was gone. Not on my fork. Not on the plate. *Where did it go?* "Sorry…" I started giggling. Then hiccupping.

Daisy's booming voice snapped me back. "Charlotte, how many gummies did you eat?"

Putting my hand up I raised one, then two then three fingers. I think Daisy said something else, but I wasn't sure. I floated swaying here and there.

Sharon asked me a question that I didn't understand. I smiled. I think.

I poked at another piece of chicken but kept hitting the table and not my plate. Swaying back and forth. Am I on a cruise ship? "W.v... ing?" "W.v ... ing?"

Daisy moved closer to me. "What? I don't understand."

Pulling the word up from my gu,t I screamed, "Boat."

Daisy's mouth moved. I felt her hand on my shoulder.

Suddenly my euphoria disappeared and a huge ache struck the pit of my stomach. I cringed as acid rose in my throat, and before I knew what was happening, I vomited. The piece of chicken I kept chewing flew across the table and landed on the woman's cheek across from me. Sharon said something, and I turned toward her just in time for the second projectile vomit to rain in her lap. Wobbling in my chair, I thought I would pass out.

I heard Sharon's raised voice, "Oh God! What a mess!"

Then I heard Daisy. "Who cares about the mess? Jesus, maybe we should take her to the hospital."

"No way. She'll be fine when she sobers up. Look at this. Look at me." Sharon stood and quickly sat down again. "Can someone bring the paper towels from the kitchen? I can't get up without tracking throw-up everywhere."

The next thing I remembered was being in the rain. No, it was the shower. I was fully clothed, sitting on the tile floor, with Daisy holding my arm.

I don't know how long it took before the water worked its magic and I grew lucid. Daisy helped me stand. I stripped off my wet clothes and she put them in a plastic bag, then ushered me into a pair of sweats. Every time I have pot in Vermont, it ends badly. Stupid. Stupid. Stupid.

*

I don't remember the rest of the night but woke up in Daisy's guest room feeling shaky and thirsty. The sun crept around the blinds, hurting my eyes. I heard my friend talking on the phone and hoped it wasn't about me.

Dragging myself out of bed, I got a whiff of a horrible odor. *Good God. What reeked?* I threw back the covers. Had I vomited in my sleep? The bed was clean, so it had to be me. Grabbing my overnight bag, I opened the bedroom door and mouthed *shower* to Daisy.

Turning the water on, I anchored myself under the nozzle and let the water beat any remaining remnants of my hangover away. My embarrassment grew as I washed my hair and found small bits of food and who knows what else in it.

What the hell happened last night? I'm a grown-ass woman, not some teenager drinking for the first time. Cringing, I hoped Sharon's gloating face would show up at the door today. I took my time trying to come up with something to say to Daisy about ruining her dinner.

I cracked open the bathroom door.

"Come to breakfast," she said.

Slithering out of the bathroom, I took a deep breath. "Daisy, I'm mortified. I'm so sorry. I know how much you were looking forward to it." Collapsing in one of the counter chairs, I said, "What can I do to make up for my stupidity?"

She touched my shoulder softly. "You have nothing to feel sorry about. I'm the one who's sorry. You should never have eaten three gummies. You're not used to that much THC in your system."

"What? I thought they were medicinal from a dispensary. Sharon said that it just takes the edge off." Confused, I stood to get a glass of water. "I didn't feel anything after the first gummy, so I took another two. All I wanted was some sleep."

"Well, Sharon's been taking them for years to help her deal with anxiety." Daisy pulled out a bagel from the bread drawer, sliced it, and put it in the toaster. "Would you like cream cheese or butter?"

"Butter," I replied, grateful she had something to eat that I liked. The last time she made me breakfast she nearly killed me with dry, bitter, organic, gluten-free granola. Just the thought of it made me shudder.

"Three gummies together had too much THC for you." Daisy slid the buttered bagel in front of me.

I grabbed a napkin from the holder on the counter as I spoke. "Thanks," I said, still feeling a little woozy. "That was probably the highest I've ever been. And believe me, I've been pretty wasted before."

Daisy sighed. "I feel awful. I should have told you to just take one."

"Did you take more than one?" I asked. "You didn't seem bothered by it."

"I've been using gummies for years to sleep at night, so I've built up some tolerance. And, yes, I had one. You didn't have any food yesterday, then you had two drinks before the edibles, which heightens the level of THC in your system." Daisy ran her hand through her hair.

"Damn. There should be warnings about edibles or at the very least some sort of instructions." I closed my eyes, massaging my aching temple.

She took my glass and refilled it with water.

I took a large bite of my bagel, hoping my stomach was ready for food.

Daisy cleared her throat. "When I first started taking them for my anxiety, the staff at the dispensary told me that you have to start off at a low dose and build up from there."

"Oh." I bit back on what I wanted to say. *Why did Sharon have to bring them at all? Weren't cocktails enough?* But I didn't want to badmouth her friend, so I left it alone.

Daisy put the butter back in the refrigerator. "I didn't think about it. Like when someone asks you for a drink, you just get them a drink. You don't think about what it may do to them. Stupid of me."

"Clearly, I know nothing. And it certainly didn't relax me."

She wrapped her arm around my shoulders. "I'm so, so sorry."

Turning toward her, I said, "Other than being embarrassed, I'm fine, and it's not your fault. I'm a big girl. I could have asked some questions. Instead, I popped them in my mouth without a second thought."

Daisy squeezed my shoulder, stepping back from the embrace. "I was surprised Sharon even brought the gummies. I wanted a lively party, not a sedated one."

I moaned. "Well, I gave everyone a good show."

"Maybe Sharon's going through something and needed a little help to relax."

Raising my hand, I said, "Doesn't matter. There is no excuse. She's probably having quite a laugh over it today." My stomach churned and I pushed the plate away.

Daisy's eyes widened. "Oh no. She's not like that."

Shrugging, I stood, bringing my not-quite finished plate to the sink. A bright, sunny day glowed outside, and I remembered another such day years ago at college, and just like today, Sharon had prayed heavily on my mind. I remembered...

*

Sitting at a picnic table set up outside the campus library, I studied in the warm spring afternoon for an exam in political theory. What a mistake this course was. The exam was in less than an hour and I wasn't ready. The library door behind me opened. Ignoring the hovering presence, I highlighted a sentence in my notes that I thought key for the exam.

"Well, look who's here."

I knew that grating voice and twisted in my seat facing her. "I don't have time for your crap right now. I have an exam soon." I turned away from Sharon and her gaggle of girls.

She walked over and looked at my textbook and notes. "Too bad you don't come to our monthly discussions. We just read The Prince. *You know, the one right here." She pointed to the textbook's sidebar where a picture of Machiavelli was.*

I rubbed the bridge of my nose. "Please leave me alone. Reading that book wouldn't help at all with this course."

"Of course, it would. Obviously, you're unprepared for the test. You're cranky and anxious. So, clearly, you need to come back to our club. We'd make sure you're ready for the next exam."

My head pounded. "Go away. Now. And stop stalking me. If I wanted to go to your club, I'd be there."

"You're not too bright, are you?" She planted her hand on her hip. "If you were, you'd know that showing up for our discussions would bolster your knowledge and get you a better grade."

I picked up my books and left. Inflexible, intolerable, and just a complete pain-in-the-ass. Why wouldn't she just leave me alone?

*

Daisy bounced off the chair quickly, scraping the floor and bringing me back to her kitchen. "Ok, then." Energized and ready for action, she patted some papers on the side of the refrigerator.

I've never seen anyone go from one mood to another so fast. Maybe I should eat a gummy every night myself.

"Hey, it's not just you who've had crazy experiences with gummies." She continued her pat down of the kitchen. She finally spotted her purse on the desk. Throwing it open, she yanked out her wallet, and then her brush. "Here," she said, pulling out her phone. "Look. TikTok is crammed with hilarious videos." She swiped to the app. "Check these out."

We sat at the counter and watched three different videos, laughing harder at each one. Pointing to one of the videos, I said, "I definitely wasn't that ridiculous."

Daisy closed the app. "I don't know. The chicken you vomited hitting Gail in the cheek would be TikTok gold."

"You're probably right. Thank God no one filmed that."

Daisy dropped her head. "Well... someone did."

"What?" I shouted and stood. "Who? Tell me now. Give me her cell. It needs to be erased right away. For God's sake, I work for the Department of Education. I'll get fired."

Daisy put her hand on my shoulder, easing me back into the chair. "Calm down. No one would put that on social media."

"How do you know?' I panicked at the thought of my boss seeing the video. *Or God, the parents.*

"Susie always films our get-togethers and sends them to everyone present. She doesn't post them and neither does anyone else. I usually watch it once and erase it." She walked over to the desk and put her phone back into her purse. "After I got you to bed, I rejoined my guests and some were watching the video Susie had just made. I asked everyone if I could delete it off of their phones, and everyone agreed. Well. Almost."

"What do you mean almost?" My heart hammered.

Daisy turned to face me raising both arms. "Kathy wanted to show her husband. I guess she found some humor in it. But I managed to convince her."

I don't give a rat's ass what Kathy thinks is funny. Acid rose in my throat but I was glad I hadn't said that out loud. "Whose video isn't erased?"

Daisy grabbed a sponge and wiped down the countertop.

I stood. "Daisy. Please stop flitting around and answer me. Whose video didn't get erased?" But I already knew.

"Sharon. She left before Susie set the video to everyone."

"We need to go to her house right now." I ran to the guest room and grabbed my coat and purse. "Let's go."

"Wait. It's okay. I'll just call and tell her to erase it," Daisy said.

"No. Give me her address. I'll go myself." I yanked out my phone and went into GPS to put in the address.

Daisy stared at me. "I'll go too. I'll drive."

I knew she thought I was overreacting. But all I could think of was the parents in my school district. Imagine the damage that video could do. *Pot! Drunk! Vomiting!* I'd get blamed for anything that happened to any of the students who watched the video for the next ten years. I quivered thinking about it.

"Breathe," Daisy said once we were in her car. "It's all right."

I did as instructed. She babbled on, but I zoned out, thinking about being immortalized forever because of a damn gummy.

"Charlotte. Charlotte."

Hearing my name, I snapped back. "Yes."

"We're here. Why don't you let me handle this?" Daisy raced from the car and sped up the front steps. A man with a full head of gray hair answered the door.

"Hi, Martin. Can I speak with Sharon for a minute?"

He turned behind and said, "It's for you."

Sharon, dressed in a bathrobe and slippers with a full mug of coffee, came to the door. "Daisy. Charlotte. Something wrong?"

"Did you get Susie's video from last night?" Daisy spit out before I could say a word.

"What? You came all the way here to ask me that? What's going on?" Sharon seemed irritated by our intrusion.

I strode up to the top step alongside Daisy. "Please get your phone. You need to delete it right now."

"Jesus, you're something. First, you vomit on me. Now you

want my friend's video erased. No hello, how are you?" She turned and entered her home, leaving the front door open. I followed her into the house with Daisy on my heels.

"Sorry about…" Daisy began.

Cutting Daisy off, I said, "I'm sorry, but I could get fired if that video is posted to social media."

We entered her kitchen. Sharon picked up her phone from the table. I watched as she clicked through her phone.

"Did Susie message it?" she asked.

"Yes," Daisy answered.

"Here it is." Sharon held it up to Daisy. "Right?"

"Yes. That's it."

I wanted to rip the damn phone out of her hand and delete it, and my arm instinctively rose to grab it, but I paused, realizing just how aggressive I was being. I watched her delete the video.

Sharon turned to me. "Satisfied?"

I nodded. *Jesus, I'm acting like a shrew.* "Thank you. I'm sorry for being such a harpy. But if that video went public, it could ruin my life."

"Being a little dramatic, aren't we?" Sharon mocked me.

Now that the video had been erased, my tension thawed and a smile formed on my lips. "Maybe?"

Sharon put her phone back on the table. "Now that you're here, how about a coffee? Come sit."

Feeling guilty, I sat and said, "Thanks. Two sugars."

Sharon brought over the coffees and sat. "Charlotte, I was going to call today and apologize about the gummies. I don't even think about anyone's tolerance level. But clearly, if I'm sharing them with others, I should have asked."

Wow. Sharon admitting a mistake? "Well, I guess I learned not to pop something into my mouth without asking some questions first." I could see Daisy's shoulders relax.

We caught up for another two hours. Sharon was not the same arrogant pest she'd been in college.

"Hey, let me know the next time Charlotte visits, and we can all go to dinner," Sharon said as she walked us to the car.

"I will."

Driving out of Sharon's street, Daisy said, "I told you she'd changed. She's become a good friend."

I turned and looked out the side window. "You were right. I don't trust people."

"I understand. Look what your ex did."

"Yeah, but... You'd think I'd be more trusting what with the whole therapy thing after the divorce." I picked some cat hair off my pants. Maxwell crossed my mind.

As the sun set, I packed up my car. "I'm so glad I came up here, even with the gummy debacle. I don't feel so anxious. I actually feel lighter."

Daisy poked me in the ribs. "Well, you did up-chuck all over the place last night."

"Ha. Ha." Putting both hands on my hips, I said, "It's just that I don't feel this heaviness I've been carrying. It's a relief."

"Told you coming up to see me was a good idea." She beamed. "Anyway, sometimes taking some time off a problem helps. If I'm not mistaken, that was your advice to me about Janice. Remember?"

I kissed her on the cheek. "No one ever takes their own advice."

We stood for a minute, neither of us wanting to move.

Daisy spoke first. "It'll be okay with Maxwell, you know. Look how you felt about Sharon, but it wasn't true."

Hugging her, I said. "You're a good friend."

*

On the drive home, I considered how worried I'd been these past weeks about Maxwell's ex-wife, Kara, moving to New Jersey. He'd told me over drinks one night that after they both graduated from Ohio University, they lived in and around Columbus to stay close to her family and friends. After they divorced, Maxwell moved back home to New Jersey. When they divorced, Kara had moved down the street to live with Roman, the man she'd had an affair with.

Now, eight years after Roman had dumped her, she decided it was time for a fresh start, accepting a promotion at her corporate headquarters. Marketing Vision had offices all over the United States. So why move here? She had no family or only a few friends in the area, and both kids were in college in Colorado.

Having gone through a divorce, I understood why she'd want a new beginning. But this felt like a step back. Who was she kidding? She ran to the man who had fought so hard to keep their marriage together. Kara wasn't interested then. Now she's looking to fill her lonely nights with the person she so casually threw away. My person.

But I'm not the naïve, gullible pawn I used to be. No, not this old girl. I don't blindly accept what someone says as true. My ex taught me that.

When I'd seen Maxwell laughing on his dock with his ex and their children, it shot me back ten years to a neighbor's pool party. Grant, my ex-husband, laughed at something our neighbor, Mia, had said, as they stood apart from the rest of us. Like it was the funniest thing he'd ever heard. I remembered watching them for a moment before returning to my own conversation. No niggle at the back of my neck that something was up. No twinges of suspicion even when I came home at lunchtime from a business trip and found Mia and Grant in our kitchen. Something about our mail going to her house? I believed them.

Only after I caught Grant in bed with my friend Eva did I finally put the pieces together. How could I not have known? I could see the same thought running through the minds of my so-called friends when they asked me what happened and I told them he'd had an affair. *Oh.* That condescending little word spoke volumes. They knew. His philandering was obvious to everyone else. Everyone but me. Christ, what a fool I was.

About a month after I found him sleeping with my friend, he came to the house to pick up the rest of his belongings. After he packed his car, he came back inside.

Trying to look nonchalant, I sipped tea at the kitchen table, flipping through a real estate brochure. Bri told me to record everything he said whenever I saw him. I had positioned my phone earlier by the cookbooks on the countertop. I wasn't interested in the video, just the audio. I still wasn't sure why she warned me to do this. New Jersey is an equitable distribution state, but Bri's lawyer husband had suggested it.

"Are you sure you want a divorce?" He sat next to me at the table. "Throw that damn brochure out. We put so much into this house; we'll never get it back if we sell." He reached for my hand, but I pulled it away. "Come on," he continued. "It's not just the house. We'll have to split up all our assets."

I stared at him incredulously. "Wait. You don't want a divorce because you don't want to sell the house?" My voice rose. "How about, I love you. I can't live without you?"

He shook his head and gave me some lip service about being monogamous in the future.

"Forget it." I stood, pointing my finger in his face. "You slept with my friend Eva. My friend. The one you always told me you hated. Why in the name of God would I want to be with someone who lied and cheated? Just leave." I turned, walking from the kitchen.

"Sure. Like you didn't know what was going on all these years," he hissed, slowly standing up. "Give me a break."

Inhaling a shallow breath, I struggled for another. "What?" I murmured, facing him.

"You knew. You always knew. Don't play Little Miss Innocent." He shrugged. "Right after our honeymoon when you came home from work and Cammy was at the house. You were so blasé about it and even invited her to dinner."

"Cammy. You slept with Cammy?" How proud he acted, puffing up his chest and standing tall. I needed air. Using the countertop for support, I walked out the back door. I breathed deeply. *Am I this fucking foolish? Or did I just ignore the signs?* Like that stupid laugh he had with Mia at the pool party. Had something been going on with them too?

I heard Grant behind me at the screen door. "Listen…"

At the sound of his voice, I whipped around and screamed, "Did you sleep with Mia too? How many women have you slept with?"

Startled, he paused. Shrugged his shoulders. "I don't know?"

"Yes, you do. How many?" I started walking toward the screen door, anger burning in my veins.

"A couple."

"Two? You slept with two women? That's a lie. I don't believe you."

His second shrug was now more exaggerated.

I stepped closer toward the door.

Grant looked smug, standing there behind the screen door. Proud almost.

The anger burning inside me erupted. Jamming my finger through the screen right at his face, I yelled, "Get the fuck out of this house or I'm calling the police." Hate consumed me. "And don't ever come back."

He stepped back, his face dark, glaring at me. "How dare you…" He punched the doorframe. "This is my house. My money. I'll make sure you get nothing." Abruptly he turned and left muttering something inaudible.

I hoped he broke his hand smashing the doorframe. I hollered after him. "You're nothing but a bully on the playground – a big loudmouth. But you're a coward. Run away. You asshole." I knew he wouldn't want to deal with the police.

God, he's toxic. And I reeked of him. I needed a shower to get all the years of his stench off of me. Walking back into the kitchen, I grabbed the phone by the cookbooks. My hands shook and I had to click the button several times to turn the audio on. But it was all there. I burned every awful thing he said into my brain so I'd never go back to him. Fuck settling this amicably, I'd get the best damn lawyer I could find.

*

The echoes and stings of my old life with Grant faded with each mile I traveled home until they vanished completely. By the time I pulled into my garage, I was back in the present. Thinking about Grant made me appreciate Maxwell more. He was my soothing balm. This patient, kind, and caring man had shown me how to love again. I had no reason to distrust him, but I hadn't distrusted Grant either. I realized I was scared. Scared to trust Maxwell. Scared to trust choosing him – or that he'd choose me. This damn little voice in my brain just wouldn't stop prattling on.

I hauled my baffled butt into the house and plopped my things in my room. It was almost eleven. Too late to eat. And I wasn't hungry anyway. Instead, I poured a glass of white wine to help stop the chatter in my head and sat in front of the fireplace. Turning the gas on with the remote, I watched the flames flicker to life. Settling back into the couch, I noticed a picture of Bri and me on the mantel. We'd been seniors in high school with our whole lives ahead of us. A warm glow embraced me. I knew what Bri would do in my shoes. She'd take a chance on Maxwell. But she doesn't have my skeletons. I could hear her now: *What do you have to lose?* Everything. Nothing. Grinning, I said out loud, "Jesus, I'm having conversations with people in my head." But imaginary Bri was right. Deep in my soul, I knew it. The chatter died down and I finished my wine in peace. Later, my final thoughts before I fell asleep were of Maxwell giving me the first edition of my great uncle's book *Topper* on his dock over the summer. Grant had never – ever made me feel that special in the twenty years we were married.

In the morning, the sun shone brightly. My mood matched it. I picked Tucker up from the kennel, and we took a quick walk around the neighborhood before I headed to work.

"Good morning," I announced loudly as I entered the office. My co-workers looked up, puzzled. They probably wondered what had happened over the long weekend to put me in such a good mood. *And it wasn't the gummies.* I texted Maxwell and asked if he'd like to have dinner.

He replied. *Love to. Tonight? When? I miss you.*

I answered. *Redwoods at 7.*

Rushing home to take care of Tucker, I felt better than I had in weeks. I finally brought the dresses I'd abandoned on the back seat of my car after seeing Maxwell with his family on the dock inside.

Rummaging around in my makeup drawer, I found that sexy red Chanel lip gloss all my friends raved about at book club. After a final glance in the mirror, I smiled confidently. Yes, I'm ready. I flipped off the light and strode towards my future, leaving my doubts and fears behind.

Chapter 18

AVA

NSWERING THE DOOR in my bathrobe, I told Neil to make himself a drink. I'd be ready shortly.

"Ava, my dad is a stickler for punctuality."

"Relax. You're early." I shut the front door. "Is that why you insisted on us going together? You were afraid I'd be late?"

He crossed his arms. "No. I told you I had a land development meeting in your area.

"What did you take, Rideshares all day? I knew he had left his car at his father's Hampton home for the summer.

"Yes," he said briskly.

"I'm fully capable of driving myself to your father's apartment. Or yours, if you insist we go together." *Jesus. Like being five minutes behind schedule was some kind of catastrophe.*

Shrugging, he went to the bar and made himself a drink.

"I'll be right back." Once in my bedroom, I rethought my outfit for tonight. Neil looked great in a grey wool Canali suit, a silk shirt, and Italian loafers, which blended together seamlessly. I grabbed my black silk wrap dress from the closet and Christian Louboutin shoes. Ten minutes later, I met Neil in the living room.

"Great. Let's get going." He put his empty glass on the bar.

He was starting to piss me off with this hurry-up crap. "I'm having a cocktail. We have plenty of time. I mixed us both a small drink.

Neil glanced at his watch but didn't say anything.

Ten minutes later, in my car driving to his father's apartment in New York City, I pointed to the dashboard clock. "Look. We've got extra time in case we hit traffic. Relax." His anxiety was rubbing off on me, so I drove faster than I probably should have.

Tapping my fingers on the steering wheel, I pondered why I had agreed to this. It's not like I needed Bruce Bass's seal of approval or even wanted it in the first place. Neil had been pressing to have dinner with his father, and I'd finally relented. But it didn't make me happy.

His father had moved into One57 on Central Park South as soon as it was completed in 2014. Despite being eighty-five years old, Bruce Bass wasn't the type to move into a senior citizen residence.

Entering the parking garage, my stomach tightened. I'd managed to avoid Neil's father since we began dating again. Now, I have to sit face-to-face with the man who threatened to have my father fired if Neil didn't break up with me. Not only was I not good enough when we first dated in our twenties, but I wasn't Jewish. This time, though, I thought, tightening my lips into a straight line, he's not dealing with a young, insecure woman.

I stepped through the thick wooden doors of his father's apartment and took a deep breath, bracing myself. My eyes widened in awe. The city's lights sparkled against the darkness, glistening across the skyline. All framed in towering windows. The night sky filled with an infinite number of diamond-like stars. It felt like I was looking down from the heavens.

"Pretty incredible, huh?" Neil asked.

"Coats, please," said the man who had opened the door.

"Hi, Stefan," Neil said.

I handed him my wrap and heard the low murmur of his father coming from the right side of the apartment. Neil walked on ahead. Still mesmerized by the cityscape, I strolled in and examined the open-concept design. The modern furniture complemented the skyline aesthetic with clean lines of smooth stone, wood, and plush fabrics. Here on the seventieth floor, we had a dead-center panoramic view of Central Park and all the skyscrapers neighboring the park. Built to maximize the views and framed in floor-to-ceiling windows, the city simmered below with all its manmade clutter and chaos. But up here the hustle and bustle were reduced to distant chatter barely audible off in the distance. The stars were out in force tonight, glittering like tiny diamonds scattered across the sky. I wondered how many people Bruce had stepped over to get to this paradise – his own private stairway to heaven.

"Ava, I'd like you to meet my father, Bruce Bass," Neil said.

Hearing my name, I rotated to my right, and there by the kitchen counter, was Neil's father. Old, but still distinguished in an immaculately pressed black suit and crisp white shirt. Bald, like his son, his waxy face was tight with fillers. I forced a smile when Bruce turned in my direction. Neither of us moved to shake hands. He gave me a curt nod before wrapping his arms around his son.

"Finally. I was beginning to wonder," Bruce said.

I looked at my watch. It was exactly seven.

"Come. Appetizers are in the living room. Dinner will be served in thirty minutes." He confirmed that with the kitchen staff by a quick glance.

Neil followed his father.

"Drink?" Bruce Bass asked when I walked into the living room.

"Dirty martini, please," I said.

His father nodded to Stefan who made my drink at the bar on the far side of the room. The drink was presented on a small silver tray. Thanking Stefan, I took a small sip. The martini was delicious. I settled into my chair as Neil and his dad talked about various business deals. The view was so hypnotic that I drifted off momentarily.

Bruce's voice snapped me out of my reverie. "Ava, did you ever sell that management business?"

Startled, I turned toward him and answered that we had.

"Neil was hot to buy it. But I didn't think it was worth the money," he said with a smirk.

I wasn't going to play this game. "Good thing you didn't buy it then." I turned back to the view. The doorbell rang.

Now what?

A loud, young woman came sashaying into the living room dragging her coat behind her. "Sorry, Brucie dear. The photoshoot went on forever. You know I must stay to the end." She slinked around him like a snake and kissed him passionately on the lips, dropping her coat on the floor.

So damn cliché – old rich man and young model. She must be close to Alysia's age. I looked at Neil, who was watching her intently. She had on a Grecian–style mini dress which looked like she was going to the beach, not dinner. It hung off her one shoulder so low that you could see the side of her tan breast. I wondered if she was tan all over her body.

"Dinner is served," announced a woman in a maid's outfit.

I sat across from Neil at the dining room table before he made the introductions. "Ava, this is my father's girlfriend, Tassy. And Tassy, this is my girlfriend, Ava."

Tassy began to talk about the fashion layout she had just finished. You'd think she was the editor of *Vogue* or the designer of the clothing line, the way she rambled on.

Turning toward me, Tassy said, "You know, the goal of any photo shoot is to tell a story while you highlight the clothes." She brought both hands to her heart. "And this photographer was so creative... he used the backdrop of some... well, poorer neighborhoods." She paused and wrapped a lock of hair around her finger, then gazed out the massive windows.

No one spoke, and the silence interrupted whatever thought was running through Tassy's mind. "Oh, I'm sorry. Where was I?" She cleared her throat and continued, "The bright colors of the designer's clothes looked so sharp against the bleak background." She twisted toward Bruce. "Just wait till you see me in the magazine."

I wondered if she even thought about the people living in those neighborhoods. My mind traveled back to when I lived in the Bronx. The money spent advertising the designer's clothing could have gone into those neighborhoods, hiring some locals and doing some good. But I wouldn't even suggest it. People like Bruce believe they're special and that they made their money the right way with hard work and ruthless negotiations. Of course, they ignore the tremendous advantages they had by building off their parents' fortune and business connections. In that, they were lucky. So different from Gabriel who became a doctor without any family funds. Spending time with him in Puerto Rico after Hurricane Maria really opened my eyes as I watched him work twelve-hour shifts. He never accepted any payment for his services – just had the hospital give it back to the community.

I watched the dynamics of the Bass household. Both men appeared completely focused on what Tassy was saying as she continued telling them about her day. Neil seemed captivated by her, and an ugly thought coursed through me. Had Neil been intimate with any of his father's ex-partners? The thought made me sick. Why did I think such a thing? Maybe it was time to let go of Neil and the false fantasy I had created around him.

Stefan opened a bottle and poured Bruce a taste of the red wine.

His face soured and he said to Stefan, "This has gone bad. Get me something else."

"I'll go, Dad," Neil said. "Is the wine room locked?"

"No, why would it be locked if we're having dinner?" he asked. "Pick something Italian around 2003."

After Neil left the room, his father turned to me.

Before he had a chance to speak, I said, "So, Bruce. How do you feel about me being back in Neil's life again?"

He sat straighter in his chair. "Were you in his life before? When?"

I sat higher in mine. "You know when. The time you threatened to have my father fired if Neil didn't break up with me. Right before you shipped your son off to California."

"My dear, Neil's had so many girlfriends and wives, it's hard to keep track of all the women. But I definitely don't remember ever threatening to fire a father from his job," Bruce said and laughed "Boy, did my son sell you a bill of goods."

Speechless, I looked away. Was he telling me the truth? Neil had lied to me when we got back together. I wondered at the time if he had thrown his father under the bus to make himself look better. And apparently, he had. Controlling, lying, and lusting after young women his father dates – Christ, I might as well be dating my ex-husband. Any remaining illusions I may have had of Neil shattered.

Neil reappeared with two bottles of red wine. "Dad, let's decanter this one and start off with the pinot noir."

"Good picks," Bruce said.

Neil smiled broadly.

What an ass-kissing idiot. Sitting there, listening to Tassy's continued monologue, I realized I didn't want either of these men in my life. I didn't need Neil's lies or his father's approval. I picked up my martini I had been nursing but then decided I didn't need it. Or Neil.

"I think I'm going to call it a night," I said, placing my drink back on the table. "Thank you for the invitation."

Bruce raised an eyebrow but said nothing.

Neil looked up sharply from pouring his father's wine, which spilled over the tablecloth.

"For Christ's sake, look at what you're doing," Bruce roared.

Tassy smiled sweetly, ignoring the mess. "It was lovely meeting you, Ava. Maybe we can have a girls' day out sometime?"

I bit back a sarcastic retort and nodded politely. "Maybe."

"Wait, Ava," Neil screeched. "Hang on!"

Without another word to anyone, I stood and made my way from the dining room and through the living room, grabbing my wrap from the closet on the way out. As I stepped into the elevator and hit the button for the lobby, I couldn't help but feel relief wash over me. I didn't need to be a part of their self-absorbed, greedy, narrow-minded world anymore. I was better off alone. Neil should have stayed in my dreams.

*

The doorbell woke me up. "Crap. If that's Neil…" I threw back the covers and yanked my phone out of my purse. Checking my security app, I saw Bri at the front door. *Oh. Shit. I forgot to set the alarm.*

I rushed to the door, opening it. "Good morning. Bri."

She just stared at me. "Oh, Ava, I didn't mean to wake you. I'll come back later." She started down the steps.

I grabbed her arm. "Don't be silly. I'm running a little behind, that's all."

She laughed. "A little? I think you just woke up. Your hair is sticking straight up in the back."

I stepped aside to let her in. "Give me five minutes."

"Did you remember the meeting today with Mother Superior?"

"Yes, of course. I did. I just forgot to set my alarm. I've been dealing with a couple of things."

Bri put her hand on my shoulder. "Is everything okay? You don't have to come with me."

"I promise I won't take more than fifteen minutes," I said and headed back into my bedroom.

Bri hollered, "I can call and postpone. We can do it later in the week."

"Don't be ridiculous. Make yourself at home and grab a coffee. It's timed to brew in the morning."

Fifteen minutes later, I appeared in the kitchen as vibrant as a freshly bloomed flower. "I'm done. Let me grab a coffee, and I'll drink it on the way."

Once we were in the car, I asked, "Are you all set for the meeting?"

"Yes. The Sisters and Aiding the Children want to let me know about their most important sponsors and where they'd like them seated. I'm sure they'll also have some final questions."

"Let's grab lunch after the meeting," I suggested.

"That sounds great," she said and drove into the entrance of Sisters of Charitable Care. "It's my treat to thank you."

*

An hour later, as we left the Sisters' parking lot, Bri breathed a sigh of relief. "I'm so glad Mother Superior approved everything and actually gave me her blessing."

"Well done. I'm so proud of you," I said, glancing at Bri who was tinkering with the in-dash navigation system. "Anyway," I continued hesitantly, not wanting to dampen her jubilant mood, but… "I broke up with Neil last night."

She peered at me in alarm. "What?"

I told her what had happened.

Bri stayed quiet for a moment or two. The only sound was the hum of the car's engine as we drove down the road. Then, finally, Bri let out a long sigh. "Are you okay?"

"Actually, yeah," I replied. "Last night was quite the eye-opener."

She patted my arm. "Do you want to talk about it?"

"Nah, not really." My phone buzzed in my bag, and I ignored it. Then I couldn't help myself, and the words tumbled out. "Neil wasn't who I expected him to be. Or, maybe who I wanted him to be – that amazing man who lived in my imagination." *Jesus, I put him on such a high pedestal! What an idiot I was.*

I shook my head, stunned at how I'd idolized him. I stared out the window of the passenger seat, reflecting on my foolish mistakes. The warm sunshine greeted me as I stepped out of the car. The clouds had vanished, replaced by a vibrant blue sky. Colors popped around me and an unmistakable scent of lilacs filled the air. Bri laced her arm in mine, and we walked into the quaint eatery.

My stomach growled at the delectable aromas coming from the kitchen, and I realized I hadn't eaten anything since yesterday morning. We placed our orders quickly.

Bri's eyes shone brightly as she leaned toward me. "You're so brave," she whispered. "Most people stay in bad relationships because they don't want to be alone. But not you. You want the real thing. And I know you'll find it."

I joked lightly. "You're giving me more credit than I deserve. Sure, I want to find love. But I won't accept being taken advantage of, controlled or manipulated any more. Enough is enough."

Bri smiled that sweet smile of hers. "You'll find him. I know it."

Maybe I had. My thoughts turned to Gabriel. However, I didn't want to rebound with him. I don't need a partner to feel whole. It's ironic that I'd even consider him romantically; we hadn't seen each other in two decades even though we were childhood friends. We'd reconnected when we both went to Puerto Rico to help our mothers after Hurricane Maria. His mom, Lola, and my Mami live next door to one other and have been friends their entire lives. My mother would like nothing better than for the two of us to date. Perhaps she's right. Gabriel was everything Neil wasn't – kind, generous, humble, and sexy with a full head of curly locks I could get lost in.

*

When Bri dropped me home, I was delighted there were no flowers waiting to greet me. And so far, no calls or texts from Neil. He was persistent when it came to getting what he wanted, so maybe this time he'd gotten the message.

Stepping into the house, my home phone rang. I almost never answer it, but I always look at the caller ID because my mother insists on calling my home phone number. She never uses the cell I bought her.

Sure enough, I picked it up. "Hola, Mami."

"Did you get the invitation to the wedding? Did you get a dress yet? I think you should get a sexy one, maybe in a bright blue color," she said, a million miles a minute.

"Whoa, Mami. One question at a time. Yes, I did receive the invite. And no, I haven't bought a dress."

"You need to hurry. The wedding is in two weeks."

"I noticed I was not invited with a plus one. Was that your doing?"

Mami cleared her throat. "I don't know what you're talking about. But please don't bring that man you date."

"You'll be happy to know that we're not dating anymore."

Silence.

"Mami, you there?" I asked. I heard another voice in the background now. It was probably Lola and they were trying not to sound too excited.

"Si, just finishing up the dishes. Don't forget to buy a beautiful dress." She ended the call.

The thought of Gabriel put a huge smile on my face.

*

I went to Bloomingdales with my daughter. She decided I should stay in the fitting room, and she would bring me dresses to try on. But I don't wear micro mini dresses with plunging necklines, clothes that look great on a twenty-something.

"Alysia, what are you bringing me?" I asked her, holding another tiny garment up. Not only was it super short, but parts of it were actually transparent.

"Why don't you just try it on?" she asked, sounding as exasperated as I felt.

"Because I've been there and worn that a long time ago," I told her. I could wear my black silk dress. but it felt tainted now – my breakup dress. I wanted something fresh and new.

It wasn't until we were on our way out that I spotted a perfect blue dress on a mannequin. The salesperson ordered the dress in my size and promised I'd have it in seven days; at least a week before the wedding. I also brought silver pumps.

"You know, Mom, Neil was okay, but you can do better," Alysia said, getting into the car.

Before I could answer, my phone buzzed. It was Neil. "Speak of the devil. He just sent me a text." It had been a week without any contact which surprised me. The text read:

Hey, just wanted to see how you're doing.

I stared at my phone for a moment before typing back a quick reply:

I'm doing fine.

Seconds later, he responded:

I bought that property in Mendham.
Why did he do that?

Another text popped up.

You'll make a nice commission. You can thank me later.

What the hell is he up to? *God Damn it.* I reined in my emotions and relaxed the taunt muscles in my face. I didn't want to alarm Alysia. This must be yet another way for him to control me and I wanted no part of it. Once his confidence, wit, and charm had been my kryptonite, but as I sat there in my car in the mall parking lot, I knew without a doubt that I never wanted to date him again – ever.

I typed out a simple reply:

I didn't do anything for a commission, and I don't want it.

Alysia looked at me as I locked my phone and shoved it into my purse. "What did he want?" she asked, starting the car.

"Just checking in," I said with a shrug. "Trying to make small talk."

"That's all he was ever good for," Alysia muttered under her breath.

We drove in silence for a mile or so. Then Alysia spoke up. "You know, Mami told me about Lola's son. How funny his name is Gabriel too. Did you name my brother after him? Mami said you were childhood friends."

Grinning, I said, "She did? What did she say? And no, I didn't name my son after him. I've just always liked the name."

*

I arrived at St. Paul's Cathedral right before the wedding party started down the aisle. I've got to be more punctual.

Slipping into a pew, I wondered how Miguel, the groom, managed to get the Catholic church to annul his first marriage. He'd been married for twenty-five years and had three children. I smirked. It must have been some type of miracle. He stood at the altar with his best man, Luis. Mami told me that they'd been friends since kindergarten.

The gentle melody of a violin flowed through the room, and I glanced around for familiar faces. Mami was up front gesturing for me to come join her, but I refused with a shake of my head.

The tempo of the music changed, and a lovely flower girl appeared, showering the aisle with scattered rose petals as she skipped to the front of the church. She couldn't be older than four, with brunette hair cascading down her back in tight curls. Her cute little pink dress matched her ballerina flats. Her lips had a soft pink gloss on them. The maid of honor trailed behind her in a fitted teal gown with such a large bouquet that it was hard to tell what the flowers were. Her black hair was cut into a shoulder-length bob that accentuated the sharp angles of her face.

The bride moved gracefully down the aisle in a gown that sparkled in the candlelight. It was probably made of silk with a subtle sheen. Her hair was up in a tight bun, stylish and chic, an embellished hair clip on one side. A tear slipped down my cheek. I always cried at weddings.

My eyes followed the bride up the aisle and locked on Gabriel's. He nodded in my direction. *Boy, he cleans up well.* His midnight blue suit was paired with a white shirt and colorful tie. I couldn't make out the tie's design, but it had deeper hues of red and purple contrasted with white.

Once at the altar, the priest spoke about marriage and God's blessing of love. I zoned out. As the couple exchanged vows, I drifted back to Paul and how my own marriage ended in failure. God, I was so wrong about him. And now about Neil. Why can't I pick the right man?

I waited in line to congratulate the happy couple and joined Mami and Lola at the entrance of the church.

"Sophia looks beautiful," I told Lola, squeezing her shoulder.

"Si," she replied, her eyes misting as she looked at her son and his new bride.

We made our way outside, holding handfuls of rice to throw. I felt a tap on my shoulder and turned around. Gabriel stood there, handsome as ever with a warm smile on his face.

"Ava," he said, "it's been too long."

My heart skipped a beat as he leaned in to give me a hug. The soapy smell from the hospital had been replaced with spicy cologne with a hint of musk. I wondered what it was. I loved it. His bronze eyes held so much empathy and intelligence, and his wild dark curls cascaded down his neck. Those damn curls will be the death of me. But I reminded myself that I had just broken up with Neil and shouldn't rush into anything.

"It's good to see you, too," I said.

We chatted about the wedding for a minute or two until it was time to throw the rice. Everyone was cheering and wishing the new couple the best. A feeling of nostalgia washed over me as I watched them drive away in an old-fashioned carriage. It seemed like yesterday that Paul and I had married. How fast it all goes.

Gabriel escorted both our mothers to the reception. I didn't want to leave my car at the church, so I drove myself. I wasn't surprised my mother went with them. It would give her a chance to talk me up to Gabriel. Our seats at the reception were arranged together, no doubt thanks to my mother's maneuvering, but I wasn't upset with her. I enjoyed being around him.

"How is your daughter doing living on her own?" he asked.

"She loves it. I don't. I wish she had a roommate."

He shook his head. I noticed a hint of pink on his cheeks as he spoke.

"Have you done any more work outside the country since Puerto Rico?" I heard our mothers chatting away in Spanish beside me, but I was sure they were also listening to every word we said.

Gabriel let out a small sigh. "No. My employer wants me to wait a year before heading out again." He ran a hand through his hair, pushing the strands away from his face.

"Do you work in other countries every year?" I asked.

He nodded. "It varies. I usually go with a team of doctors from around the Tri-State area."

I couldn't help but contrast his selfless dedication to helping others with Neil, who would never do anything if he didn't get anything out of it personally.

The corners of Gabriels's mouth lifted into a genuine smile. "It may not seem like much, but if I can make even the smallest difference in someone else's life, then it's worth it."

His words tugged at my heartstrings, and I knew he meant every word.

Those sultry Latin songs with their sensual beats made me want to move. Grabbing Gabriel's hand, we danced song after song. Until the DJ played a slow song. Gabriel carefully placed one hand on my waist and the other on my hip. I turned my head to him and our cheeks brushed. Tingles shot up my spine. I knew Mami and Lola were looking and loved it. Forgetting all about Neil, I moved in time with the rhythm of the song. Gabriel leaned in close. "You know," he whispered into my ear, "I've always had a crush on you."

My stomach fluttered. "Really?" I asked, breathless.

Gabriel nodded; his eyes fixed on mine. "Really." He leaned in and kissed me.

As our lips met, a jolt ran through my body. I wrapped my arms around Gabriel's neck, deepening the kiss.

I could just imagine my mother and Lola grinning from ear to ear.

Chapter 19

STACI

As I GAZED out the window of The Busy Bean, my mind drifted back to the morning after George's heart attack. I could vividly recall struggling to get out of bed after just one hour of sleep. Even splashing cold water on my face didn't clear the fog in my head. The drive home from the hospital was a blur. It seemed like it happened just yesterday, but it was actually a week ago.

The door to the coffee shop swung open, sending a chill through the air. *Brrr!* I shivered. So much for spring. It felt like a freezing February day. I took another sip of my coffee and added an extra packet of sugar to try and sweeten it. When that didn't work, I walked up to the counter and asked for a little more milk before finding a table in the back of the shop, away from the drafty door.

Madeline and Bri were meeting me here in a few minutes. I needed to vent. My life felt like it was spiraling out of control. Both of my sons called me the morning after George's heart attack, and what did I do? I avoided conflict like always. My sons wanted to know how I was. Did I tell them I was devastated? No. Did I tell them how wrong my mother was to say what she did? No. I explained to them that I thought their grandmother was tired and cranky and didn't mean what she said. What crap – she meant every word. What the hell is wrong with me? Why do I keep trying to pretend everything's okay – when it certainly isn't?

Lost in my thoughts, I didn't see my friends approaching the coffee shop. I looked up when a cold burst crept up my spine. Even in the back, I shuddered and wrapped my coat around my shoulders.

"Hi, Staci," Bri said.

"Good morning," Madeline said.

"Thanks for meeting me." I rose, giving each a peck on the cheek. "You're always so punctual."

"Of course we are, dear." Madeline took off her coat and laid it over the chair back neatly folded. "Bri, I'm buying, what do you want?"

"Hot tea – English Breakfast." Bri slung her purse and coat over the chair and sat. "What a nice way to start the day," she said, patting my hand.

When Madeline returned with the drinks, Bri said, "You mentioned on the phone that your mother said something unkind to you?"

I squirmed in my seat. "Try vicious."

Madeline raised her eyebrows. "Tell us."

My throat tightened. "Basically, my mother accused me of causing George's heart attack. In front of my sons."

"What did she say exactly?" Madeline asked. "Do you remember?"

"Yes, the words are burned into my mind. 'My loving mother said, 'This is all your fault! You gave George that heart attack. By taking up with that hobo of yours and shoving it in his face. He worked so hard so you could have everything, but apparently that wasn't enough. You should be ashamed of yourself.'" My stomach cramped. Her biting words were still so fresh and painful.

Bri covered her mouth with her hand, and Madeline's face turned pink.

"That's horrible," Bri said. "I can't believe she'd say such a thing?"

"She blindsided me. I can't think of a better word than that. I walked into that hospital room and her loathing came at me in waves. I started to ask her what her problem was but stopped. My sons didn't need to see us fighting. But what my mother said was unforgivable. She destroyed any hope I might have had that we'd be able to fix our relationship. Instead of supporting me when I was most vulnerable, she attacked me in front of my sons." A tear slid down my cheek. "I never cared about that damn house or any of the crap George insisted I have."

Madeline grasped my hand. "You're the least pretentious person I know. Don't take what she's said to heart."

"Aren't moms supposed to love unconditionally? I showered my kids with it. But not her, not for me."

Bri patted my shoulder reassuringly. "No, that can't be. I'm sure she loves you."

"Hanna working things out with her mother made me hope that maybe we could work out our differences. But…" I dropped my head. "Nothing I ever do is right. Except when I married George. He's the one she loves."

Madeline shook her head. "Some moms just suck. Mine sure as hell did."

A couple more tears fell. I wiped them away. "I guess." I remembered an incident when my mother's mom died. Dad went to console her, but she pivoted away from him like a child fleeing an annoying adult. The look she gave him froze the blood in my veins. I knew then that a coldness spread through her veins, freezing her from within. Even my father's warm and compassionate heart couldn't melt the ice in her.

"I think you need to address this with her," Madeline said. "Just like you did with that bitch up in Vermont. Nothing's going to change until you do."

"I know." The door opened. A group of people walked in, and I heard a familiar voice speaking loudly over their babble. *Damn.*

My mother stood proud as a peacock and just as colorful in another new winter coat of teal wool with a bright lavender and blue scarf.

Madeline leaned onto the table. I thought she was about to say something but instead she sat back again.

Praying she wouldn't notice us was futile. She had eyes and ears like a hawk. Sure enough, I heard her say, "Oh, my daughter's here. Let's say hi to her." Her eyes narrowed as she focused on me and my friends.

My mother approached and air kissed the top of my head, her friends in close pursuit. "Well, Staci, I see you're not too busy from all your writing to while away the day with your friends. It's nice getting a large divorce settlement, isn't it?"

Madeline swiveled to face my mother.

Placing my hand on Madeline's knee, I said, "Mom, how nice to see you too. And you're so right, that settlement check is amazing." Anger spurred me on. "Is that another new designer coat? It's a Burberry, right? How many is that this year? Can you afford all those new coats?"

Her friends gasped.

For a moment her face flushed but she recovered just as quickly. "That's so typical, dear. So typical." She swiveled away and left, her posse in toe.

I watched her get her coffee and sit with her friends in the front of the little shop. "I'm sorry you had to witness that," I told my friends. "I just want to slap her."

My mother's table wasn't far enough away. Her gang was whispering and pointing. Mother's voice picked up, and we heard her say, "Her father spoiled her terribly. Who speaks to their mother like that?" She shook her head dismissively.

"Wow. She's harsh," Madeline said.

I sighed a slow exhale. Why did she have to be here today? "With her it's all about the money and what other people think. She drives an expensive car and spends lots of cash on everything, dropping designer names and prices. That's her soft spot, and I go for it every time we argue. What the hell is wrong with me? Attacking her doesn't solve anything."

Madeline pursed her lips. "You can cut off that pain right now. Walk away and don't look back."

"Hey, that's a bit extreme. Don't you think?" Bri interjected.

"Is it?"

"I don't know." Fidgeting in my chair, I thought of my sister. "If I left, my sister would get the brunt of it. I can't do that to her."

"Why don't you and your sister talk to your mom about the way she treats you? Double team her so she knows you mean business," Bri suggested.

I rubbed my hands together. "This makes me miss my dad so much more. I feel all alone." My voice broke.

"You have us." Bri leaned forward and put a hand on my elbow.

Mother's harsh voice fired through the air like an arrow finding its mark. "She had a great husband that she threw away. Can you imagine? He gave her everything and asked for nothing in return. She's always been ungrateful."

"You don't need that sanctimonious ass in your life. Get rid of her." Madeline's voice turned strong and deep. She clearly meant the ladies to hear her.

Licking my parched lips, I sank into my chair. Rage gripped me and I sat up perfectly straight, repeating Mother's words in my head, "She's always been ungrateful." I could barely contain myself. Years of her telling me *don't be so stupid. Why can't you be more like your sister? If you keep eating, you'll be the size of this house. It's no wonder no one wants to be your friend.* Acid rose and burned in my throat. No one needs this much toxicity in their life.

Madeline stood. "I'll put a stop to this right now."

"Sit down," Bri said loudly.

Startled, I looked from Bri to Madeline. "Sit, Madeline, please.

I'll deal with her later." I didn't want my friends getting mixed up in this mess.

Mom and her cronies gathered their coats and their drinks and left without looking back. Had Madeline scared them off? Everyone in town knew she'd be ruthless. Relief flooded me, and I took a deep breath, calming down.

Madeline inched forward on her chair. "I know it's easier said than done, but you don't need her in your life."

I looked at Madeline and shrugged, unable to think of anything more to say. Exhausted. All I wanted was to go home.

Grabbing my hand, Madeline said, "Well, if you can't completely let go then you have to set boundaries. It won't be easy, but it's better than going through this every time you see each other. I have a great therapist, Dr. Evelyn Mann, and she can help you. She's done wonders for me."

Bri turned her head. "You're going to her too?"

"I've been to therapy in the past to deal with my childhood and, unfortunately, I've returned because of Sarah." Madeline rummaged around in her purse and handed me a business card.

"I absolutely agree," Bri said. "Counselling would give you guidance. And you sure need it with that mother."

"When I was younger, I twisted myself into a pretzel to please her, but she was always cold as ice. Now, it's just a war between us, always lobbing insults at one another. Which just makes it worse." I rubbed the back of my neck.

"Call my therapist today. She can help," Madeline insisted.

"Let's talk about something more cheerful," I pleaded.

"Okay. How's John?" Bri said, finishing her tea.

I bowed my head. "Not exactly cheerier."

"Why, what's wrong?"

I shifted in my chair. "Nothing."

"Yes, there is. Out with it." Madeline folded her napkin, placing it on the table.

"Shouldn't John have offered to drive me home from Vermont when George had his heart attack?"

Madeline sat back in her chair, biting her lower lip.

"I wouldn't have expected him to actually drive me home. He has his farm to run, but I wanted him to ask me. Am I way off base here?"

Bri gave Madeline a sideways glance, but neither said anything.

I continued, "It seems to me that he's the one in charge of this relationship, and I don't have much of a say. Not like George, but... oh... I don't know. Maybe I'm just whiny because I'm not getting what I want."

"It's a bit of a red flag to me," Madeline finally said. "You need to tell him how you feel."

Bri nodded.

I finished my coffee. "So, the takeaway here is I have to talk to Mom and I have talk to John. I don't know. Seems like way too much talking in my future. And I suck at it."

Madeline smirked. "You know, I could coach you."

I laughed. "You sure could. I just might take you up on that."

*

I called my sister the next morning and told her what had happened with our mom at the coffee shop.

"I think your friends are right. Give me the therapist's name. I'll make an appointment for myself also," Savannah said.

After hanging up, I went to get groceries. Driving by the baseball fields where my sons used to play reminded me of a day in my late teens when my dad and I went to a Mets game at Shea Stadium.

We ate too much greasy junk food and licked our fingers clean. It was something that would make Mom cringe with disgust. We cheered when the Mets brought in a run. The game slowed, and we talked about work and friends. I desperately wanted to raise the subject of Mom, but I didn't know where to start. *Hey Dad, why in the name of God did you marry her?* He wouldn't appreciate my asking. Around the bottom of the eighth I said, "Shouldn't we leave now so we don't get stuck in traffic?" No runs had been scored in the last six innings.

"But the game isn't over yet. What if the next man hits a homerun? You'd miss it." He sat back in the stadium chair. "You have to believe in people. They can do the most amazing things."

Sure enough, after two strikes and three balls, Mookie Wilson hit a home run. We stood screaming as Mookie ran the bases, touching home plate. My dad jabbed me in the arm. "See? Don't give up on people. They'll surprise you."

Pulling into ShopRite's parking lot, I wondered why I had remembered that just then. Was Dad trying to tell me not to give up on Mom? *Shit!*

*

After a restless night, I called Madeline's therapist, Dr. Mann, to schedule a date and time. A patient had canceled for the next day, so I took that appointment. She emailed me an assessment to fill out. I did and emailed it back to her within the hour.

I'd been to couples counseling with George but none of those sessions ever helped us. I knew there wouldn't be a quick fix for this problem with my mother.

Surprised at how nervous I was when I entered Dr. Mann's office, I wasn't sure I'd be able to express my feelings properly. Maybe sensing my anxiety, she reviewed the assessment quickly and asked, "Is this problem with your mother new? Or has it always been there?"

I paused before answering. "I think it's always been there."

She tilted her head. "You think?"

"Ah. Yes. It's always been there."

Dr. Mann glanced at my assessment and asked, "Can you tell

me something you remember from childhood that would help me understand your relationship with your mother?"

"I… well… my dad was so wonderful that I didn't fully understand how offensive my mother was until after he died." I searched my memory for an example of something, but nothing popped into my mind. I twisted my hands together.

Tapping her pen on the pad, she asked, "Then can you think of something that happened recently that would help me understand your relationship?"

"Sure." I told her what my mother said when we left the hospital after seeing George. "And she calls my boyfriend, or whatever he is, all sorts of demeaning names."

"What do you mean by 'whatever he is?'" she asked. "Wait. We'll come back to that. Let's stay with your mother."

"Okay." Once I started, I couldn't stop. All those nasty interactions with her since my father's death came bursting forth.

Then I recalled something that happened in high school. "My parents had a small party with their friends to celebrate my father's promotion to consulting manager for the CPA firm he worked for. I wanted to talk to him about one of my grades but never got a chance. What I didn't know was that the teacher spoke with my mother earlier in the day about my grade. She never mentioned anything to me that afternoon." I closed my eyes, massaging my aching temples. "I came up from the basement to go to bed after my TV show was over. Mother called me into the living room. I remembered waving to everyone and saying hello. I'd known most of them my entire life. Mother stood by me and called my father. 'Richard, our darling daughter failed Chemistry. She is grounded.'"

Dr. Mann interrupted. "She said that in front of everyone?"

I nodded. "Loudly. I was mortified. My father shot up from the couch and grabbed my arm and we went into my room. Funny, I can't remember anything he said to me that night. And you know what? I didn't fail. I was missing a paper and had an incomplete. Dad and I spoke with the teacher the next day."

"Did your mother undermine you often in front of your father?"

"Umm… maybe. Dad had a way of softening her harsh remarks to Savannah and me most of the time. We listened to him and ignored her. But I didn't fully realize how vicious she could be until after he died."

By the end of the therapy session, I felt drained. Utterly drained. I'd spent almost an hour talking about my mother. Dr. Mann had scheduled another appointment for me in a couple of days. I guess she felt I needed it.

I called Savannah. "The session was intense. Once I started talking about Mom, I didn't stop."

"Did it help?"

"I don't think so. Probably too soon to tell."

"Keep me posted," she said.

Clicking off the phone, I drove past Alstede's Farm on my way home. I thought about John and the time he visited me and the apple walnut pies we bought there. I missed him.

*

The return of warm spring weather brought a chorus of cheerful chirping as I stepped outside to fill my front door planters. The air was filled with the sweet scent of new beginnings. I was more than ready for a change. I attended four additional sessions with Dr. Mann and spent half the night organizing my thoughts for a meeting with my mother about our relationship.

"You have the power. You are completely in control of the way you react. Understand your mother may not be capable of having an authentic conversation about these issues," Dr. Mann said, at my last session. Deep down, though, I was hoping for the outcome

Hanna had with her mother: a mutual understanding and a genuine desire to work it out.

We met at Broad Valley Country Club, my mother's favorite spot. George and I were members when we were married, and he insisted that I keep the membership when we divorced. I only met my mother there, so it was a complete waste of money.

She was late as always, and I soaked up the sunlight by the large picture window, trying hard to keep myself calm.

"Darling, you've got my favorite table," Mother said, air kissing the top of my head.

"I'm glad you approve."

"Are we celebrating something special? Have you come to your senses and decided to remarry George?" She sat and motioned for the waiter.

Taking a deep breath, I said, "No, Mom. I want to talk to you about our relationship." I let the words sink in.

My mother told the waiter to bring her a Chardonnay. "What's wrong now? You know, dear, you simply have to accept the mistakes you've made and try to do better the next time."

I dug my fingernails into my palms trying to squelch my anger. I wanted to scream and tell her off.

The waiter brought my mother's wine and asked if we were ready to order. "Not yet. Give us a few minutes," I said.

"Well, I think I'll have that salad with the beets," she said, looking at the menu. "Isn't it great how fast George is recuperating? He'll be going back to work next week."

"Yes, I'm happy for him, but…"

Mother placed the menu on the table. "You'd better get it together before George finds somebody else."

"Mom. Enough. We need to talk."

"What is it, dear? What now?"

"Well, you're right. I'd like to fix some things in my life. And one of the things that needs fixing is our relationship."

"Oh, please. Is this about your terrible mistake with George? That's on you, not me." She sipped her wine smugly.

I shook my head. "I dread going to family gatherings. I leave feeling worse about myself than when I got there."

"Why? Because you see how wonderful your sister's life is? You had every bit of that until you threw it all away."

I bowed my head and closed my eyes, working up the strength to continue. "Mom, you need to hear me. Please."

She huffed, blowing out her lower lip. "Oh, for heaven's sake – go on."

"You dismiss my feelings every chance you get. You try to manipulate and control me and are constantly criticizing everything I do." I swallowed and tried to modulate my voice, keeping it soft and steady. "I'd like us to try family therapy and see if we can work out these issues."

"Therapy? What for? You'll find anything to waste George's money." She scoffed.

"I have a great therapist…"

"Forget it. These are your issues, not mine. Why would I go to therapy? Enough of this silly conversation. Let's order." She took off her readers and cleaned them with the napkin.

Anger gripped me. But I listened to the lines my therapist had repeated over and over. *I have the power over how I react and the ability to define this relationship. It's not all about her.*

"No, Mom. If you won't go to family counseling, then I will set boundaries for this relationship. I deserve to be treated with respect. First, I never want to hear another word about George," I said louder than I intended.

My mother glanced around the dining room, then shooshed me.

"Second, I don't want to hear any more of your criticisms. You know the old saying – if you have nothing nice to say…"

"Oh, for pity's sake, I'm your mother. It's my job to correct your mistakes. You make enough of them."

The base of my skull throbbed. "You know, if it weren't for Dad..."

"Of course, your hero. Dad this and Dad that." She raised her hand, motioning for the waiter who promptly came. "Can I have another wine? And I'll have the beet salad."

"I'll have a wine too, but nothing to eat."

The waiter left.

"I knew Dad loved me, but I was never sure you did. You've always been so cold to me."

When she spoke, her words and tone were direct with no crack of emotion in her voice. "So, all this is because you don't think I loved you. Okay, I love you. See, you don't need therapy and can stop spending George's money on it."

As condescending as ever. She wasn't listening. "Mom, this relationship is toxic to me. I'd hoped you'd agree to therapy. But until you're ready to work on this, I won't have any contact with you." I stood and grabbed my coat. "Enjoy your lunch, Mother."

I heard her say, "Staci, where are you going? We haven't eaten yet."

The therapist was right, I do have control over how I react to this, and I'm simply not going to take it anymore. By the time the valet brought my car around, clouds blotted the sky but not my mind. My path was clear now.

*

Walking around my new townhouse, I noticed how quiet it was. No children, no workmen, no sawdust or calls from George – just silence. It unnerved me after living in chaos for so long. I flipped up my laptop and checked my emails. There were some small assignments from various clients not due until next month, freeing me up to help Bri with the Aiding the Children fundraising event.

By the time I got to Bri's home in the early afternoon, people on phones were walking around her house, some in her dining room studying papers, some using calculators. Ava and Bri were at the kitchen counter on the speakerphone with a wholesaler of paper goods.

I waved to both. When the call ended, I approached them.

"Stace. What's happening?" Ava asked, marking figures on a pad.

I gave them both a kiss on the cheek.

"Hey. Thanks again for all your help. Am I pulling you away from anything today?" Bri looked flustered.

"Just my too – quiet house. Here's the press release for the event for your approval." I handed it to her.

"Approved," she said, handing it back to me.

"I wish all of my clients were so easy." I chuckled. "How's it going?"

"Well, actually. We're just confirming last-minute details now." She paused, "Let's get some coffee and sit outside on the patio for a moment away from the chaos. You too, Ava."

We filled mugs with coffee, grabbed our coats and headed outside.

Bri inhaled deeply. "What a beautiful day." She lifted her face to the sun. "Feel how warm the sun is. I just love spring."

"Me too." I looked up and enjoyed a moment of peace.

"Me three," Ava said.

"By the way, how are things with your mother?" Bri asked. "You know you can call me anytime. Event or no event."

"I know. Things are the same except that I don't feel responsible for her bad behavior anymore. I haven't heard from her and I haven't reached out. But we'll see one another at the next holiday or grandchild's birthday. And she'll be socially friendly, as will I. It's never going to turn out like Hanna and her mom. My mother will never be what I want her to be. And I guess she's going to have to accept that I won't either."

*

A couple of days later, I was on my way to see John. I longed for him in my arms. With my mother center stage for a while, I had put what I felt about John on the back burner. After I canceled my trip to Vermont weeks ago, John called every day. Funny how that works in a relationship. When you're not available, that's when they want you. I've tried not to think about him, but I can't seem to help myself.

Dr. Mann was definitely helping my anxiety about this relationship as well as my continuing angst about my mother. She emphasized that no one could put a timetable on someone else's emotional healing. John needed to grieve the loss of his wife in his own way, and the fact that he was dating again was a sign that he was recovering. But it wasn't all about John. She made me focus on my own healing from my divorce. Her words still resonated with me as I made the long drive, feeling confident and excited to see him.

By the time I crossed into Vermont, everything seemed perfect, even the weather. I lowered my window to breathe in the sweet, musky scent of the spring blossoms on the trees lining the road. Snow still lingered on the mountain tops, but everywhere I looked yellow daffodils and purple crocuses speckled the land. It was a glorious day, just like I did the first time I made this trip, and I drove up and over the hills on Rt. 22A singing at the top of my lungs.

Twenty miles up the road, my phone buzzed. A text. I didn't recognize the number and waited until I pulled into a small convenience store/station. As I filled the car with gas, I looked at my phone.

Rose had a great time with you last night. She can't wait to see you again. I gave her your phone number. You can expect to hear from her soon. John, I think she's perfect for you. Carl and I are so excited.

I sank deep into the car's seat as the air expelled from my lungs. My hand shook holding the phone. I swiped down the text and realized it was the original message John had sent to his daughters, his friends, and to me thanking us after his accident. That bitch, Maryanne, deliberately sent this to me.

Shaken, I pulled my car into a parking spot at the station. I didn't want to drive feeling like this. I kept looking at the text over and over. I sat there for an hour or so trying to decide if I should confront John or just go home. Proceeding slowly with a relationship is one thing; dating multiple people is another. At least for me.

My phone rang. I looked at the caller ID and cleared my throat. "Hello," I squeaked out.

"What's the matter?" Madeline asked.

"How do you know something's wrong?" I barely choked out. "All I said was hello."

"I can hear it in your voice. I'm a speech therapist. Remember?"

I dissolved into tears.

"Staci, are you driving crying like that?"

"No," I blubbered. "I'm sitting in a gas station."

"Calm down. Let's talk about this. Breathe."

"What's there to talk about? John went out on a date last night with someone called Rose. It's all here in Maryanne's text that she sent out to John's daughters and me."

"Read it to me," Madeline commanded.

I slowly enunciated every word as it seared into my brain.

"That woman is pure evil. If John went out on a date with this Rose woman, wouldn't he have her number?" Madeline paused. "Think about it. Mary, whatever that bitch's name is, deliberately used that group message to upset you."

"And she did." I started to cry again.

"Stop it. Don't let her win."

I blew my nose. "So, you think I should still go to John's?"

"What's the matter with you? That shrew couldn't scare you off by blindsiding you in bathrooms, so she's turned to more surreptitious tactics. Do not let her ruin your relationship. Talk with John about the text calmly and forget about the other issues you mentioned to Bri and myself. You can talk about them later. This is more important than John not offering to drive you home after George's heart attack. Just focus on the text."

I wiped under my eyes and looked at my face in the visor mirror. Mascara streamed down my cheeks and intersected with red splotches. What a mess! "That's a good idea. You think this was just Maryanne causing trouble and not John going out on a date?"

"I do. The text gives you an opportunity to talk. Make good use of it."

I inhaled deeply then exhaled. "I'm not as brave as you."

"Yes, you are. And don't let that gnarly woman push you around up there. Call me if you need some pointers, or better yet, send me her phone number." Madeline laughed. "I'll take care of her permanently."

After I ended the call, I touched up my makeup and tried telling myself that everything would be okay. But it wasn't working. God almighty, what would I ever do without my friends? I'd have turned tail and run home.

My happy spring vibe from earlier had vanished with a single text. Clutching the steering wheel with white knuckles, I drove on.

*

Pulling down John's driveway, anxiety hung over me like a dark, dense cloud. I saw him out in the field on Chance, his back to me in the setting sun. They made quite a team. They moved together with such grace and fluidity as they cantered up a small hill. It was clear they were a great team. I hoped we'd be like that someday.

At the top of the hill, he turned quickly in his saddle, almost as if he felt my presence. Waving, he turned Chance and galloped toward me. I hoped my face didn't show any worry.

"Hi. How was the ride?" he asked, dismounting.

My hands shook as I closed the car door, so I put them in my coat pockets. "Easy. It's a beautiful day and not much traffic." My voice cracked as I shivered.

"Oh, honey, you're cold. Go into the house. I have a fire started. I'll be in in a minute." He smiled and kissed my cheek. Tugging Chance's reins, he led him into the barn.

The warm day had turned chilly, but I wasn't cold. I dropped my overnight bag in the foyer by the front table and noticed John's cell and keys were there. He probably hadn't even seen the text. *God. This is awful.* My stomach rolled in knots. How do I address this? Do I let him bring it up? I curled up in a chair in the family room in front of the fire, but its warmth didn't ease my trembling.

Fear gathered at the back of my mind. But I was determined to carry this through even if it meant losing him. I'd had enough of walking on eggshells around his friends. I heard Dr. Mann's voice in my head: I have a right to feel secure too.

The front door opened. My heart fluttered.

"How's the fire?" he asked, throwing his coat on the foyer chair. "I made a smaller one to take the chill from air but not overheat us. It's not that cold today."

"It's perfect." I managed to say.

"I'm getting a beer. Would you like a glass of wine?"

Turning to face him, I said, "Sure." My voice steady. I watched as he picked up his phone and put it in his pocket.

He brought the drinks out quickly, handed me the glass of wine, and said, "I'm so happy you're here. It's been a while. I was starting to think you were having seconds thoughts about us." He sat in the chair next to mine.

Me? Second thoughts? I looked at him and bit my lip, squelching any too-hasty words.

He must have sensed something. "Is everything okay?"

Inhaling, I plunged ahead and blurted out, "Well, I was upset when I saw Maryanne's group text earlier today about you and Rose."

His brows furrowed. "Who? What?" He took his phone out of his pocket and looked through the texts. "Oh. Staci, this isn't... this didn't... happen. I was at Carl's and they had a bunch of people over for dinner. I barely talked to Rose. I don't understand why Maryanne gave her my number or sent this text to you and my daughters."

"Maybe it's time we talk about us." I steeled myself, tamping down my pent-up emotions. "A couple of months ago, you wanted to take this relationship slowly. I understood. But if you'd like to see other people, I don't think I can do that." My free hand clutched the armrest so hard I thought I'd break a nail.

"What? No, no." He twisted in his seat toward me. I'm not dating anyone but you. I don't understand. Why did she send this text? I barely talked to her."

"All I know of Maryanne is how much she hates me. Why else would someone corner me in bathrooms and tell me to get out of your life?"

"Wait, what? She did what? Start at the beginning."

I recounted every restroom encounter and what had occurred before I left to see George at the hospital.

Sitting on the edge of the chair, confusion streaked his face. He turned toward me and said, "Why didn't you tell me about this? I would have said something to her."

My heart hammered in my chest. "How could I? It started on our first date when we ran into them in the restaurant. I didn't want to put you in a position where you'd have to choose between me and your old friend. How could I possibly have competed with her when we were so new?"

John slid back in his chair, staring at the text. "This doesn't make sense. Maryanne was always trying to set me up with someone she knew."

My pulse kept up its frantic rhythm as some moments passed in silence.

"I'm so sorry," John continued. "My daughter mentioned that she heard raised voices between you and Maryanne at the wedding. But when I asked you about it, you said that she just missed Jess. I had no idea she was so horrible to you."

"She also blamed me at the hospital for your accident," I said softly. He snapped his head up. "I can't believe that. Why did no one tell me?"

"I don't think anyone wanted to upset you right after your accident."

John rose. "This is awful." He slid his phone back into his pocket. "I don't get it. Neither Maryanne nor Carl has said anything to me about you at all."

I shrugged.

"Are you sure about what she said? Maryanne has a mean sense of humor. Maybe you misunderstood?"

My jaw clenched. "Oh, I see. It was me." I put the wine glass down hard on the table.

He knelt down in front of me. "Damn it. I'm sorry. I didn't mean that… I just don't get it."

"Well, neither do I."

"You should have told me," he said, a note of discomfort in his voice. "She must be grieving still. Jess's death broke her heart too."

I paused, thinking. "Maryanne's grief seems to have manifested into anger against me," I said. "And I'm sorry she's having such a hard time. I truly am. Maybe someday getting accosted in the ladies' room will be a joke among us. But right now, it isn't."

With his gaze fixed on me, he gently grasped both of my hands and held them. "No, it was wrong on so many levels. I'll speak with her tomorrow."

"I don't want to come between you and your friends. Maybe I should speak with her?"

"Let me try first." He bowed his head, gently kissing each hand.

When his head raised, I peered into his beautiful green eyes. Our bodies were so close that my thoughts went blank. His smell washed over me, and then his lips were on mine. Warmth surged all around as we swayed with the pulse of the kiss.

Catching my breath, I pushed back from the embrace. I hadn't finished talking yet. "It may not be grief. Maryanne may be in love with you."

Shock registered on his face. He stood and stepped back to the fireplace. "No. Absolutely not. She's my best friend's wife, for God's sake. We've known one another for years. No way."

His strong reaction made me think Madeline was right all along and that John also suspected it. "I hope you're right." I let it hang in the air. He would have to have a difficult discussion with Maryanne – the sooner the better.

It grew quiet except for the crackling of the fire.

His shoulders sagged as he leaned against the mantel, staring into the crackling fire. "This isn't exactly how I imagined our evening going," he murmured with disappointment.

Shaking my head, I uttered, "Me either. I just thought I should say something."

"I'm glad you did. And I'm the one who's sorry." His voice was heavy and slow.

I rose, touched by how troubled he was. Wanting to comfort him, I touched his shoulder. "It's okay."

He reached his arm around my waist, pulling me to him tightly. His head nestled next to my ear. "You shouldn't have had to go through any of this." John leaned back and kissed my forehead then nuzzled his head next to mine. He whispered, "Ah, Staci."

I loved the way my name sounded on his lips. God, it felt good to be in his arms again. I lifted my head off his shoulder. Our eyes met. And there, at that moment, I saw it. That quiet intensity as he looked deep into my soul. My breath caught. Could it be?

My body tingled as his lips devoured mine. A sense of urgency drove us, and we collapsed onto the couch, lost in our need and each other.

*

Later in the evening, we strolled down his path to Lake Champlain. Holding hands, walking with the water's current as the moonglade followed us. Its luminous glow lighting our way.

John stopped. "It's kind of magical. Isn't it?" He pointed out over the lake.

"It is," I slid under his arm and smiled up at him.

"I don't want to date anyone else." He tilted his head, looking down at me. "I want to get to know you, really know you. I want to enjoy life with you." He stepped back and grasped both of my arms, looking directly into my eyes. "I'll always love Jess. But right now, I'm falling in love with you."

Excitement coursed through me, and I jumped up and wrapped both arms around his neck like a crazy teenage girl, almost knocking him off balance. "I'm falling in love with you, too."

Laughing and kissing, we sealed our love in the glimmering light of the lake. The world faded away suspending us in the moment – that magnificent moment. Just John and me.

Chapter 20

BRI

MY FATHER IS *alive!* All this time I'd heard nothing from him. Felt abandoned and betrayed. Standing by my kitchen counter, I tried to focus on all the details I had to deal with for the upcoming event, but all I could do was stare at an invoice for linens until the amounts blurred together. Giving up, I threw it back into the expense folder.

I have half-brothers and sisters. I ignored the tear creeping down my cheek as I looked over the schedule on my kitchen desk. I pushed it away and slumped into a chair. Just a few days away from Aiding the Children's annual fundraiser. Not the time for my husband and son to surprise me with brothers and sisters I never knew I had. *And with my dad.*

Laying my head on the counter, I wrapped both arms around it. To make matters worse, I couldn't forget that my ex-boss was hell bent on seeing me fail. If I mess this event up – I'm done. No one will ever hire me again.

All this crap at once. I stood too quickly and wobbled. I grabbed the counter, easing myself back into the chair, suddenly realizing I hadn't eaten anything all day.

I concentrated on my breathing until I felt steady. My thoughts drifted back to my father. *My damn father.* A week after my mother died in a car accident, he dropped me off at my grandparents and I never saw him again. When I was six years old! Years later, therapy helped me understand the full impact of my father's action. My therapist called it compounded grief – losing my mother, then my father, plus my home and friends all in a single week. For years, I yearned for him. I'd played all sorts of scenarios in my head, where he'd show up and tell me he loved me. Give excuses why he'd done this awful thing. But year after year passed, and he never came. I finally stopped torturing myself and let him go. At least, that's what I told myself.

My stomach growled. I opened the refrigerator. Yogurt was the only thing that looked appetizing. Leaning on the sink eating, my father crept back into my thoughts again. *Damn it.* I didn't want to think about him. Not even for a second. But the loop kept spinning over and over.

The doorbell rang. *Now what?*

When I opened the door, Madeline said, "We've come to help with the event. It's almost here, and we'd figured you might need some assistance." She stepped inside.

I shook my head. "You came to help? Or did you hear from Charlotte about my new family?"

Staci wrapped her arms around me and said, "Of course, we heard. Are you all right?"

I melted into the hug for a minute. Stepping back, I said, "No, I'm not. Come on in."

Madeline's eyes focused on mine. She spoke softly. "Do you want to talk about it? We're here to listen or just help. Whatever you need."

"You're right. There's plenty to do." I'd been so focused on my family issues, acting on autopilot for days, that I'd left too much undone. "Thanks."

Once in the kitchen, I asked if they wanted a glass of wine. I definitely wanted one. I poured myself a large pinot grigio and set the bottle and two glasses out. "Let's go into the dining room where we'll have more space." I picked up the expense folder, schedule, and my wine glass. "The rest of the stuff is already there."

In the dining room, Staci sat down next to me. "You must be shocked."

I plopped my glass down on the table harder than I meant to. "Blindsided, startled, absolutely stunned. To name just a few." My hand clenched the glass stem tightly.

"Charlotte told us that you have four half-siblings. Are you happy about that? Or not?" Staci nervously twisted her fingers together. "I can't imagine how you're dealing with this."

Christ. I don't want to think about it, much less talk. What I wanted was to be in bed with the covers over my head. Instead, I looked at the event planning board situated on the top of my breakfront. "I'm not dealing with it. Listen, if you are going to be here, then help me with the seating plan."

Staci patted Madeline's back and said, "Sure, we can do that. Where do you want us to start?"

Madeline's restrained demeanor grated on me. Why was she pussyfooting around? Acting so reserved, so unlike her usual intrusive self? My anger flared, and I turned away. I wanted to scream and lash out. Flipping around, I said, "What, Madeline, no quick tips on how I should feel or deal with this situation?" My voice rose in pitch. But as soon as the words left my mouth, I regretted them.

Before I could apologize, she said, "No. I have no advice. I'm here…" Madeline looked at Staci. "We're both here because we care about you. We're happy to help in any way we can."

I released the death grip on my wine glass. "I'm sorry. I sounded like a real bitch just then. I'm not in my right mind."

"It's okay. You've had a huge shock on top of all this." Madeline pointed to the table crowded with event material.

Nodding, I grabbed the folder with the guest list and pulled out the seating table layout I had previously created. "Okay. Some sponsors bought tables and have listed the people they want seated with them. I'll place those names at the appropriate tables. Why don't you two do the rest?"

Staci lifted a stack of RSVPs and rifled through them. "Just great. George bought a table. I don't remember him donating to Aiding the Children in the past. He typically gave money to charities when there was something in it for him. I bet he doesn't even know Sister Mary Joseph." Her eyebrows shot up. "I hope he doesn't make a scene when he sees John."

"That heart attack didn't stop him from being a pain in the ass, did it?" Madeline peered over Staci's shoulder and pointed. "Who is Anna Pine?"

Looking at the names at George's table, Staci said, "I don't know her. The other guests listed are our old neighbors from Cromwell Drive."

"She must be his date." Madeline snorted. "Ha! That ass wants you to know he's moved on too. How petty."

"Yes, he is. Hopefully, she'll keep him amused and far away from John and me." Staci shook her head, her lips pursed.

I touched her arm. "Ava's ex-boyfriend is coming, and he bought a table too. She's not happy about it either."

"Jesus. What's up with these guys?" One side of Madeline's mouth rode upward. "Can't let go?"

I shrugged. "Seems not."

"I don't care who George brings as long as it isn't my mother. She'd pick John and me apart all night." Staci shivered.

"Maybe someday you'll work things out with her," I said.

"Right now, I don't care." Staci threw up her hands. "I'm sick of George's and my mother's superior attitudes. And quite frankly, socially, they're both imbeciles." She paused, looking over the names. "Wait, my mother's name isn't on the list, is it?"

I shook my head.

"Thank God." Staci noted the name of her old neighbors on the table layout. "Hmmm, like I said, George doesn't understand people as well as he thinks. Look – he put our old neighbors the Sandlers and the Rooses together at his table. We need to switch one of them."

"Why?" I asked. "He wrote them on his table selection."

Madeline smirked. "Oh, come on. Everyone knows the story. Their children dated for a while, and after the breakup the parents took sides. When the couples happen to be at the same game or the same party, there's always an issue."

My head ached. "What do you mean, issue?"

"Loud conversations and some finger pointing, nothing too terrible." Staci reached for the name cards. "I'd move one of them to another table. If I were you."

"No. Let's not. Could be amusing," Madeline cajoled.

"You're incorrigible!" I looked at the table configurations. I would definitely move one of them. I don't need trouble.

Madeline chuckled. "I'm glad my girls didn't date any of my friends' sons. That probably wouldn't have ended well."

I laughed out loud. "No, I don't think it would have." For the first time in days, I sensed a slight weight lift off me.

We decided to leave the quarreling neighbors alone and moved onto the next table.

"Here." I handed Staci an RSVP I held separately. "Please put my half-sister and her husband at the table with all of you."

"Don't you worry – we'll take care of her." Madeline snatched the card from Staci. "Lori and Liam Williams, huh? Easy names to remember."

I shuddered watching her write their names. "Anybody else?" I asked massaging my aching temples.

"We've filled up all the tables but the two left by the entrance to the driveway. Not the best spot. Who do we have left?" Staci asked.

Madeline held the last names. "You're not going to believe this."

God. Now what?

"Out with it. Which lucky people got stuck with those tables?" Staci said.

"What did you call her before?" Madeline began. "Nasty Nicole and the gang? How apropos."

"No. We can't put them there. They'll think I did that on purpose. Let's rearrange some of the tables." I studied the list.

"How about we put her in the pond on a float?" Madeline mused.

"With spotlights," Staci roared.

Madeline snapped her fingers. "And pink flamingos."

"As amusing as those sound, I don't think it would be wise." Looking over the seating chart, I decided to leave Nicole and Shelby's group at the entrance. "I've changed my mind. Why should I worry about where they're seated? That table is as good as any of the others." I wrote the names of the last remaining guests at the two tables and looked over the entire chart. "That's it. Done. Thank you."

Madeline just snickered.

*

An hour later after we'd cleaned up the dining room, boxing the programs and supplies, Madeline cleared her throat. "We can leave now, or we can talk. Whatever you're up for."

Clamming up had never served me well in the past. "All right. But I need another glass of wine. Let's go into the kitchen."

Staci and Madeline sat at the island. Neither wanted any wine. "Would you like some tea or coffee instead?" I asked. Tea won, and I put water into the kettle. After my woozy episode earlier, I certainly didn't need any more wine.

Putting the boiling water into a tea pot to steep, I started the story. "Logan and a friend at college decided to send in their DNA for testing in the fall. A match was made that showed close family on his maternal side."

"Charlotte told us. Crazy that all this angst came from a swab," Staci said.

"Logan didn't leave it alone, of course." I pushed myself to continue. "He reached out through that DNA company and started talking to one of my *alleged* half-sisters."

"So, your father had another family?" Madeline asked.

My stomach churned. "Now I know why he never came looking for me. He had a new and improved family."

Staci smacked the counter. "What an asshole. What does Eric think about all this?"

I shrugged. "I'm not speaking with him right now. He knew Logan had done this and never told me. Said I was stressed out enough. I confronted Logan myself. I almost passed out from the shock. Eric's staying out of my way right now and playing more tennis than usual."

I thought back to the surprise on Logan's face when I almost fainted that night. His beautiful smile transformed into a frown of concern as he bit his lower lip. He kept pacing, telling me he thought I'd be so happy and how sorry he was to have upset me. I hated seeing my son in such distress, so I calmed down. I convinced him I was okay, and he should go to his friend's party. I told him it was just a big surprise and plastered my face with a toothy grin, hoping it looked more authentic than it felt. But it did the trick; he went to Kevin's party.

Eric, on the other hand wasn't my child and the next few days were fraught with arguments. I felt betrayed. No matter how hard that conversation might have been, if things had been reversed, I would have told him. Hell, he'd had weeks to tell me, and he didn't.

Madeline popped up and gave me a bear hug. Staci followed her.

"We'll be there and will help you through this. I promise. You won't be alone," Madeline said. "Why doesn't Logan tell her not to come to the event? It's too much with everything else. You can meet her another time."

I rubbed the bridge of my nose. "Maybe I will. But… I just don't know how to feel. Excited, definitely, but I'm also anxious. And sad. This mess has almost made me forget all about nasty Nicole. But she still appears every night in my nightmares along with this new set of characters. Christ, it's almost too much to bear." I took a deep breath and exhaled. "On the other hand, I have brothers and sisters and that's something I've always wanted."

Staci and Madeline remained quiet. A chill snaked up my spine, and I wrapped my arms around myself. "I've decided to see how my conversation goes with my half–sister, Lori, tomorrow night on the phone before I make any decisions."

*

What do I say to this half-sibling who I never knew existed? Wandering around the house, I couldn't find anything to distract me. I'd completed everything needed for the event.

My phone rang. Charlotte. When I went to pick it up from the counter, it slipped out of my sweaty hands. *Yuck.* My hands never sweat like this. I scrubbed them in the sink and wiped down my phone before calling her back.

We talked for almost an hour, and she helped calm me down. I wasn't ready to start singing *Que Será Será*, but I knew that I'd be able to speak with my sister tonight without freaking out.

Eric came home early. He stood at the garage door, looking haggard.

"We need to talk," he said putting his briefcase on the kitchen desk.

My good mood slipped away as I exhaled loudly. "I have enough on my plate. I don't need anything else. Nothing to say anyway." Turning my back, I entered the dining room and sat pulling out my list of final details from a folder.

He leaned on the doorframe. "I'm sorry. I should have told you. Honestly, I just didn't know how."

"That might make you feel better, but it does nothing for me," I spat out.

Eric's eyebrows rose high. "What kind of thing is that to say?"

I didn't know what I was saying. *Shit, I'm starting to sound just like Madeline.* I diverted my eyes.

An uncomfortable silence settled between us.

He sat next to me. "When Logan told me he found your dad, I was speechless." He touched my arm.

I shook it off.

"You were clear over the summer when you told me not to search for him. But I never mentioned that to Logan or Julianna. Never occurred to me that one of them might actually look, much less find him."

A vein throbbed in my forehead. "It's not the finding. It's the secrecy. We're a team. Remember?"

"You're right. But once Logan did find him, all I could think of was how this would affect you, especially with this crazy-ass event hanging over your head. I wanted to tell you afterward." Eric's voice softened. "I'm…"

Cutting him off, I said, "No, you're controlling the situation. You're controlling me." My hands shook. "The very day Logan told you what happened, you should have told me. I'm your wife – equal partners. Remember? I want to be treated that way."

My nerves were taut, like a wire pulled around a fence. Did Eric deserve my wrath? Maybe. But I was tired and anxious and scared.

Too many variables were coming at me and I didn't know if I was capable enough to handle them.

I stomped into my office and shut the door. The clock read 8:01 pm. One hour to go until my phone call with my half-sister, Lori. I watched the minutes pass on the clock, then picked up the picture of Eric and I in Italy with our kids. That was a great trip. God knows, Eric is nothing like my father. But still. He should have told me.

Calming myself, I looked on Facebook and Instagram to see if I could find my half-sister. Hundreds of women shared the name Lori Madison. I narrowed my search to New Jersey, and ten women popped up. Just looking, I knew which one was her. She looked just like my father, with his dark curly hair and eyes. Goosebumps prickled my arms. How could my father do this to me? Scrolling through her pictures, I stopped at what looked like a family party in someone's backyard. The banner above the table read Sammy's Fortieth. My half-brother was named Sammy. Look at them. I touched the screen and stroked Lori's image. All this time, I was a member of this big family and never knew it.

My posture sagged and my head rested in one hand. *How could he...*

My cell rang. It was Lori. My heart hammered. "Hello."

"Bri, this is Lori." Her voice sounded kind and a little like mine.

"Hi." So many things I wanted to ask, but I could manage a single word.

"I feel I know you from everything Logan's told me." She paused. "This is awkward. I'm sorry."

"No. I mean. yes, it is. But I'm glad you called." I hesitated, then blurted out, "Did you know about me? I never knew about you." The moment the words popped out; I was mortified. What a thing to say. I wanted to explain, but she answered first.

"No. Nothing. Not until Logan reached out to me," Lori said. "I... this must be hard for you?"

Choking, I barely squeezed out, "It is."

"I can't say I understand any of this. Dad told me what happened, and I still don't believe it. That's not the dad I know... knew. I don't know what to say except I'm sorry you haven't been part of our lives all these years. You should have been. That's why I'm reaching out. We all - your brothers and sisters – want to meet you and your family as soon as possible. We can meet in the middle or at your home or at one of ours. We are so excited to have another sister. We really are."

I twisted a strand of hair around my forefinger, over and over, until it was a perfectly tight corkscrew. "I'd like that too." It came out as a whisper, so I repeated it.

"Oh, and by the way, I have to tell you that your son is so proud of you. He insisted we come to the event you're having next week. He thought it was the perfect time to meet you. I wasn't so sure. But when he told us it was for Aiding the Children, I couldn't believe it. We've been supporting them for years. So, I bought two tickets." She paused. "That's if it's okay with you." Without letting me answer, she pushed on. "We are all so excited that we have a new sister. But I thought meeting the whole family at the event might be overwhelming. Just let me know if you're uncomfortable."

Uncomfortable. Try traumatized or heartsick. *Maybe you shouldn't come.* "Sure, that's fine. I won't be able to spend much time with you though." Is this what I really wanted? Did it matter? My mouth went dry.

"Great. I'm so excited. Logan told us you're running the event. Don't worry about us. Just a quick hello and we'll be out of your hair."

"He did mention you were coming, and I put you at the table with my friends." Of course, Madeline had suggested that seating arrangement. She would manage it so that my friends could keep them occupied and out of my hair if she wanted more attention than I could give right then. "They'll keep you entertained." I hoped she couldn't hear the strain in my voice. *Stupid.* She doesn't know me or my voice. Stop worrying.

My cell started buzzing. First, a call from Madeline, then Charlotte, then Staci. I smiled, knowing they had my back. "Well, I have some calls to finish tonight, but I'm looking forward to meeting you, and your husband." This time I meant it. A sister. Siblings. Wow. It's not them I'm angry at.

"Me too," Lori said. "See you next week."

After clicking off the phone, I sat still for several minutes. I heard Eric walking outside the door, but he left me alone. My anger toward him had subsided, and I decided to fill him in when we went to bed. I called my friends on a group chat so I didn't have to repeat the story over and over. When I hung up, I sat there for a while. Thinking. I even said a prayer before venturing upstairs to sleep. Lots of irons in the fire. I prayed I wouldn't get burned.

Chapter 21

MADELINE

SARAH AND I had an appointment with Dr. Mann, the first one since her hospitalization. She wanted Sarah to come weekly for the next four months, and more if she felt she needed it.

Upon our arrival, Dr. Mann requested to speak with me first. I entered her office while Sarah waited in the reception area.

She gestured to a seat that I had occupied many times before. "Let's start by discussing how you are handling Sarah's recent developments."

I crossed my legs and thought for a moment. "It seems to me that Sarah is finally listening to what I have to say rather than huffing out of the room. At least she appears to be listening. I think being hospitalized knocked some sense into her."

Dr. Mann put her pencil down and fixed her gaze on me. "That's not what I asked."

I lowered my head. "I haven't thought about me. I'm trying to save my daughter from the miserable existence my parents had."

The doctor leaned forward. "Sarah must make her own choices and even her own mistakes. She is the only one accountable for her actions. You must be supportive in a healthy dose. You can't control her or the disease, if in fact, she has an addiction."

Frustration bubbled up. "Oh, come on. What else could it be?"

"Sarah may be abusing alcohol but..."

I cut her off. "Of course, she's abusing alcohol. That's how she landed in the hospital."

Dr. Mann paused and looked directly at me. "Madeline, please let me finish. Alcohol abuse occurs when drinking becomes an issue that has negative consequences. But alcoholism happens when a person forms a mental reliance on it. And it's early in this process to know if Sarah has that reliance. Do you know if she is under a lot of stress at school?"

I take a moment to gather my thoughts and remember my conversations with Sarah recently. "No. She hasn't mentioned anything."

"Okay, I'll speak with her."

"I don't think I can just butt out. I mean, what wouldn't you do for your own child? It's my job to protect her."

Dr. Mann reclined in her chair. "If you push too hard, you will isolate her, and she won't share her feelings with you. Sarah's fragile right now. Let her breathe."

Despite wondering how practical that was, I agreed and left the office. While Sarah spoke with the doctor, I stepped outside and strolled around the park across the street. I loved walking, but with the recent move and Sarah's struggles, I hadn't done so in months. My thoughts turned to the challenges my family had faced over the past year, and I wondered if I had somehow contributed to the turmoil. Probably.

An hour later, I flipped through magazines in the doctor's waiting room. The room was quiet, aside from the soft murmur of voices coming from inside. When Sarah finally emerged, she didn't utter a word. As we rode down in the elevator together, her silence felt deafening. Was something wrong? I had so many questions. But, trying to take the doctor's advice, I held my tongue.

But it was impossible. I broke the silence when were in the car. "So, how did it go in there?"

"Well, that was something," Sarah uttered.

"What's that mean?" I asked.

Sarah let out a deep sigh, her gaze fixed on the passing scenery. "It's just more of the same. Talking about my feelings, trying to understand why I do what I do."

I nodded. "Well, that's important, isn't it? Understanding your triggers and learning coping mechanisms?"

Sarah shrugged. "Yeah, I guess." Clearly, she wasn't in the mood to talk, so I stopped asking questions and focused on driving us back home. As soon as we arrived, Sarah headed straight to her room and closed the door. I expected her to be upset; it's hard for anyone, especially someone that young, to admit they have a problem. Following Dr. Mann's advice and stopping my helicopter parenting would be a struggle, and I wasn't sure if I could do it.

In the kitchen, I turned my phone on. Scrolling through texts from my friends put a smile on my worried face. The texts wished us luck with Sarah's therapy appointment. They offered their support and offered to bring us some dinners. Normally, I kept my struggles to myself, but having these amazing women in my life comforted me. I wasn't alone.

Sitting at the kitchen table, I typed out responses to my friends while thinking about Bri's upcoming event. I was excited for it, anticipating the drama between her former boss and the awkward dynamics of the guest list, which included exes and current partners. Not that I enjoyed seeing my friends in uncomfortable situations, but I would be there to support them. And, if needed, I'd gladly offer a couple of well-deserved jabs.

Chapter 22

BRI – THE ANGELS IN THE MIDST EVENT

I MADE MYSELF AN espresso and settled at the kitchen counter, sipping it slowly. Except for some last-minute items, everything was in place for the event. At least, I hoped it was.

My cell buzzed. Madeline.

"Hey. What's up?" I asked.

"You mentioned over the weekend that you had a light day today. Well, surprise! You now have an appointment at two o'clock for a facial with my dermatologist," Madeline said.

"What? Why?"

"Because, darling, the facial I booked for you is simply fabulous. I've had it twice, you know. It does wonders for your skin. Just go. Don't you want to dazzle everyone at your event?"

"Are you saying I look dull?"

"No, silly – you're beautiful. But a little extra pizzazz never hurts. The vampire facial makes you look more alive, you know refreshed."

I scratched my head. "Wait a minute. You want me to get a vampire facial to look more alive? Do you hear the irony in that?"

"Trust me on this. Don't you think my skin glows?"

"Yes, it's simply ethereal." With a theatrical sigh, I walked to the powder room, I stared at my reflection. "How did you get an appointment so fast?"

"To tell you the truth, it's actually my appointment, and I've already contacted the doctor's office and told them you were going instead of me. The facial was a present from James and Vivian for my birthday, you know, Stan's ex-partner. I was raving about it to Vivian months before James was arrested. When she gave me the gift, I was shocked because the facials were expensive, and we never gave each other such pricy gifts. I should have known something was up then."

"You keep it, Madeline. Especially if it's expensive," I said. "Why waste it on me?"

"I can't bear to use it after what James did." Madeline's tone turned serious. "I asked the doctor's office to give me cash in lieu of the service so that I could make a donation to the Sister's charity. They said I can either use it toward another procedure or pass the gift on to someone else. No refunds."

"I'm not sure what to say."

"Say you'll go. You'll love it, I promise. Get there a bit early to fill out the paperwork. You'll look stunning by the weekend, and you'll be doing me a huge favor," Madeline urged me.

Reluctantly, I agreed, though I had no clue what she meant by "the weekend." Then my phone chimed. I spent the next hour trying to calm Susan from the catering company from their menu-related woes.

With the menu crisis resolved, I showered quickly and was out the door by one thirty. As soon as I got in my car, I realized that I hadn't bothered to look up anything about vampire facials. Eric's words echoed in my head. *Why are you doing something you know nothing about?* But then I thought, "Why the hell not?" Madeline's skin was so dewy and beautiful. Maybe this was just what I needed. A little time to myself. It might even help me relax and forget all about my newfound family and the drama surrounding the event. And Madeline was right – I wanted to look my best for both.

The nurse showed me into the procedural room. I nervously asked what I'd look like after it was over. She assured me I'd look great by tomorrow morning. There isn't as much downtime with this procedure, she said – not like you'd have with a facelift.

I was still processing what she said when the doctor entered and explained the procedure in detail.

"First, I'll draw blood and put it through the centrifuge to separate the platelets. Then, I put a numbing cream on your face before using the DermaPen to create tiny holes in the skin. It's usually referred to as microneedling. The final part of the treatment is to place the platelets on your face. The process uses your body's natural healing ability to reduce wrinkles by encouraging new collagen growth."

Barely understanding half of what he said, I was concerned with how much time it would take me to heal. "I have a big event this Saturday, and I want to look like myself, not some ballooned version of me."

The doctor chuckled. "You'll have a healthier overall look by Saturday. No swollen cheeks, I promise."

As they covered my eyes with a cushy pad, I took a deep breath. How bad could this be?

When it was over, the nurse asked, "Did you bring a hat?"

I panicked. "No. Was I supposed to? Why?"

"You don't need it. Most women wear one to shield their faces from view due to the blood on your skin," she explained, handing me a mirror.

"Jesus. Don't you wipe it off?" I complained. "How do I go out in public looking like this?"

"It's just the platelets that we cover your face with after the microneedling. Just don't wash it off until tomorrow morning," she explained. "The platelets will continue to work overnight."

"What? How am I supposed to sleep?" I kept staring into the mirror. Why did I listen to Madeline? I'm gonna kill her.

The nurse must have noticed my concerned expression. "By tomorrow this will mostly be gone. Don't worry. By the weekend, you'll look great."

I looked again into the hand-held mirror and grimaced. "I hope I don't run into anyone I know. I look like I should be in a horror movie."

She laughed.

I sprinted to my car. Thank God, I didn't have any other appointments today.

Looking at my face in the rear-view mirror, I turned left out of the parking lot and proceeded up Route 206. Not a minute later, blue and red lights flashed behind me, accompanied by a blaring siren. *Shit.* I pulled over to let them by. But instead, they pulled in behind me. *What?* I didn't do anything. Then it dawned on me. In my haste to get home, I'd exited the parking lot through an entrance-only lane.

I grabbed my license and insurance card from the glove compartment. My heart raced as I waited for the police officer. He came up to the passenger side window, and I rolled it down. Christ, he was just a kid. He couldn't be much older than my own son.

The officer took one look at my face, his eyes widened as shock registered on his face. "Ma'am, are you alright? You have blood all over your face!" he exclaimed in alarm.

Without giving me time to respond, he radioed his partner. "Larry, call an ambulance. This woman is bleeding from the head."

My heart skipped a beat. Stammering, I tried to tell the officer it wasn't blood, but before I could get the words out, I saw the other officer leave the patrol car.

"Larry, what's the ETA on the ambulance?" the young patrol-man asked.

My stomach churned. *This can't be happening.*

"Ma'am, did you hit something?" He dashed around my car. "I don't see any damage."

"Stop. Please don't call an ambulance. I'm fine. It's just a facial," I shouted, waving my arms like a crazy woman.

The young officer held up his hand to Larry. "Hold off a minute on the ambulance." He returned his attention to me. "It's a what?"

"A facial. I'm fine. Really. Just completely embarrassed. You can call the doctor's office. It's right down the street." I quickly explained the treatment. "Nothing to worry about."

"Ma'am, are you okay to drive? You exited out of the entrance and made a left turn. Both of which are illegal. Did you have anesthesia?" He sounded concerned.

I shook my head vigorously. "No, of course not."

"Is there someone who can pick you up from the police station?"

"What? That's not necessary. Please, I'm fine. The doctor's office will explain everything."

"Can you step out of the car? Do you need help?" he asked, his hand on the door.

I quickly clicked on the doctor's number and the nurse answered.

"Hi. This is Bri Lambert," I said quickly. "I have you on speaker phone with a police officer, who is worried about the blood all over my face. Can you explain it to him? He's alarmed that I may have had anesthesia, which means I shouldn't be driving."

Of course, she hooted. Uproariously. But after a moment, she got control of herself and explained the procedure. The young police officer relaxed. He was clearly trying not to laugh. Larry, however, didn't restrain himself.

"All right. I'm not going to give you a ticket. But you should go home right away. You don't look so hot. If your head starts to hurt, go directly to the hospital."

Nodding, I tried to smile, though the skin around my mouth felt sore and tight. "Thank you, officer."

With that, they let me go. The police car followed me for a

couple of blocks, then decided I was driving fine and turned off. I waited a couple of minutes – I didn't need them to see was me on the phone. About a mile down the road, I called Madeline. "I have blood all over my face. And I just got pulled over by the cops, and they started to call an ambulance," I screeched into the phone.

Madeline responded with a fit of laughter. "That's hilarious! Absolutely hilarious."

What am I, everybody's joke today? "It's not funny. Why didn't you warn me that I'd have blood all over my face? I'm so embarrassed. I don't even get Botox. There I was stopped with all of rush hour traffic inching by. I wonder how many people I know passed me. So many people stared at me with this damn bloody face. Now, I'll be the laughingstock of Chester."

"Calm down," Madeline said. "No one's laughing but me."

"Oh, really. How about the cops? And the receptionist at the doctor's office. Plus, it's Monday, and my event is on Saturday. For God's sake, what if my face doesn't heal fast enough? Now, on top of everything else, I have my damn face to worry about and all these tiny little red holes." My jaw clenched. Then a thought crossed my mind. "I hope no one took a picture. God, what if I end up on social media."

"Stop. You're killing me. You must see the humor in this. I can't wait to tell everyone at book club," Madeline said giggling.

"This is *not* funny," I protested.

"Calm down," Madeline said in a softer tone. "Don't get all worked up. No one took a picture of you. Well, except for the officer's video cam."

My chest tightened. "Oh, my God! What if they share it at the police station? With a reporter? I'll be on the local news – Chester woman in horrific accident ends up with blood all over her face."

"Relax, for heaven's sake. You're getting hysterical. Breathe."

I inhaled and let it out slowly.

"Listen to me. You'll look back at this and laugh. And just wait till you see your skin tomorrow morning. You'll be beautiful by Saturday. Trust me. I'll call you tomorrow." She clicked off.

Madeline's infectious laughter echoed through the air. I guess it was kinda funny. The patrolmen's expression was priceless. I started to laugh just thinking about it – a good, deep belly laugh. And for a couple of precious moments, my worries drifted away.

*

My good mood carried me home. When I opened the garage door, I saw Eric's car, and glad we were in a better place now, was surprised he was home early. . I don't know what I'd do without him.

I didn't want him freaking out when he saw me, so I called him on my cell.

"Why are you calling me? Didn't I just hear the garage door open?" he grumbled.

"I wanted to give you a heads up. This facial I had today… well… it made my face kinda bloody. It's not blood – blood. It's platelets from my blood, and they smeared them all over my face. I think it helps with collagen growth or something. In any event…"

Before I could elaborate, Eric opened the side door and stepped into the garage. "Jesus, Bri. Are you sure you're okay?"

I stepped around him and went into the house. "Yes. I'm fine. Don't stare at me. I'm self-conscious enough. My face will be back to normal by tomorrow." *Allegedly.*

Eric trailed behind me. "I guess I better cancel our dinner reservations."

Putting my purse on the kitchen desk, I opened the refrigerator. "You made reservations on a Monday night? I thawed two steaks this morning." Handing him the meat, I said, "Why don't you grill these, and I'll get a salad together. You know I like mine rare." I winked at him.

He grimaced, looking at the steak and then at my face. I guess he didn't appreciate my attempt at humor.

*

Five days later, volunteers, mostly from church, zigzagged their way through my home, sidestepping each other as they took the decorative items, tables linens, and the carefully packaged auction items to be displayed at the venue. The busy beehive now moved from my house to the Sisters of Charitable Care at the top of Bernardsville Mountain.

Warm rays of sun shone down on me as I led the caravan up the winding road. The weather was perfect. Unseasonably warm with no rain in the forecast. I'd set up the larger items like the tents and patio heaters, yesterday, so today I could focus on the smaller details.

My friends arrived right after I did. They had enough food, coffee, and water to feed a small army. But mostly they provided me with tons of emotional support. Madeline and I were unloading some boxes from the car when a loud screeching noise jerked our heads up. There, in the belfry of the chapel, three large, ugly birds stared at us. Their screech turned into a raspy, drawn-out hissy sound that made me shudder. "What the hell are those?"

Madeline hissed back at them, flapping her arms. "Vultures."

"What? No way. I'm calling pest control right now. Those things can't be foraging around this event."

Madeline mumbled something and left. I looked up at the belfry again. Those hideous birds stared down. I couldn't help but feel it was a bad omen.

A group of nuns came out the front door. "Aren't there bells in the chapel that we could ring to scare away those vultures?" I asked them.

The group collectively shook their heads. "They don't work anymore," one said.

"Oh." I looked for Dave's Pest Control's number. Before I clicked it, I asked the nuns, "Do the birds actually live in the belfry?"

"No. They visit and usually leave the same day. They will be gone by tonight," Mother Superior answered unexpectedly. I wasn't expecting her to be standing behind me in the door's entrance.

Startled, I jumped.

"Sorry. Didn't mean to frighten you."

"Are you sure? I found the number for pest control."

Just then, two loud clanks pierced the air and made us all look up.

One of the nuns pointed at the belfry. "I think your friend managed to shoo off the birds." Madeline stood in the bell tower and nodded down at us. I couldn't figure out how she got there so quickly with a set of frying pans in hand. She is simply unbelievable.

There was certainly no mention of vultures in the event planning manual. They seemed to have overlooked the black beasts. But my friend had figured out a solution. *God*. Madeline to the rescue.

"Bri!" I heard Charlotte yell. Staci and Charlotte were in the main tent setting up the tables.

Staci ran from the tent. "Bri, come quick. Those ugly birds shit right in the middle of the tent."

"No. No. No." I darted in to see. A white fluid mess spread out from the middle of the tent. I had used translucent tents so people could stargaze while eating, but I hadn't counted on bird crap. Did Madeline have a remedy for that too? The tent was forty feet high. I doubted the nuns had a ladder that tall.

Staci and Charlotte crowded around me. All of us stared.

"Any suggestions, ladies?" I asked.

Both shrugged.

"Ew." Shaken, we turned toward another loud screech.

Ava clamored into the tent, hopping on one foot. "Bri, why the hell are all these geese here?" She pointed outside the tent. "I just stepped in poop unloading boxes from your car. It's all over the driveway."

I sighed.

Ava plopped into a chair, dangling a filthy shoe from her foot.

"You don't realize how things work in the countryside, do you, city girl?" Madeline miraculously reappeared by the tent's opening. "Here, use these to wipe your shoes. I'll take care of the driveway. Bri has enough on her plate already."

Ava accepted the paper towels. "Thanks. But I'm not a tourist. This is my town too."

Madeline arched an eyebrow and replied with a sly smirk. "Then you should know that if there's a pond, it's probably full of ducks or geese. Or both."

"Always the smartass." Ava wiped her shoes. "I don't think the guests want to step in bird shit. Just saying."

Mother Superior appeared at the tent entrance. I wanted her to think I had everything under control. But vultures and bird shit cleanup weren't in my purview.

She grinned knowingly and gestured for me to follow her outside. She went over to a shed and opened it, revealing various hoses. "This should help clean up the driveway. Not so sure about the tent. I'll get Emmanuel to help."

Madeline didn't wait. She grabbed one of the hoses and sprayed a steady stream of water. That driveway sparkled by the time she was done. She even tried to angle the hose in an arch to attempt to wash off the bird poop. It helped somewhat.

All the bird-related incidents seemed to be over. At least for now. I prayed those vultures would stay away. But I could see Madeline in a silk dress with a set of frying pans climbing up to that belfry fast, if an issue arose. The vultures gave me the creeps. I was so glad my friend was here to handle it.

By the time the techs finished setting up the PA System and projector, most of the volunteers had left, and just Charlotte remained behind with me. As I was doing a final check for tonight, she asked where Hanna was.

"She picked her parents up from the airport and settled them at Ashley's. She'll be here tonight."

"That's great," Charlotte said, reaching for her sweater. "Please let me know if you need anything tonight. I'm so excited. I'm sure everything will be fabulous."

I stayed behind to do one last walk–through. Everything seemed to be in order. I hoped for the best, but unease lingered in the pit of my stomach. Just as I opened my car door to leave, a shadow fell across the driveway. I looked up and saw those three nasty vultures circling. God, I really hope they weren't a bad omen.

*

Pushing my anxiety aside, I raced home to shower and change. After wrapping my wet hair in a towel, I examined my reflection in the bathroom mirror. Madeline was right, my skin had healed nicely and looked lovely. My cheeks glowed pink, and my skin's texture seemed softer, though I didn't look any younger. The one negative was that the area around my mouth was still sore. Had it been worth the money? I don't think I'd pay for another. But I appreciated the gift.

As I finished dressing, my mind reviewed the sequence of events and possible problems that might arise. Nothing ever goes off without a hitch and I expected some hiccups, but if something major happened while my awful former boss, Nicole, was there to gloat, she'd undoubtedly revel in my failure.

A shiver ran through my body, and my thoughts drifted towards Lori. Jesus, I was still so blown away that I have a half-sister and other siblings. It was probably a blessing in disguise that I'd been so busy since finding out about them and my father. Being preoccupied prevented me from obsessing over it. I looked forward to meeting her tonight. Hopefully, I'd meet the rest of my half-brothers and sisters soon. My father, on the other hand, well, that was way too much for me to think about.

As I hurried from the house, a sudden thought crossed my mind – should I research vultures and their behavior? I checked my watch. I didn't have time. Hopefully, Madeline did. She's always prepared.

Eric drove and I tried to calm myself with deep breathing. I didn't hear a word Eric said during the entire ride. When we pulled into the Sisters of Charitable Care's parking lot, Madeline and Stan were already there. I could always count on her. On time and dependable, that was my dear friend.

"I can't wait to see how the big tent looks with all the lights on. I couldn't get the full effect this afternoon. But we can now that it's twilight," Madeline said, kissing my cheek.

I snaked my arm into hers. "Let's go find out." We walked toward the tent. "By the way, thank you so much for all your help. You were so impressive scaring those vultures away." I squeezed her elbow. "But I don't think that Mother Superior was correct that the vultures only stay around for a couple of hours. After everyone left today, I saw them fly over the parking lot."

Madeline stopped walking. "Don't worry about them. I'll deal with their sorry asses."

Somehow, I knew she would.

I went to the back of the main tent and pulled the generator lever. Hundreds of small twinkling lights snapped on.

Positioned at the tent's entrance, Madeline exclaimed, "Wow. It's stunning. Your vision for the Angels in the Midst event is spot on." She strolled through, pausing to appreciate the all-white fresh flower centerpieces of gardenias, roses, and hydrangeas arranged in a fluffy white container as if nestled on clouds, subtle touches of silver running through. "It was beautiful this afternoon, but in the evening light, it's magical."

I wandered around, illuminating the flameless candles at every table and the candelabras positioned around the tent. Sheer white fabric cascaded from the ceiling poles, creating a frame around the stage. Long white garlands adorned the fabric, catching the light with glimmering tiny crystals.

"You've captured the theme perfectly," Madeline remarked. "Such an ethereal atmosphere. It's truly enchanting."

"Thank you. That means a lot coming from you," I said.

Headlights poured into the parking lot. "Fantastic," I said, watching as the caterer and their staff pulled up to start setting up for dinner. They were using the convent's kitchen, which saved us money as we didn't have to rent another generator and an oven. "I'm going to check in with them. When the A/V techs arrive, please ask them to double-check the microphones and the projector." Without warning, I pulled Madeline into an embrace. She blushed, obviously not expecting it. I was so grateful for all her help. For her always being there when I needed her.

Before I entered the outside door to the kitchen, I saw three geese walking through the parking lot. I tried to shoo them away, but they just honked at me and walked toward the back of the building.

The kitchen was pure pandemonium. Pots clanked, dishes clattered, silverware clinked. Everyone was yelling.

In the midst of the culinary chaos, the chef shouted above the rest, "Jesus Christ Almighty," while slamming the oven door.

I wasn't sure if he was swearing at the stove or having a personal crisis, so I walked over to see what was happening.

As I got closer, I noticed Mother Superior standing at the side door. *Oh no.*

"God damn it." He swore.

"Lord, have mercy." Mother Superior made the sign of the cross.

The chef looked up from the stove and nervously wiped the sweat from his brow. "Forgive me, Sister. I shouldn't have been taking the Lord's name in vain," he stammered, noticing her disapproving look. "I was told there was a working stove here. And I just can't get it to work." He rose to his full height, towering over the petite Mother Superior. "Most of the dinner is ready and in portable warming cabinets. But I need the stove for the sauces."

"That's why I stopped by. Because of the building's age, we have a specific gas shut-off just for the oven. It must be turned on for it to work," she explained calmly. Without missing a beat, she reached into a nearby drawer and effortlessly pulled out a massive wrench, passing it to the chef. "You might need this," she added.

The chef snatched it from her in a frenzy, not realizing its weight and smacked the countertop with his hand. "Frickin' ouch!" he exclaimed, rubbing his injured hand.

"I didn't think the wrench was that heavy," she said with a sly smirk. "Are you okay?"

The chef squeezed out a breathy, "I'm fine."

She stared at him for a minute, then opened a cabinet near the oven. "The valve sticks sometimes so we use the wrench when it gets stuck." She pointed to the valve. "Don't forget to light the pilot." With that, she turned and sailed out, leaving the chef staring at the wrench.

I offered my help, but the chef shook his head. So, I followed Mother Superior out of the bedlam.

Once outside, I heard the chef screech, "God damn it. Someone get me some ice. I think that fuckin' wrench broke my finger."

I chuckled. Such a typical male reaction to a little pain.

My phone vibrated, and I pulled it out of my pocket, answering with a bemused "Hello." I didn't recognize the number and usually wouldn't have answered. But the craziness all around me made me careless.

"Brianna, this is your... this is Henry Downs."

Everything slammed to a halt like brakes on a big rig before a collision. "I... I know who you are." My father. Who decided, tonight of all nights, to contact me. "I can't talk. I'm running an event right now."

He interrupted. "I know. I just wanted to wish you good luck."

For a second, I contemplated throwing my phone into the nearby woods. How dare he call me?

Like a good angel, Madeline came around a corner of the building, noticing my distress. She reached out to touch my shoulder. "Are you alright?"

I nodded, but tears threatened to spill from my eyes.

She grabbed the phone. "Hello. Who is this?" She paused, then in a harsh voice added, "And you thought tonight would be a good time to make a call you should have made thirty years ago?"

"It's all right," I assured Madeline, gently patting her arm as I reclaimed my phone.

Drawing a deep breath, I said to my father, "Tonight isn't the night for a conversation," cutting off any further exchange.

"Yes. Of course. I'm sorry," he said. "Another time…"

I clicked the end call button.

Madeline clasped her hands tightly, her knuckles turning white. "The audacity of him."

"Let's not talk about this right now. Let's stay focused," I said, trying to control my emotions. "We have an event to run."

Madeline nodded, relaxing her hands. "The bar is getting set up. I'll go supervise."

"Yes, thank you." After she left, I leaned against the steps outside and took a moment to steady myself. The call felt like a punch in the gut, and I gasped for air. How did he even get my phone number? Was it Lori or Logan who gave it to him? But now was not the time to dwell on that. I needed to push him out of my mind and regain my composure. I could deal with this later. There was no way he was going to ruin this event like he ruined my childhood.

*

The sun set over Bernardsville Mountain, leaving the sky awash in the subtle hues of evening. The parking lot teemed with cars, and guests had comfortably settled into their seats within the tent. The constant smiling and talking as I greeted all the guests left my sore mouth aching.

Lori and Liam appeared right before the festivities started. I was still at the entrance to the tent when they arrived. I knew what she looked like from the pictures on social media. She apparently also knew what I looked like because she pulled me into a tight bear hug.

Lori released her grip. "Wow. I still can't believe I have a sister."

"Me either," I said. I had so many questions, but this wasn't the time. "Come. Let me get you settled and introduce you to my friends. I'm sitting with Mother Superior and the honoree, Sister Mary Joseph. But you'll be in good hands."

The entire book club was seated together with their significant others. Madeline and Stan, Ava and her new boyfriend, Gabriel, Staci and John, Hanna and Mark, and Charlotte and Maxwell. Gabriel, John, and Maxwell seamlessly integrated into our tight-knit group.

Lori and Liam settled in with my friends. Relieved, I let go of the anxiety I had felt about meeting her. She was lovely. As I stood by their table, I glanced around the tent. Even the guests that my friends and I didn't want to come seemed to be in good humor. George was laughing and entertaining the people at his table, and Neil was schmoozing with anyone that came close.

Suddenly, I spotted a woman donning a dreadfully outlandish hat. As she approached, I realized it had an animal coiled around the crown that looked like a fox and was accentuated by lurid plumage bursting out from the side. The hat was hideous. It would have been laughed out of the club room at Churchill Downs or any royal wedding.

When the crazy hat lady approached Shelby's table and raised her head, I knew at once it was my ex-boss, Nicole. I stiffened at the sight of her. My stomach twisted as I watched her take her seat with a smug smirk plastered on her face. I knew she was just waiting for me to fail.

Madeline, who never missed anything, followed my stare and must have sensed my unease. "Is something wrong?"

Ava, who was sitting next to Madeline, looked up.

"That nasty ex-boss of mine has arrived. Don't look now, but she's at Shelby's table by the entrance."

Of course, they both turned around immediately. I rubbed my forehead, feeling a headache start, hoping Nicole didn't notice.

Ava popped up. "I'm going to say hello to my friend Shelby."

"Please, Ava, don't cause a commotion," I pleaded. "I want this to be as professional as possible without any drama."

"Not to worry, I'm going with her." Madeline stood and followed closely behind.

Now my head really throbbed. Madeline was anything but a peacekeeper. I just hoped Charlotte, Staci, and Hanna were too preoccupied with my sister to join them.

Someone touched my shoulder and I jumped.

"Sorry, Bri. Didn't mean to scare you," Sister Mary Alice said. "The tech standing by the stage needs you. Something about a dead mike."

Oh God. We're ready to start the program. *Damn it.* That mike worked perfectly before.

"Seth, what happened?" I asked when I got to the stage.

"I can't figure it out. It won't turn on," he said. "I replaced the batteries. But still nothing."

"There must be a spare mike. Where would it be?" I asked.

"I'll look in the containers behind the stage," Seth said.

I went with him. "There's three hundred people here. We need a mike." I hoped no one noticed the delay, especially Nicole. Then I remembered that Ava and Madeline had gone to her table. I peeked around the curtain and saw that my friends were back with my sister. Thank God. I didn't want them poking at Nicole and getting her all riled up.

Combing through the cables and drives, Seth found another mike that worked. One small catastrophe avoided. I prayed there'd be no more.

Retrieving my notes from my table, I signaled to the presenters that we were about to start. Stepping on stage, I took a deep breath. Seth turned the spotlight on me.

Looking out into the audience, my eyes first fell on Nicole. Her presence seemed to taunt me but also strengthened my resolve to do well. My gaze then shifted to my friends, and my tension slowly dissipated.

I introduced the first speaker, Evelyn Woodall of Aiding the Children.

Evelyn began, "We are so blessed to have worked with Sister Mary Joseph over the years. She has single-handedly created a network with vast connections in South America for us to identify children who need life-altering medical procedures. She has also created a network of host families in the tri-state area to give those children and their families a place to stay while they heal. We'd like to share a video that shows more detail regarding her inspirational work."

When Evelyn pushed the remote for the video, nothing happened. *Shit!*

Seth was pushing buttons and turning things on and off. This video had to work. They'd spent so much time preparing it. Probably no one noticed the mike mix-up, but this was different.

So, he shut down the entire system and rebooted it.

It screeched to life with a God-awful noise. Half the audience covered their ears. Seth quickly turned down the volume. I looked at Mother Superior. Her eyes closed and she was muttering something – maybe a prayer. Finally, the damn thing started to play. Alleluia. Mother Superior must have some good friends up there. I relaxed slightly but felt Nicole's piercing gaze upon me. I refused to look at her, shaking the feeling of doom away.

The video showcased the Sister's journey of faith and service helping hundreds of children and adults. When it ended, Evelyn spoke once more to the audience. "Everything you just saw was all made possible by the efforts of Sister Mary Joseph."

A standing ovation with roaring applause followed. I wiped a tear from my cheek. The Sister remained seated; her face flushed. She wasn't used to the spotlight and while I was sure she was touched by the honor; she probably wished the event was over.

I returned to the podium, and the audience hushed. After clearing my throat, I announced Jose Arenas, who, as a nine-year-old, was brought to this country to have his cleft palate fixed. He stepped on stage. You couldn't tell he'd once been deformed.

As Jose spoke, I surveyed the crowd, who were clearly captivated by this young man's story. When I looked at Sister Mary Joseph, all I saw on her face was her pride in him. When Jose completed his remarks, some of the patrons dabbed at their cheeks with a napkin.

I breathed a sigh of relief. The first half of the event was over. I signaled the pianist to play soft music as waiters bustled about with the salad.

Eric put his arm around my chair. "Great job."

"Thanks, but it's not over yet."

"Stop thinking something's bad is going to happen. You should be proud of yourself," he said. "I am."

I squeezed his hand. "We'll see."

Just then, I noticed some commotion at the entrance to the tent. My friends' table was positioned between mine and the tent flap. Madeline was already standing. I scooted over to her. *Now what?*

As soon as we reached the tent entrance, I saw the problem. Four geese had entered and were honking at Nicole's hat, which rested on a chair beside her.

"What kind of event is this?" she screeched when she saw me

walking over. "Get these filthy animals out of here. You're serving food in a place where dirty birds are spraying their feathers, feces, and God knows what around. I knew they should never have let you organize this event." Her face bloomed red.

Madeline swiftly grabbed a plate and knife from the table, clanging them together loudly. The geese weren't fazed. She laughed out loud. "Well, look at that. I don't think they fancy that dreadful fox hat."

Nicole spat out, "How dare you mock my hat." She turned to me and pointed an accusing finger. "These pests are here because of your incompetence."

Shelby tried to calm Nicole by placing a hand on her arm, but Nicole yanked away from Shelby and leapt up from her seat, snatching the plate and knife back from Madeline. "For God's sake, do any of you do anything correctly? I'll show you how it's done." She smashed the knife into the plate but instead of making a loud noise to scare the birds, the plate broke into pieces. For a moment, Nicole was frozen in shock before turning back to me and shouting, "What kind of cheap dishes did you use?"

Madeline couldn't help herself. "Well, you certainly showed us how it's done."

The people around Nicole's table burst into laughter, infuriating her more.

A loud honk caught my attention as I looked toward the geese. One of them was pecking at the hat.

"Do you see what that creature is doing?" Nicole shrieked, pointing. She picked up the hat and placed it on her head. Then, without hesitation, she grabbed Shelby's plate and raised it as if to strike the bird on its head.

"Stop," Mother Superior's authoritative voice rang out, causing even the piano player to halt in mid-song. "What are you doing?"

Nicole twisted around, her face contorted and her mouth tight, about to pounce on whomever spoke. But upon realizing it was

Mother Superior, she stepped back and started to say, "Mother, I'm... ."

Mother Superior raised her hand to silence her. "This is an outside event, and we are guests in their house. There's no need to hurt them." She grabbed a napkin and tried to shoo them away, but the geese didn't move. So she removed Nicole's hat from her head, "I'll return this in a minute." She turned to the geese and said, "Come on, let's go back to the pond." The geese obeyed and followed her outside the tent.

"Wait a minute. Where are you going with my hat?" Nicole protested loudly and began to follow us.

I turned and saw Shelby grab Nicole's arm and say, "Stay here. Mother Superior will return the hat. What has gotten into you?"

Me, I thought as I trailed behind. I closed the flap at the entrance when all the geese were outside. Mother put the hat on her head and waved at the geese. "Go now. Go on." The geese padded off to the pond.

"I apologize, Mother Superior," I said.

"Stop it. You have nothing to apologize for. But I doubt the flap will keep the geese out," she said. "They can be stubborn when they want something."

Mother Superior took the hat off her head. "And heaven only knows what the attraction is for this hat." She turned the hat around and shrugged. "I'll return this beast to its owner."

As we passed by her table, Mother Superior stopped and gave Nicole her hat back. Shelby stood and thanked her profusely while Nicole glowered at me. I walked on.

Madeline motioned for me to join their table as I passed by. "I wasn't close enough to get any of that on my phone. But we have to video that snooty ex-boss of yours if those geese come back for her ugly hat." She laughed loudly. "It's social media gold."

Ava and Staci both grabbed their phones. "We're all set," said Staci with a giggle.

Charlotte added, "I can stand by the flap and give it a nudge."

Hanna joined in the laughter, saying, "Yeah, let's do it!"

"Let's just behave ourselves, okay? Don't instigate anything, please," I pleaded.

"Hello, ladies." A man's voice interrupted me from behind. Turning, I saw George standing there with a woman. "I'd like you all to meet Anna Pine," he announced proudly. Her slender frame was engulfed in his embrace. I wondered why he was holding her so tightly. Was she a flight risk? I glanced at Staci, who just rolled her eyes and turned back to John. I felt sorry for George's new girl-friend. Staci's ex-husband was poison, pure and simple.

Madeline whispered into my ear, "She must be an escort."

"Stop," I said, swatting her away. "You're certainly enjoying all this mayhem tonight."

She winked at me, a huge grin crossing her face.

As dinner was served, I excused myself to return to my table. The dinner was delicious and quite warm, so the chef must have finally wrestled with that wrench to start the oven. And there were no more birds, old boyfriends, or nasty ex-bosses to deal with while I ate.

After dinner, Mother Superior spoke about the honoree, thanking her for all she had done and continues to do.

The melody from the piano was soon accompanied by the rest of the band, and the night was now in full swing. People rose to dance, and even Mother Superior joined in, swaying to the beat with a smile on her face.

Eric and I strolled to the bar for a drink. "Been a hectic couple of weeks," I said, lifting the Cosmopolitan to my lips.

"It has," he agreed. "But it all turned out well."

As I sipped my drink, I gave the tent a once-over. "I guess it did. Well, most things, at least."

Neil swaggered up to the bar, flanked by two women hanging onto him. "Bri, great event," he slurred. He proceeded to kiss both women on the lips and handed each a hundred–dollar bill. "Get whatever you want and grab me a martini."

I rolled my eyes at Eric and tugged his hand, signaling to leave. I couldn't care less about anything Neil might have to say.

But just then Madeline bounced over, always one for stirring the pot. "Neil, good to see you again. Couldn't decide which date to bring tonight, or are you compensating for something?" She fluttered her eyelashes at him and stepped closer. "You do realize this is about helping people, God, etc.?"

"As charming as ever," Neil mumbled. The women brought him a martini, which he promptly spilled.

Madeline gave the women a thorough once–over. "So, Neil, have you had the pleasure of meeting Ava's new boyfriend, Dr. Gabriel Ruiz? He's a surgeon in Manhattan and spends his vacations traveling the world to perform surgeries for those in need. Quite an altruistic soul. And, in case you didn't notice – he's devilishly handsome. I'd be delighted to introduce you."

"I just bet you would," he replied, swaying and dripping drops of his drink. "But no need to introduce me. Ava will come crawling back to me when she's done playing with him." He gestured nonchalantly with his free hand. "I always get her back." Neil raised both arms, and the women nestled into the crook of each elbow.

Before they could take a second step, Madeline intercepted them with a sly grin on her face. "Well, Neil, I hate to break this to you, but Ava has moved on. She's upgraded to a surgeon with a heart, not just a guy with deep pockets."

Neil's face flushed with anger as he scowled at Madeline. "Who asked for your input?"

"No one," she responded smugly. "But someone should let you know that Ava won't be coming back."

With that, Madeline strutted away, leaving Neil fuming behind her.

Eric and I shared a chuckle and watched as he stumbled back to his table. There probably wouldn't be any drink left in his glass by the time he reached it. I was glad Madeline called him on his bullshit. What an ass. Ava deserved someone better, and it seemed that Gabriel might just be the one.

As we sat at our table, I said to Eric, "You know, I think my single friends have finally found loving partners." I pointed to Staci, Ava, and Charlotte, all dancing with their new boyfriends. "I'm so happy about that. Don't we all deserve to be loved?"

Just then, Nicole stormed over to our table, looking livid. "You think you fooled everybody with this travesty," she spat out, pointing around the tent. "But you haven't fooled me."

I stood.

Eric rose from his chair and draped his arm around me protectively. "Watch how you speak to my wife."

Turning to Eric, I said. "Honey, would you mind getting me a coke from the bar? Please?"

He glanced at me before and bent down whispering, "Do you really want me to go?"

I shook my head. "I do. I've got this."

Eric left, and I gestured for Nicole to sit down.

She paid no attention. "You stole all my ideas for this event, and I finally figured out how you did it."

"I did not steal anything. Everything you see here is my own creation, not yours," I argued.

"You're lying. Shelby didn't understand why I was so mad, but I told her what you did." Each word dripped with hostility.

"And what exactly did I do?"

Madeline and Ava approached.

Nicole pointed an accusatory finger at Ava. "It was her. Your little sidekick. She copied my proposal because she's friends with the Sister. Then you undercut my price."

I could sense the anger radiating from Madeline and Ava. They were ready to pounce on her like vultures on roadkill.

"You're completely insane. You need to see a doctor for treatment." Ava said.

Nicole stood straight, her eyes narrowing as she stepped closer to Ava. "How dare you speak to me like that," she hissed.

"That's enough." I intervened, stepping between my friends and Nicole. "Can the two of you please go help Eric at the bar? I'd like to talk to Nicole alone."

They both glared at me but grudgingly left.

When they were gone, I turned to Nicole. "I don't have any idea what you're talking about. Let's speak with Mother Superior and have her straighten this out."

"You'd love that, wouldn't you? Show me up," she spat, her face beet red.

I took a deep breath and tried to keep my cool. "Nicole, I'm sorry if you feel like I've somehow hurt you or copied your ideas for this event. But I can assure you that everything here is my own work."

"I know your lame–ass work, and it isn't anything like this," she sneered.

"How would you know what my work is like? You never gave me the chance to do anything on my own. Everything was done your way. Period."

She scoffed and rolled her eyes.

I shook my head. "I'm not going to argue about this anymore. We can go see Mother Superior and clear this up or you can stew all you want, but far away from me. This event was all me. Not you. Me." I folded my arms across my chest defiantly.

Behind Nicole I saw Charlotte, Staci and Hanna coming toward us. "If you don't mind, I have an event to run." I left her standing there.

I met my friends by the stage and asked if they were having a good time.

"Of course, we are. What was that all about?" Charlotte asked.

Staci looked around me and Nicole was still standing by my empty table. "Is everything okay?"

A grin stretched across my face as I pulled them close, wrapping my arms around their shoulders. "Couldn't be better, " I said, tightening my grip. "I finally stood up to Nicole. I feel incredible."

Madeline and Ava approached us with concerned looks on their faces. "What's going on?" Madeline asked.

I beamed, recounting the details of my confrontation with Nicole.

"Good for you," Madeline said. "She needed to be put in her place."

We all shared a laugh. As the event ended, people began to leave. The kitchen and technical team cleaned up, while my companions and I stepped outside, leaving the men at the bar enjoying their final drink. The moon glowed brightly above us in the dark sky.

A noise like slapping flip flops came from the corner of the parking lot. We all looked toward it. At least forty sets of webbed feet were smacking the pavement and closing in on a person. Honking furiously.

I started to run in that direction. Next to me, Madeline was fumbling with something in her purse. She must have realized before I did that it was Nicole.

"This is going to be epic," Madeline said, whipping out her phone.

I held her arm. "Don't. She's an awful person, but we don't need to be like her."

As we approached, Nicole started screaming, "Get away from me, you filthy beasts."

Just as she reached the safety of her car and opened the door, a large shadow loomed overhead. Before I had a chance to warn her, vulture shit rained down on her car, her hat and her arms from all three birds.

Madeline stopped dead in her tracks and said, "Oh, my God!" She tried to hold back her laughter but failed.

I didn't laugh. In that moment, I noticed Nicole looking

completely deflated, mortification written all over her face. My anger melted away, and I couldn't help but feel sorry for her. "Nicole, let's get you cleaned up." I put my hand on her back to lead her. And to my astonishment, she willingly let me take her to the bathroom. Stunned, she didn't say a word.

"I'll get a bucket so we can wash off your windshield enough for you to see. Would you like me to follow you home?" I asked.

She shook her head. Walking to her car, she asked me, "Why are you helping me?"

I thought of a couple smartass remarks, but it just wasn't my style. "Because someone needed to help you."

As we approached her car, I noticed that someone had kindly washed Nicole's windshield, and I immediately knew it was my friends.

As she climbed into the car, Nicole rolled down her window and looked at me intensely. I prepared myself for another angry tirade, but to my surprise, she simply said, "Thank you."

My friends watched and waited as I saw Nicole off. When I approached them, they all talked at once.

"Wow. That's all I can say," Madeline began. "The event was awesome. Nicole got shit on by some big ugly birds. What more could you ask for?"

Everyone laughed. "It was kinda funny," I agreed. "But in the end, I felt sad for her."

Charlotte said, "That's because you're a nice person."

Her comment started all my friends buzzing.

I put my hand up. "Thanks, guys, for having my back. You're the reason I made it through this." My father entered my mind. Now I would have to deal with him. My stomach cramped. But I willed the thought away. I wanted to enjoy the moment a little longer. "Come on, ladies. Let's go collect our men from the bar."

Chapter 23

BRI – A FAMILY AFFAIR

ERIC STOOD NEXT to me, his hand holding mine tightly as we waited for my half-sister Lori to open the door. My stomach was in knots, my heart pounding. I had talked to Lori every day since meeting her at the charity event, but now that I was about to meet the rest of my new family, I couldn't help but feel anxious.

Behind that door were my half brothers and sisters, the family my father had after he left me behind and never thought of me again. Would they accept me or feel sorry for me? Would they even want to get to know me?

When Lori finally opened the door, my heart leapt into my throat. But before I could even say hello, she pulled me into a warm hug, wrapping her arms tightly around me. "Welcome to the family," she whispered, tears in her eyes.

In that moment, I realized that my fears were unwarranted. These people *were* my family, and they were ready to accept me. Just as Eric had said they would. As we walked into the house, my smiling brothers and sisters lined the foyer.

"Bri, this is David," Lori said, gesturing towards a tall man with strikingly familiar features. He had my father's jawline and piercing blue eyes. I was momentarily taken aback by how much he looked like my memory of him.

David offered his hand for a handshake, but then changed his mind and pulled me into a hug instead. "It's so good to finally meet you," he said, patting my back

Emotions overwhelmed me as I hugged him back. My oldest brother. I still couldn't believe I had brothers and sisters welcoming me into the family with open arms and hearts.

"I'm Emma." A bubbly voice interrupted our embrace. I turned to see a younger version of Lori standing next to us with the same dark hair and dimpled smile.

"Number three in the lineup," she said, giving me another big squeeze before stepping back.

"And I'm Sam," the youngest chimed in from behind us. He had a playful glint in his eye.

"You just had a birthday?" I asked. "I saw a post on Lori's social media."

He nodded. "So happy to meet you." He kissed me on the cheek.

I couldn't believe how similar they all were to my father in appearance. It was almost like looking at him through different stages of his life. Stages, of course, I had missed.

As we settled in the family room, Lori brought out some snacks and drinks for us to enjoy while we talked. I met David's wife, Sally; Sam's wife, Sophia; and Emma's husband, Oliver. And talk we did – about everything from how we earned our living, our favorite hobbies, and our children. My head whirling, I realized I had a whole slew of new nieces and nephews.

Then we finally shared some memories of our father.

Sam popped up from his seat. "Hey, remember when we went skiing in Park City and Lori got stuck on the chair lift on the way down?"

Her face reddened. "I couldn't get the restraining bar up. What was I supposed to do?"

David grabbed a cracker. "Don't get me started on all your screwups over the years."

"Hey, I never screwed up anything," Sam said.

His expression told a different story and it made me grin. As I listened to them share stories from their youth, I couldn't help but feel a twinge of regret for all the moments I missed out on when my father left. I could have been part of this close knit, loving family.

It was bittersweet. But at the same time, I felt incredibly grateful to have them in my life, and I decided not to dwell on what could have been – just to enjoy the now.

"You're going to see Dad tomorrow," Emma said, breaking the silence that had fallen over us after they showed us some old photos from a family photo album. Pulling out my phone, I gave them a glimpse of their new niece and nephew, as babies, young children, and now as new adults.

Emma's comment made me purse my lips, not sure what to feel. "Yes. I don't remember much about him. I was only six when he left."

Lori reached out and squeezed my hand. The room went quiet.

"Well, we have each other now," Sam chimed in. "So we'll have to make up for lost time. I can't wait to meet my niece and nephew."

"And I can't wait to meet all of your children." Tears filled my eyes, not from sadness, but from overwhelming gratitude. *Wow, I have siblings.* Ones who have given me such a warm welcome. I looked over at Eric, who had been largely silent this whole time, giving me the space I needed to absorb all the emotions I felt. I blew him a kiss.

Tonight marked the start of a new chapter in my life. A wonderful, exciting new beginning. Only one more hurdle – tomorrow I would see my father for the first time in more than forty years.

*

Eric insisted he come with me to the restaurant where I was meeting my father. Lori would bring Dad and leave with Eric to give us some time to talk. I didn't utter one word on the hour drive to the restaurant. My hands shook. My wonderful husband kept trying to engage me in conversation to help settle my nerves but I ignored him. Finally, he left me alone, and I hoped he understood. As we pulled into the parking lot, my stomach roiled.

I had secretly longed for my father for so long. Would he accept me? Like me? Even love me? I looked around for Lori's car but didn't see it. I was glad we were here first.

Goosebumps rose on my arms as I kissed Eric on the cheek. "I'm going in by myself. Lori and my father should be here shortly, and I want to be by myself for a few minutes."

"Are you sure?" Eric asked.

"Yes. Don't worry so much. After this, I'll be fine, and I'll call you when we're done."

The restaurant was slow. It was after the lunch crowd and before dinner. I took a seat by the big bay window looking out to the parking lot. I saw Lori's car pull in a minute later. My heart pounded.

I watched a white-haired man get out of the passenger seat and amble through the parking lot. Bile rose and I held back my tears. He opened the restaurant door and looked around. He didn't recognize me. I mean, of course he didn't. I was just six when he left me. But I had taken the time to go through Lori's social media so I could identify him. The fact that he hadn't bothered shouldn't have bothered me, but it did. Why couldn't he do the same? I stood, and he must have noticed movement and looked in my direction. He stood still.

After a few seconds, he came over to the table. "My God, you look just like your mother."

I held out my hand to shake his. He grabbed my hand, wrapping it tightly in his.

"Hello," I said, my voice shaking.

He looked down at my hand and released it. "Hello, Brianna," he replied.

We stood there just looking at each other. His once dark hair was now almost completely white, and wrinkles lined his face. But despite the years that had passed, I could still see traces of the father I remembered in his features.

After what seemed like forever, we finally sat. The little girl inside me, who had longed for her father all these years, was finally facing him. And it took everything I had not to burst into tears.

A waitress came over, but we waved her away.

"I couldn't believe it when Lori told me Logan had reached out to her," he said, his voice tentative.

I nodded, trying to hide the pain in my eyes. "Yes, it was quite a surprise."

"I never told my kids about you," he admitted quietly.

Anger surged within me. "You just tossed me aside like garbage."

"No, that's not..." He reached once more for my hand, but I placed both in my lap.

"I don't want to hear it," I interrupted, feeling tears welling up in my own eyes. "You hurt me deeply. You can't imagine how much."

He flinched at my words but remained silent. We sat in uncomfortable silence for a while.

Just as I was about to get up and leave, he said, "The accident was my fault. I was drunk that night. And your mother..." Tears streamed down his cheeks.

He wiped away the tears with the back of his hand. "You cried a lot, and kept calling out for your mom," he said, his voice heavy with regret. "I just couldn't cope, so I decided to give you to your mother's parents. They were just as heartbroken as you. No one knew that I'd caused the accident; there weren't any sobriety tests back then. Looking back now, I realize I acted like a coward – I ran." He hung his head in shame.

My father's words hit me hard, like a ton of bricks. The crash that took my mother's life and left me without parents was my father's fault. And yet, he never faced any consequences or took responsibility for his actions.

"You ran?" I couldn't contain my anger.

He nodded, looking remorseful. "I was scared and didn't know what else to do."

I felt betrayed and enraged that he could just abandon me without looking back. Had he cared nothing at all about me? "How could you leave me like that?" I demanded, my voice quivering.

"I'm sorry, Brianna. I was foolish and immature. I simply couldn't face the reality of what had happened."

He was clearly upset, but I couldn't bring myself to feel sorry for him.

I held back tears. "You could have at least checked up on me," I managed to choke out.

He shook his head, a look of shame on his face. "I was afraid to face you and your grandparents. I didn't want them to hate me for what happened."

"They did hate you," I replied bitterly. "And so did I."

The waitress came over again, took one look at us, and backed away. Out of a corner of one eye, I saw her gesturing toward us, conferring quietly with the hostess. Usually this would have embarrassed me, but right now, I simply didn't care.

He spoke softly, "I understand if you never want to see me again or forgive me. But I want you to know that I'm truly sorry for the pain I caused. I tried to be a better person and father."

"Well, that's great for my siblings," I retorted, resentment rising within me. "But it's not that easy where I'm concerned."

We sat in silence, lost in our own thoughts. I was filled with conflicting emotions – anger, confusion, and anxiety. What was I supposed to feel? Say? Do?

After a few minutes, my father cleared his throat and spoke again. "It took years of therapy for me to start forgiving myself. I hope someday you can forgive me too. Maybe we can try to build a relationship now, despite the past."

I looked at him skeptically. Could we really start over after all these years? Was it possible for me to let go of the hurt and anger I had buried for so long?

But then I thought about Logan – my son who reached out to my family all on his own. He wanted a relationship with this part of our family. And maybe, deep down, a part of me does too.

"I can't make any promises," I finally said, surprising myself with my response.

The waitress, possibly seeing something resembling calm between us, came back over, and this time we let her take our drink orders.

My father's lips formed a faint smile as he reached across the table to take my hand once more. In that moment, I felt a glimmer of hope for our future.

Epilogue
MADELINE – BOOK CLUB

S I PLACED the ice into the crystal bucket, the doorbell rang. Checking the clock, I saw that it was exactly seven o'clock. Surprised, I thought to myself, *Wow. Someone actually arrived on time.* Opening the door, I was shocked to see everybody. "You're all here on time? I can't believe it."

Charlotte walked in and joked, "I guess your persistent nagging finally paid off."

Bri eased in next. "Don't mind her. We're here because we have so much to talk about." She kissed my cheek hello.

Charlotte twirled around. "We sure do. Just talking about Bri's event will have us here until two in the morning.

Staci laughed. "Yes. Forget the book discussion tonight. We have more immediate things to discuss, like that poor woman dating my ex-husband. That's good for at least an hour of conversation. Although, I really enjoyed *Lift and Separate* by Marilyn Simon Rothstein. Let's do that book next month."

Hanna slipped in with a big plate. I wondered what was underneath the beautiful wrapping.

Ava entered last and pecked my cheek hello. "And let's not forget Neil. God, where to begin?"

I ushered everyone into the kitchen.

"I can't believe you have this place organized and decorated already," Ava said, looking around.

"It's beautiful," Bri said.

"Thanks. But you know I crave organization. I had everything in its place in a week," I said.

"Of course, you did," Charlotte interrupted. "And it really does look great."

"Thanks." I motioned to Hanna to put the tray she was carrying on the counter. "You didn't have to bring anything."

"It's nothing, really. A little of this and that," she said.

Ava helped her take the wrapping off. "It's a chock-full charcuterie board."

Hanna blushed. "Thanks. My sister helped me. She's really into food presentation, and she's a great cook."

I walked to the counter. "You two should start your own catering company. Your platters are beautiful," I said, picking up a piece of prosciutto and a pepper-seed cracker. "And delicious."

Ava popped a square of cheddar into her mouth. "Very good. What kind of cheddar is this? It's so creamy."

"It's Irish cheddar. Ashley gets cheese from Ireland, France, and Italy," Hanna said.

"Well, Madeline's right. You and Ashley should definitely start your own business," Ava said.

"I'd be happy to use you as caterers for my events business," Bri offered.

Hanna beamed. "I'll speak with Ashley and get back to you. Thanks."

"Okay. Let's all grab some food and drinks and meet in the family room," I suggested, gesturing toward the door. We settled onto couches and chairs; plates precariously balanced on our laps.

"Now that we're all settled," I called out, silencing the chatter. "Bri, let's get down to business. How are you managing with your new family?"

All eyes focused on Bri.

"Hmmm. Well, first let me say thank you for all your calls and texts last weekend when I met my new family and my father," she began.

Staci accidentally dropped a cracker on the floor and knocked her empty wine glass over while reaching to pick it up. I caught the falling glass before it shattered.

"Oh gosh, I'm so sorry, Bri. I didn't mean to interrupt you." Staci turned to me. "Thank you for catching it. I'm such a klutz." She sat back on the couch, a vivid blush crossing her cheeks.

I waved my hand. "Don't worry about it. We all have something."

Bri smiled and said, "I don't know what's going on, but everyone's so civilized tonight. No snarky remarks."

I smirked. "Well, the night is young."

Charlotte clinked her fork against her wine glass to get everyone's attention. "Back to what we've all been waiting to hear about. How do you feel now about meeting your family?"

Bri placed her plate on the table. "Good. These past few days, I've had some time to reflect and try to understand. And forgive, I guess?"

Shaking my head, I said, 'Forgiveness. That's a hard one."

"Did your father tell you why he abandoned you?" Hanna asked.

"Guilt. He was driving the night of the accident, and he was drunk." Bri paused. "He told me that he couldn't look at me. I was so upset after my mother died, and his guilt grew every day because of it until he couldn't handle it anymore. He was the reason I was grieving. He thought I'd be better off with my grandparents."

"I think you're a better person than me," I interrupted. "His excuse for leaving you was he couldn't stand the guilt. His own damn guilt. What crap!"

"That's some lame-ass excuse," Ava uttered angrily.

Bri shook her head. "It is."

Not hiding her irritation, Charlotte grumbled something no one could understand.

"What?" I asked.

Charlotte grabbed her wine glass. "It's awful."

But I thought she was probably swearing at him under her breath. I was glad she didn't translate.

Staci asked gently, "Can you forgive him?"

Bri looked up. "Honestly, I don't know if I can ever fully forgive him for what he put me through," she admitted, dabbing her cheeks with a napkin. "But seeing him now... he's old and frail and seems genuinely remorseful about what happened." She took a breath. "The best part was meeting my brothers and sisters. They genuinely welcomed me into their lives. We're all excited to build a relationship with each other and with our families."

Charlotte rose from her seat. "I think this calls for a toast," she declared. "And luckily, I brought a bottle of champagne that I stashed in the fridge when you weren't looking, Madeline."

I stood, "Great idea. I'll get some glasses."

Ava popped up also and we brought back six full flutes.

Bri stood and took a glass from me. "I'd like to make a toast first."

"Hey. This is our toast to you. Not yours," Charlotte replied.

Bri laughed and waved her hand, conceding.

Charlotte cleared her throat, drawing everyone's attention. "Bri, my oldest and dearest friend." She put her free hand over her heart. "I'm so glad that you have the siblings you always wanted and a whole new family to love and support you. God knows, you deserve it. You were always there for me when I needed comfort, or compassion, or just an ear to listen to my rants."

Ava cut her off. "Boy, forty years of Charlotte rants. You may need the whole bottle of champagne."

Bri laughed with everyone else.

Charlotte gave Ava a look. "Yes, well she probably does. So, here's to you Bri. I'm thrilled that you've been in my life for so long. You're my sister, my best friend, and I love you. Just don't forget me now that you have real sisters."

Bri walked to Charlotte and wrapped her arm around her. "I could never forget you. You are my sister. You are all my sisters."

We clinked our glasses together and took a sip of champagne. I could see tears prickling at the corners of Bri's eyes as I looked around at my friends.

"Okay, enough mushy stuff. Let's talk about the event," I insisted as only I could.

We sat and started talking all at once about the vultures, the geese, and anything else that happened to meander into the tent the night of the event.

After the laughter died down, Ava told us she thought George, Staci's ex, had been better behaved than Neil. "Those two women hung on him all night. He flaunted wads of cash around and got really drunk. At a friggin' charity event. I mean come on. What's he, a rap star now?"

I threw my hand in the air. "Wait. Did you hear what I said to Neil?"

Ava shook her head.

"Well, you're going to love this." I retold the story of my encounter with him. Another round of laughter ensued. We must have sounded like a cackle of hyenas.

Charlotte poured another round of champagne, then brought up Nicole.

Bri sipped her drink and said, "I think she's had enough of us for a lifetime. Let's leave her be."

"After all the shit she put you through. Why?" Hanna asked.

Before Bri could reply, Ava asked, "Why did you help Nicole

when the bird shit came raining down from the heavens at the end of the night?"

Bri played with her necklace, thinking. "Why beat someone who's already down? I just don't have that in me."

I started to say that she should be less empathetic, but Bri spoke over me.

"Think about all the books we've read and all the many different situations those characters have faced. It's all a reflection of real life. We all have problems, misfortunes, and tragedies. Life is difficult. We get through that with love. Without it, we have nothing. It doesn't matter how much money you have or what your title is. And when someone is constantly spiteful, nasty and angry, something deeper must be going on behind the scenes. By the end of the night, Nicole's bravado crumbled, and I saw the vulnerable woman underneath – someone broken. I couldn't and wouldn't add to her challenges. She has enough of her own."

"Jesus, Bri, you should be on a pulpit," Ava said.

Hanna interjected. "It's so noble of you."

Bri shrugged. "No, it's just human of me."

"Bravo, Bri," I said. "That's why I love you. But I can always go back and give Nicole a piece of my mind if I think she hasn't learned her lesson."

She winked, then batted her eyelashes at me.

"No need." I stood. "I'd like to make a toast but we need more bubbly."

"There's another bottle in the refrigerator," Charlotte said.

I opened a fresh bottle and ventured back into the family room.

"My turn to make a toast," I said, and started pouring champagne into our glasses.

Charlotte held out her glass. "How nice. More bubbles."

I cleared my throat. "Last summer was our book club's tenth anniversary, and what a year it's been. As we approach our eleventh year, I want to reflect on how far we've come. It all started with our shared interest in reading, but it's become so much more. We started just discussing books but now we're a support system for one other." Turning to face each of my friends, I thought about our shared journey, all the highs and lows and the strength we found in each other. "From the bottom of my heart, thank you for being there for me when Stan was going through his business problems and helping out when we downsized. And thank you especially for lending an ear when I needed to vent about Sarah. Your support has meant everything to me." I raised my glass. "Cheers to you and to many more years of book club and friendship."

We clinked our glasses.

Bri stood and said, "Let's have a group hug."

We all gathered around the fireplace and embraced.

Staci pulled away from the group hug first and said, "You know, I think I'm gonna write a book. How does *Navigating Your Older Years for Dummies* sound? Maybe AARP will feature it."

"Not sure I'd want to read that. Maybe a better title?" Ava commented and sat down.

I inquired, "So, what do you want the book to be about?"

Staci sat and pondered for a moment before replying, "I don't know. Maybe a guide to help us navigate this stage of life. Something like that."

I sat down with the rest of the group. All of us quietly thinking.

Hanna suggested, "Sounds promising. So, like a self-help, non-fiction book?"

Charlotte snorted. "Forget that. Write a novel about older women. I'm sick of reading books about young women with perfect bodies. Yuck! Not interested. What you should write is a story about some hot older women. We're not dead yet. We're not invisible. Hell, I'm sick of being ignored."

I burst into laughter with the rest of us. "Nobody ever ignores you, Charlotte. You wouldn't let them."

She grinned mischievously, "Exactly. That's why we need some strong, attractive older women in literature."

I chimed in. "I like Charlotte's idea. I'm tired of reading about all these pert, perfect, and boring young women. Writing about older women would be refreshing."

"I've got it," Bri interrupted, looking excited. "Write a book about a book club. Aren't you supposed to write about something you know? Well, you know book club."

Staci stood up excitedly, "That's a fantastic idea. What if we all write it together?"

Everyone jumped up at once. Ava grabbed her phone while Charlotte snatched a pen and paper from the desk. Staci and I huddled together.

"We need a catchy title. You know, one that sells books," I said.

"How the hell do you know what sells books?" Ava retorted.

Charlotte started scribbling titles as everyone threw out ideas.

Bri gently placed her hand on Charlotte's to stop her from writing. "Guys, I think we already have the perfect title. Our book club – Novel Women."

Everyone cheered.

"That's perfect," I exclaimed again. "After all, aren't all women novel in their own way?"

Acknowledgements

As I sat down to write this, I reflected on the journey that brought me to this moment. The countless hours spent scribbling in notebooks and typing away at my computer, the hundreds of meetings with my co-authors and collaborators, the numerous workshop classes attended, the rejection letters, and the moments of self-doubt were all part of the process. But so were the moments of pure joy and inspiration when the meetings went well, and the words flowed onto the page. It has been an incredible adventure working with my friends to complete what we started eight years ago. I owe a huge thanks to my fellow collaborators, Fran and Jeanne, and to Patty and Denise.

As I reflect on the completion of this trilogy, I am filled with gratitude for all those who played a role in its creation. At the forefront of my mind is my editor, Michelle Cameron, who has been with me every step of the way through all three novels. Her expert guidance, insightful feedback, and unwavering commitment challenged me as a writer, making this story the best it could be.

A special thank you goes to my Tuesday night workshop class for their patience and guidance. You are all such accomplished writers, and your help and encouragement have been invaluable.

I also want to express my gratitude to all those who supported me in bringing these books to life – from friends and family who listened to my ideas and offered their support, to fellow writers who inspired me with their own work. To my family, especially my sister, my daughter, and my wonderful husband who listened to all my ideas endlessly. And to my son, Alex, I don't know if I could have attempted this without your unwavering support and kind words. You always knew the perfect thing to say to lift me up or make me laugh, and boy, did we laugh.

Thank you to every reader who picks up these books. It is an honor to share these stories with you, and I hope you enjoy them as much as I enjoyed writing them.

Kim

Made in the USA
Middletown, DE
21 September 2024

60828125R00159